THE COLUMBIA CONSPIRACY

A HAWK & HUNTER THRILLER

LIAM BONNER

WWW.LIAMBONNER.NET

First edition 2023

Paperback ISBN: 978-1-7389626-1-7

Large Print Edition ISBN: 978-1-7389626-3-1

eBook ISBN: 978-1-7389626-2-4

CHAPTER 1

IT WAS SUPPOSED TO be a celebration. A long awaited, much need-ed, and highly anticipated celebration. Owen Reid, his best friend Eddie, and a few other friends had intended to celebrate their grad-uation months earlier. Turns out being valedictorian at NYU meant people were keen to steal him away the moment he doffed his tasseled cap. Admittedly, it was Owen's dream job, so he wasn't about to say no when the UN offered him a position as an interpreter. His only regret, not seeing Eddie and the others before he left. But here they were now, at some overpriced club full of trust fund kids and rich tourists looking for a taste of New York at night.

"Remind me why you chose this place," Owen called over the music. They had chosen the most secluded corner of the club. Only a few booths tucked next to the bar, away from the writhing mass of the dance floor. But the thumping, repetitive tracks still made the table shake and the next booth over was full of more people shouting to be heard.

"Because," Eddie began, pausing to down a shot of tequila and grimacing like a kid tasting his father's beer for the first time, "we're moving up in the world. You aren't a kid anymore, Reid." Owen rolled his eyes and took a sip of his rum and Coke. It had been a running joke for four years that he was the youngest of the group.

Having started at NYU a year earlier than most had meant he'd been forced to sit out of the typical club hopping when the others had turned 21. Not that he had minded. Nor, it seemed, had Eddie and the others. They were quite content to stay back at the dorms, drink their smuggled beer, and poke fun at Owen for being a kid.

"So, what's it like?" shouted one of the others, a very petite girl named Cassie, struggling to be heard over the din of the club. Cassie had strawberry blonde hair that cascaded down her shoulders, sparkling green eyes, and a slightly crooked smile. All in all, Owen's vision of perfection. He felt suddenly uncomfortable under her intense stare and he swallowed hard.

"What do you mean?" he asked.

"Working at the UN, dummy," she said with a little laugh, "I bet it's amazing."

"Oh right," Owen said, smiling easily, "yeah it has been amazing so far. Lots of translating documents and I've even sat in on a few sessions to interpret live."

"How do you keep up with something like that?" asked the other girl, Emily, who had been glued to Eddie's arm since they had sat down. Owen had not met her before that night, but he had certainly heard everything about the newest girlfriend. Owen met Eddie's eyes for a moment and the latter immediately cut in.

"Oh no, don't you dare!"

"What is it?" asked the girl, looking at Eddie in shock.

"Every time this bastard starts speaking other languages, all the girls forget I even exist," Eddie complained. This was something of an understatement. Owen was thin and awkward looking. With his messy black hair and glasses, he was simply the epitome of nerdy. Eddie, meanwhile, was the football quarterback to Owen's nerd. Tall, broad, chiseled jaw, and longer blonde hair. How they had ended up friends, Owen still didn't know, but he knew he liked Eddie just fine.

"Oh come on," Emily said, slapping Eddie's arm playfully, "I wanna see this for myself. Please?" she added to Owen who simply shrugged. Grinning, Emily leaned across Eddie so that she could be heard clearly and said, "So how do you do it?" The words had barely left her mouth when it fell open in shock. Owen had repeated every word in perfect Spanish with hardly a delay. Eddie groaned at the look on Emily's face and Cassie burst out laughing.

"See?" Eddie said, "I told you; it happens every time." Owen merely repeated this in fluent Mandarin. This only made Cassie laugh harder.

"How many languages do you know then?" Emily asked, punching Owen in the arm when he repeated the question back in Portuguese.

"Ow," Owen complained, grinning as he rubbed his arm, "alright, alright, including English I can speak seven languages."

Emily's eyebrows shot up in surprise as she fell back into her seat and played with the straw in her daiquiri. "Why bother to learn so many? I speak exactly one and feel that that's plenty."

"You can thank my mother for that," Owen replied with a slight smile, "she was a French teacher at one of the public schools in the city. She made sure I grew up learning at least two languages and encouraged me to learn as many as I could."

"I bet she's proud of you now then," Emily said brightly. This statement swept over the table like a chill wind, silencing the laughing Cassie in an instant and making Eddie frown deeply.

In response to the panicked look on Emily's face at this reaction, Owen waved away the sentiment like a swarm of mosquitos and said, "My mother passed away when I was little, my dad too. Car crash."

"Oh, I'm so sorry," Emily said earnestly, pouting slightly and thrusting her chest out as though that would make it better.

"Come on," Owen said, shaking his head, "there was no way you could have known. It's not like you're dating my best friend who knows all this." He turned an artificial glare towards Eddie who blushed slightly and made Emily smack his arm again. The moment passed smoothly as Owen and Cassie laughed at Eddie as he tried to stammer some sort of apology. Cassie flagged down a passing waitress to order another round and Owen relaxed into the booth a bit deeper. It was nice, going out like they were still in school. It had been ages since he'd even slowed down enough to realize he had no life outside of his work.

Then it happened. The current song faded slightly, and the roar of the crowd was more audible and the shouting at the next booth rang clearly in Owen's ears.

"...*not messing around, we will kill you if...*" and just like that the music was back and the voices were drowned out. Only as he whipped around to look at the group next to them did Owen realize that what he had heard had not been English. It was French, specifically, Provençal French. Three people sat in the booth, two were rather brutish and menacing, the other was clearly a very drunk, very rich man of about twenty-five. His dark suit alone could have probably paid for Owen's entire education. Not to mention the five-hundred-dollar haircut and gold Rolex watch. This third man looked frightened, though the alcohol seemed to make him think whatever was happening was some sort of prank.

"What's the matter?" Eddie asked, thumping Owen hard on the arm. When he looked back, it was to see Cassie and Emily heading off towards the bathroom together and Eddie looking at him with concern.

"I...I thought," Owen stammered, pointing vaguely at the table next to them.

"Are you alright, dude?" Eddie asked, apparently thinking that Owen had just had too much to drink. Before Owen could say another word, the three people at the adjacent booth got to their feet. One of the bigger men was half dragging the drunk one along, while the third followed with a hand inside his jacket. Owen frowned at the man. Wasn't that the sort of thing you saw in spy movies and stuff? The sort of thing you did when you wanted to keep your weapon close. The man with a hand in his jacket glared down at them as he passed, and Owen felt his face go cold. Did they know what he had heard? Had he really heard it? Maybe they were just friends of the drunk guy coming to pick him up after partying too hard. Deep down, though, Owen knew exactly what he had heard.

"I think that guy is gonna be killed," Owen said after the large man had left.

"What are you talking about?" Eddie asked, looking around at the guy being led out like this must be some sort of game.

"Those two big guys were threatening him, and I think one of them has a gun."

"I didn't hear any threat," Eddie said reassuringly, looking away as the trio left the club.

"You don't speak French," Owen retorted, "come on," he added, acting on a whim and sliding out of the booth.

"Whoa, Owen, hang on, you aren't a cop," Eddie said, grabbing his arm, "what exactly are you planning on doing?"

"I just want to see what they're up to. If it looks shady then I'll call the cops." He pulled himself free of Eddie's grip and wove his way through the crowd towards the door. The stench of sweat and booze hit him like a wave as he ventured farther from the booth and he had to dodge a very drunk girl, evidently looking to get laid, before he could duck out of the doorway. As soon as the door shut behind him the blaring music was reduced to a dull thumping. Owen took a breath of the fresh air, not realizing how stuffy it had been in the club. Summer was passing by now, but it was still muggy from the day. As he looked around for a sign of the three men, the door to the club opened behind him and Eddie stepped out.

"What are you doing?" Owen hissed at him.

"You know my mom would never let me hear the end of it if I let you get shot," he said sarcastically. Though, Owen reasoned, there was some truth to that. Eddie's mother had taken Owen in as a kid and loved him like he was her own. "Where did they go?"

"No clue," Owen said, listening carefully for any sign of them.

"Yo!" Eddie called loudly, turning back to where the club's bouncer stood like a brick wall, "Did you see three guys come out this way? We just wanna make sure they make it home alright."

The bouncer, at least three hundred pounds of muscle and fore-head, looked Eddie up and down for a moment before answering. "Yeah, I saw 'em," he grunted in a low boom, "turned down the alley, probably headed for the subway." The man nodded towards the alley next to the club and Eddie inclined his head in thanks. Owen was already headed towards the indicated spot, recognizing in the back of his mind that this was the sort of place you went to get shot. The alley housed a handful of dumpsters, more than a few rats, and a slowly leaking steam grate that left a haze in the air. Eddie caught up to Owen as they stepped into the alley, squinting through the gloom.

"Last chance," a voice called gruffly, and Eddie looked at Owen in confusion. It was definitely the same French speaker as before.

"Come on," Owen whispered urgently, quickening his pace slightly. Blurry shapes slowly resolved as the drunk man slurred an unintelligible response. The two larger men loomed over a crumpled figure on the ground. The unmistakable silhouette of a gun swung out from one of the hulking figures and Owen's heart seemed to stop at the sight. Some sort of autopilot function seemed to switch on in his brain and he ran forward a few more steps as the man began counting backwards from three.

"Three..." Owen took a deep breath, *"two..."* Eddie tried to grab at Owen's wrist, *"one..."* the gun lowered slightly to find its mark.

"HEY!" Owen shouted, surprising himself almost as much as the men who both whipped around in alarm. Something heavy slammed into Owen, there was a bang, and then only the sound of running footsteps. Owen hit the ground, unable to breathe and sure he had just been shot. Once the shock wore off, however, and he took a grateful breath of the steamy air, he almost laughed with relief. Until he looked back at Eddie. Standing exactly where Owen had been a moment before, Eddie was blinking rapidly, looking slightly puzzled as to why his chest was bleeding.

"Eddie?" Owen asked quietly, equally confused by the gaping hole that had been punched through his best friend. Eddie fell backwards, almost in slow motion, and hit the ground with an awful finality. Owen crawled into the slowly growing pool of red and tried feebly to put pressure on the wound. Someone was speaking near him, someone with a very deep voice, but he couldn't hear them.

All he could hear was a ringing in his ears and his own soft begging for Eddie to wake up. After the flashing lights had filled the alley, Owen had to be pried away from Eddie for the paramedics to decide he was already dead. They placed Owen on the ground next to the drunk Frenchman who was looking around in confusion and someone put a blanket around both their shoulders. Why, though? Owen wondered. He didn't feel cold. He didn't feel anything at that moment. But putting a blanket on someone's shoulders was just something that happened.

Vaguely, Owen heard the sound of Cassie calling out to him, but the police line was already up and she couldn't get any closer. "Can you tell me what happened?" someone asked right next to him and he looked up blankly to see a pretty young woman with flaming red hair in an NYPD uniform. The look of utter sympathy seemed at odds with the blue eyes and dusting of freckles on her cheeks. This was someone who should be smiling, not looking like the world had ended. When Owen failed to do more than stare at her for a moment, she patted his arm reassuringly.

"Don't worry," she said gently, "we can do this later." She then moved on to the Frenchman and Owen did everything he could not to look at the body now covered by a bloodstained sheet a few yards away. When the officer asked the Frenchman what had happened, he immediately launched into an enthusiastic recount of the events, complete with wild gestures. By the end of this, the officer looked like someone had just explained it to her in a foreign language. Then, Owen realized, it was because they had.

"I'm sorry, sir," she said gently, "could you repeat that?" Owen closed his eyes and leaned his head back against the bricks behind him. She had just thought the man was too drunk to speak properly. As the man started talking again, Owen relaxed his brain and began translating without thinking.

"There were two guys," Owen said, following the Frenchman only a few words behind, "they came up to me in the club and started buying me drinks. Then they wanted to know about my father's next shipment and got angry."

"What shipment?" the woman asked, turning back to Owen, "Who's your father?"

"Not mine, his," Owen said, jerking a thumb at the Frenchman before asking those very questions to him. Seemingly impressed that Owen could understand him, the man immediately brightened. "My father is Pierre Lambert," Owen went on as he answered, "an attaché with the French member of the UN Security Council, and he was expecting a shipment of drugs at the docks." The man suddenly slapped his hands over his mouth, realizing what he had said.

The officer blinked a few times and then looked back at Owen. "How did you do that?"

"It's my job," Owen said simply, closing his eyes again.

"And what was your name again?" she asked, flipping to a new page in her little notepad.

"Owen Reid, I'm an interpreter for the UN."

"Hi Owen," the officer said kindly, "I'm Officer Caitlin Hunter, and I think you just blew the lid off a smuggling ring."

CHAPTER 2

"Hunter!" a detective barked as he crossed the bullpen of the station. Owen had been loaded, not unkindly, into the back of the cruiser driven by Officer Hunter and her supervising officer and taken to the station half an hour earlier. He had already been subjected to thirty minutes of enduring the supervising officer, a man Hunter called Boone, chewing her out for breaking protocol. Apparently, she was only a few short months out of the academy and seemed, according to Boone, to have a real problem remembering she was a lowly patrol officer. Now came the detective in charge of Eddie's murder, a thought that Owen still could not cope with. This man was not exactly the hard hitting, get to the bottom of it sort of detective you saw on TV. No, this man looked to be one street hotdog away from his fourth heart attack. The smell of cheap cigarettes and even cheaper whiskey seemed to be used exclusively in place of cologne. The thinning, greasy hair clinging to his head seemed to quiver independently from him as he marched to where Officer Hunter stood meekly next to Owen sitting in a sad little plastic chair beside a desk.

"Sir," Hunter began, but the detective held up a pudgy finger to silence her.

"You were on the scene for all of two minutes before you threw protocol out the window and started your own little investigation. Tell me right now why I shouldn't have you manning a tip line for the rest of your career!"

"Maybe because she actually showed up," Owen snapped as Hunter mouthed silently, a blush obscuring her freckles. "I thought detectives were supposed to actually attend a crime scene and, you know, detect things." Hunter gave a little warning shake of her head as the detective rounded on Owen, onion and tobacco laced breath spewing like the world's most disappointing dragon.

"You shut your mouth; I'm still not convinced you weren't in on this. You seem to know an awful lot about this French bastard they dragged in here with you, even speak his language. How I run my investigation is none of ya concern."

Owen knew he should have kept his mouth shut. He knew that retorting would only make things worse. But the thought that he had been involved in his best friend's death? That was too far. "Just because I have mastery over more than just English while you clearly struggle with it does not mean I was involved." He held up the hands that still had traces of Eddie's blood on them. "I felt my friend die tonight, detective, and I would kindly ask that you get off your fat ass for long enough to acknowledge that the killers are still out there."

The detective's doughy face transcended red and shot straight to a blotchy purple as he seemingly swelled with rage. "That's it," he roared, "you and me are going to have a little chat and you can look forward to a night in lockup. Let's go." He grabbed Owen roughly by the elbow and hauled him painfully to his feet. Hunter was still there, frozen with what looked like shock, when the detective barked again. "Hunter, you stay right here, I'm not done with you yet."

Hunter nodded morosely and stood at attention until the detective had left her line of sight. He banged open the door of an interrogation room, complete with the mirrored glass and metal table bolted to the floor. Owen was nearly thrown into one of the chairs before the detective actually cuffed him to the bar set in the middle of the table.

"Now then," he said, his voice still shaking with rage as he closed the door and collapsed into the other chair, "why don't we start with a confession and speed this right along."

"What?" Owen demanded, too incensed to manage anything else.

"Listen, kid, you might have Hunter out there all dewy eyed with your story, but here's the facts. You were found after the bouncer at that swanky club heard shots. He saw you enter the alley with your 'friend' only moments before. You had his blood on your hands and were the only one able to speak to that rambling moron. Looks to me like your friend intruded on your business, you shot him, and felt guilty. Simple as that."

Owen's face went cold again as he stared at this man, reclining lazily in his chair as he picked at his teeth with a fat pinky finger. The number of curses and names that flew through his mind made him dizzy as he reeled from this wild accusation.

"Look," the detective went on, leaning forward as he flicked a piece of his last meal onto the table and wiped his finger on his shirt, "if a confession is too much right now, why don't you start with where you tossed the weapon. That'd go a long way in making this less of a headache for the boys down at the scene."

Owen was on the verge of bursting to his feet and shouting at the man, when the door to the interrogation room opened. The man that stood in the doorway held himself with a grace and power that the detective certainly could not have managed. He was tall, black, with a shaved head and round glasses perched on his nose. The suit he wore was well tailored, but lacked the obvious signs of value like those at the club and he carried a samsonite in both hands in front of himself. "Good evening," the newcomer said in a slow, articulate voice.

"Who the hell are you supposed to be?" the detective asked indignantly, then turned back to Owen. "Don't tell me you lawyered up already."

"I fail to see how that would matter," the man said from the door, "though I could see your worry as it seems you have arrested

Mr. Reid here without advising him of his rights. I was under the impression he was here as a witness."

"So, you are a lawyer then?"

The stranger merely checked his watch, straightened his tie, and cleared his throat before saying, "Detective Alcona, you are about to receive a call that will tell you to leave this room, go back to your desk, and forget ever meeting with Mr. Reid here."

"What the hell are you..." Alcona was cut off by the muffled ringing of his phone in the depths of his pocket. He frowned as he turned red again and yanked the phone out, still staring at the man as he held it to his ear. "What?"

The speed at which Alcona's face turned from red to white was almost alarming. Owen could do nothing but stare between the detective and this newcomer in slight amazement. Alcona muttered a few "Yes sirs" into his phone before dropping it to his side, his hand shaking slightly.

"I don't know who you think you are," Alcona began, but the man cut him off in an instant.

"Detective Raymond Alcona, you grew up in the Bronx where your mother still lives and you visit every weekend, usually to borrow money. I've been in this hellish building you call a precinct for less than five minutes and I already know people hate you. So, to answer your slack-jawed question, I'm the man who will happily break each of your fingers should you fail to follow the orders of the lovely commissioner you just spoke to. The best part, perhaps my favorite part, is that not one of those officers out there will do a damn thing to stop me."

Owen's eyebrows shot up at this statement and his eyes slid to the detective who looked suddenly very small. There was a silent power emanating from the newcomer that made it very clear he could not only get away with the threat but follow through on it easily. Alcona said nothing else as he shuffled forward and the stranger stepped aside to let him pass. He then gestured into the room and Officer Hunter entered ahead of him. What followed startled Owen far more than the fat detective trying to coerce him had. The man closed and locked the door before pulling the cable out of the camera and sitting in the seat vacated by Alcona. Caitlin stood uncomfortably in the corner, equally as frightened of the man as Owen was. The man set the briefcase on the table and glanced up at Owen before tutting softly.

"Officer Hunter, could you please release Mr. Reid here? There's no need for him to be shackled like this." Hunter stepped forward at once and unclipped keys from her belt before undoing the cuffs. "Excellent, thank you, now please have a seat." Hunter grabbed a chair from the side of the room and slid it over to sit beside Owen, sensing that she was not to join this man.

"Who are you?" Owen asked.

"My name is Morris and I'm very keen to talk to the two of you. Now let's start with a name." Morris clasped his hands and leaned forward as though nothing in the world would make him happier than hearing his answer.

"My name is Owen Reid, but you knew that already."

"I did know that, yes."

"So, what is it you want?" Owen asked, looking over at Hunter in confusion but she was staring blankly at him.

"I merely wanted to meet you; you seem interesting."

"You aren't going to accuse me of murder too?" Owen asked sarcastically, his heart still racing from the rage he felt towards Alcona.

"Okay hang on," Hunter interjected, looking a little nervous as Morris fixed her with a hard stare for interrupting, "why aren't you speaking English?" It took Owen a full five seconds to understand that he had been answering Morris in whatever language he happened to be using. They had cycled through Russian, Japanese, and Italian within the last thirty seconds all without him having to think about it.

"I was just seeing if his skill was exaggerated," Morris said in English again as he unlatched his briefcase and opened it, removing a plain looking file folder from it. "Let's see here," he went on, licking a thumb to leaf through the documents in the folder, "Owen Alexander Reid, twenty-one years of age and graduated three months ago from NYU with a four point oh GPA and a degree in both linguistics and political science. You speak seven languages fluently, three more conversationally, and you recently began work as an interpreter for the UN. Hardly the stuff of a hardened killer, wouldn't you agree? Besides, we already know who killed your friend despite what Detective Alcona is ready to think."

Morris reached back into the briefcase and withdrew two full sized photos, placing them on the table with a dull slap. They showed the two men who had taken the Frenchman outside at the club. "We?" Hunter asked and the man smiled.

"Yes, we," he said calmly. "You two stumbled your way into an investigation that has had our friends at the DEA, FBI, and the State Department puzzled for months. In a matter of minutes, you recovered information that two professional hitmen were unable to, all because you happened to speak French. Information, moreover, that is already being used to dismantle an international drug smuggling ring."

"You're telling me a hitman killed my best friend?" Owen asked, trying to decide if Eddie was about to burst into the room to admit this was all some stupid joke.

"I'm afraid so, Mr. Reid," the man said gravely.

"So, where's my file?" Hunter asked, somewhere between morbid fascination and sarcasm. Morris simply smiled again as he withdrew a second folder and Hunter looked startled that there was indeed one in the briefcase.

"Officer Caitlin Amelia Hunter, twenty-two years old and recent addition to the NYPD. Top scores on all tests at the academy including hostage negotiation, stunt driving, and even bomb disposal. Daughter of retired police chief Lucas Hunter and quite honestly, far too intelligent to be a lap dog to ass wipes like Alcona out there."

Hunter frowned at the unsettling amount of detail that had clearly just been a portion of the first page, but asked anyway, "How is it that you know what the Frenchman said? I only wrote it down and even Boone didn't want to hear it until I'd told a detective."

"May I see those notes?" Morris asked calmly, closing Hunter's file. A little nonplussed, Caitlin reached down to where she kept her notepad, but only groped at an empty spot on her belt. Morris reached back into the case and withdrew the notepad.

"Apologies," he said, "but I had to know what he told you. I saw the three of you talking down at the scene and thought it might have been what we were looking for. Turns out I was right. Now, let's discuss how we proceed."

"Not a chance," Hunter said sharply, making Owen look around at her in surprise, "I want to know what's going on here, who you really are, and why you stole from me."

Morris frowned for a moment, pushed his glasses farther up his nose, and laced his fingers together. "Yes, I suppose that's only fair. The man you saved tonight," he nodded to Owen, "is Marc Lambert and as you know, his father is an attaché for the French member of the UN Security Council. It turns out that Pierre Lambert has been using his connections to smuggle drugs from New York to France. DEA agents have long suspected that there was a connection to the French personnel in the UN, but the State Department has been blocking efforts into the investigation. Pierre Lambert has, regardless, been under surveillance for the past six months."

"You said the FBI was involved as well?" Hunter prompted.

"Yes, well you haven't been on the force long enough to know that the FBI likes to poke their noses into anything and everything they can. They really have nothing to do with this but like to think they do. What amazes me, however, is that no one ever thought to go to Lambert's son. Then, you two come along and hear a single sentence that confirmed everything we had suspected. This same insight is what led me to come here and read you in on an operation that is not only top secret, but also threatens our relationship with France."

"And what," Owen said, "you're here to silence us? Maybe even kill us?" The question had been burning within him since the moment Morris had walked in. That's how it always went in the movies. If someone knew too much, they were kept quiet, usually with a bullet.

"No, Mr. Reid, your skill with languages surpasses anyone I've ever met, I'm here to offer you a job."

CHAPTER 3

OWEN LOOKED AT HIMSELF in the mirror of his room. He inhabited a somewhat sparsely furnished room overlooking the forested areas of Camp Peary or, as the CIA referred to it, The Farm. The simple bed, chest of drawers, tiny wardrobe, and mirror were the only things that made this place more than an empty house. Having lived for four years in the NYU dorms, he wasn't about to complain about having an actual kitchen in exchange for fewer possessions. As he looked, he noted the muscles through his chest and arms that had certainly not been there a year before. New, too, were the handful of scars on his back, upper arms, and hands. Of course, if anyone was to ask about the scars, Owen was to simply explain he'd gotten them while free climbing in South Africa. He had just pulled on a pair of sweatpants when Hunter opened his door without knocking. She crossed the room and fell onto his bed, long red hair cascading around her like a starburst. A year of living together, not to mention a litany of exercises designed to make them trust each other, had certainly made them close. It was thanks to this that Hunter apparently felt perfectly at ease striding into his room unannounced wearing nothing but underwear and a tank top.

"If you've come to seduce me," Owen said dryly as he pulled on a cotton t-shirt, "you'll have to do better than that."

"Oh please," Hunter said into his pillow, "I could have you any time I wanted, Hawk."

"Mmhmm," Owen mumbled idly as he forced his hair, which had grown several inches, into a reasonable place. "So then why are you here?"

"I started packing, but I felt weird. I can't believe we're actually going back to New York. It feels like it's been forever and I keep waiting for one last emergency drill or attempted home invasion or whatever."

"I know what you mean," Owen said before sitting by her feet, "I've never been away this long...did you get in touch with your father?" He watched as Hunter seemed to deflate slightly and felt a pang of regret for bringing it up.

"He still thinks I've given up too easily. He thinks I saw one body and ran for a cozy job in rural Virginia."

"Yeah," Owen said softly, "but think of his reaction when you return to the NYPD as a detective. A promotion like that after only a year in uniform should slap him upside the head nicely for you." Hunter chuckled into his pillow then sat up next to him.

"At least I get to go home as myself," she said, "I'm still not calling you Andrew, by the way."

"It'll be my name as of later today," Owen commented, "Andrew Hawkins."

"I'll stick with Hawk, thanks. Suits you better. Besides, I think you've called me Caitlin all of twice since that night." Owen nodded, his face darkening dramatically.

"Hunter," he said after several long moments of silence, "there's something I need to ask you."

"Ok, shoot, but I get to ask something too."

"Are you afraid to go back? Knowing what we're going to be doing and everything we learned that night, are you afraid?"

"Of course I'm afraid," Caitlin said at once, "I was afraid from the day I joined the academy, and I was afraid every night I went out on patrol. Seeing Eddie like that...well it's every cop's nightmare. What scares me more, though, is knowing there would be more bodies out there because I decided to give in to that fear. If I've saved even a single life in my time as a cop and if I save even one with what we'll be doing, then I can handle some fear. I take it you're afraid?"

Owen didn't even bother to lie, he knew that they both knew each other well enough to detect a lie, especially an obvious one. "Yes. I've been thinking a lot about that night lately. No matter how I play it out in my head, even if I'd known everything I do now, I don't think I could have saved Eddie. He died for me and because of me, I can't let that happen again."

"You won't," Hunter said quietly, resting her head on his shoulder, "I'll be keeping an eye on you too. Trust me." She let the silence linger a while Owen steadied his breathing which he hadn't noticed grow faster. "My turn," she said finally, and Owen raised his eyebrows at her.

"I do believe you asked me if I was afraid, question used, answer given." He stood from the bed quick enough that Hunter fell over in surprise, catching herself on an elbow.

"No fair," she whined, springing to her feet and pursuing him out to the kitchen, "reciprocating the same question you asked me is not me asking my question."

"Fine," Owen said, stopping and whirling around to poke her forehead, "one question."

"You promise to answer honestly?"

"Yes," Owen replied, smirking, "what a waste of a question." He then turned on his heel and marched on. The footsteps that foreshadowed the attack were nearly silent and he didn't react fast enough. Owen had only just turned around when Hunter was on him, her legs latched around his waist, and she delivered slap after slap to the top of his head.

"That's not my question and you know it!" The all-out assault of slaps was halted suddenly as Owen dug his fingers into Caitlin's sides and she froze. Turns out that no amount of CIA training can take away being ticklish. "Don't you dare," she said before performing a neat little backflip off his chest, springing to her feet at once.

"Fine," Owen said, pouring them both coffee as though nothing had just happened, "one more question that I really will answer honestly."

Hunter narrowed her eyes at him, trying to sense the loophole. When she could detect no such trap, she slid into one of the chairs at the little kitchen table while Owen added cream and sugar to her coffee.

"You could have walked away that night. Signed Morris' NDA and gone back to your life. Why didn't you? Why agree to all of this?"

"I think I can answer that with a question of my own. What if I'd never gone outside? Marc Lambert would have died like he was supposed to, the hitmen might've stolen the drugs like they wanted to, and the UN would continue to be used for a greedy man's petty desires. I was there for three months and I overheard things that made my skin crawl. Yes, they play nice with each other in the sandbox, but when it comes down to it they are all prepared to do whatever they need to do for themselves. I was never going to make a difference as a translator. But maybe I can make a difference now. I owe Eddie that much for what he gave up."

Hunter was frozen with her mug halfway to her lips, staring at Owen who sipped his own coffee casually. She had been asking the same question for a year and he'd only ever given vague answers or made jokes about hot cop partners. This, though, was so similar to her own reasons. The desire to join the NYPD had been instilled in her by her father. That drive to help others. But she never would have guessed Owen felt the same way. He'd been such a nerdy, scrawny guy when they'd met that she never would have believed he had what it took. But here he was. No more glasses, his frame filled out, and he stood with such purpose now.

"Plus, I got to live with a hot cop," he added, making Hunter throw a coaster at him, though she laughed. This was just a part of who he was. Why talk about feelings when you can joke about them.

"We're really going back," Hunter said eventually.

"Yep. Ready to be a detective?"

"I was ready when I was twelve, they just weren't ready for me." Owen laughed and drank more of his coffee, looking around the house with a sort of nostalgia. Would he miss this place one day? No, he thought, if it hadn't been for Hunter, he would have quit months ago. Her sleepy face in the morning and hauling each other out of the mud had been an inexpressible comfort. Owen knew that she didn't have to come with him, not really. She could have promised not to tell anyone too, gone back to being a regular cop, but she seemed to feel responsible for him now.

"Why are you staring at me?" Hunter asked, grimacing over her steaming mug, waiting for the sarcastic jab or joke.

"I was just thinking how much I appreciate you," Owen said simply. The blush that crept up Hunter's face turned her freckles invisible as the skin slowly tried to resemble the bushy hair.

"Shut up," she mumbled but Owen smiled. Hunter was awful at taking compliments, probably thanks to a father who never thought her good enough. Hunter got up from her chair, still glaring at Owen and passed through the sitting room to her own bedroom. They were to leave in an hour and everything Owen knew about the woman suggested that she hadn't even opened her bag to pack yet. About a minute later, Owen was downing the last dregs of his coffee when a creak outside the front door made him freeze. He counted to three, waiting for the pressure on the deck board to shift. If it did, then whoever was there was not trying to be quiet. If it didn't, then someone was waiting to hear if he reacted. React he did. The table flipped over as he kicked it, sending the mug flying like a grenade. The kitchen had a direct line of sight down the short hallway to the front door, so he crouched behind the overturned table and drew the gun secured to the bottom. He settled into position; his arms braced on the table with the gun as he poked his head up to watch. The mug hit the ground and shattered into a hundred splinters of porcelain. As though this was a secret signal, the door burst open and Owen fired a shot at the shadowy figure standing there, backlit by the rising sun.

Apparently anticipating the shot, a black samsonite briefcase shot up to intercept what would have been a bullet to the head. Paint splattered across the leather, bright green marking the black. Morris stepped into the house and examined the damage to his briefcase.

"Not bad," he admitted, "that would have killed me for sure. You still have a hard time aiming for the centre of mass I see."

"Your organs matter a whole lot less when your brains are sprayed across the lawn," Owen replied, dropping his arms to his sides as he stood. Morris shrugged as though he had a point and pulled a handkerchief from his pocket to wipe a speck of paint from his hand. Two more shots echoed from Hunter's room and she emerged in jeans and a leather jacket over her tank top followed by a disgruntled looking man with two paint splotches on his nipples. Owen snorted and held out a fist which Hunter bumped with her own, grinning, and clearly pleased with herself.

"I'm certainly not sorry to see you two leaving," the man with the painted nipples said gruffly. He had a much more militaristic look than Morris. Complete with crew cut gray hair, tan shirt and cargo pants, and tightly laced boots.

"Aww come on, Sarge," Owen said teasingly, "won't you miss us even a little?"

"You realize that that's the fifth time she's shot me like this?" the Sergeant asked sarcastically, but a slight grin was spreading across his face. "You two have certainly been interesting to train. Keep an eye on each other and try not to die out there." To those who didn't know Sergeant Major Tom Bakowski this may have seemed like a typical thing to say. To Owen and Caitlin, however, it was the closest he ever got to saying he liked someone. The man had given up several promotions to stay in the action as long as he could and when his military retirement had come around, he insisted on maintaining his rank for his new training role. Something about being a sergeant for too long to give it up now.

Owen extended a hand and Bakowski shook it with a bone crushing grip. Hunter had thrown her arms around the man before he could stop her so imparted an awkward, one-armed hug in return.

With a brief nod, which was all the real goodbye they were going to get, he left the house through the still open door.

"I'm afraid this is goodbye for me as well," Morris said without a trace of regret, "I have my own assignment to get back to. Good luck to you both."

"Thank you, sir, especially for smoothing things over with the NYPD," Hunter said gratefully.

Morris waved a hand idly through the air, "Please, pushing around Commissioner Roberts is a unique pleasure." They all shook hands and Morris made his way over to the door again before pausing on the threshold.

"Sir?" Owen asked.

"I nearly forgot," Morris said, reaching a hand into the pocket of his charcoal suit and retrieving something, "a little reminder, Mr. Hawkins, of the life you lost."

Owen frowned slightly but caught the small object instinctively as Morris threw it. Sitting in the palm of his hand was a crumpled bullet. It only took a moment to realize what it was, after all he'd seen it in Eddie's case file a dozen times. Silently, Owen slipped the bullet into his pocket and nodded to Morris in thanks, but the man was already gone.

CHAPTER 4

THE SMALL PRIVATE JET took off smoothly from the Camp Peary landing strip and soon they were well on their way. Hunter lounged in one of the spacious seats across from Owen, her feet up and her nose buried in one of the paperback books she always had. Owen, meanwhile, kept playing with the gold cufflinks he wore with the crisp black shirt beneath a slate gray silk vest. His black cashmere coat had been thrown casually over another seat. Everything, right down to the tailored pants and far too shiny shoes, undoubtedly cost more than his entire wardrobe put together. No more ratty hoodies and bleach-stained jeans. From that moment on he was to only be seen in the clothes selected for him.

"Run it for me again," Hunter said, turning a page of her book.

Owen cleared his throat and sat forward a bit to recite the now deeply memorized details. "My name is Andrew Hawkins. Parents were Melissa and Richard Hawkins. Mother's maiden name was Harvey. I grew up with private tutors in our house upstate or in Paris depending on the season until I was thirteen and was shipped off to boarding school. I attended Oxford, though never finished as I'm taking a break following the tragic death of my parents."

"How'd they die?" Hunter asked with disinterest, she had heard it so many times already.

"Helicopter crashed while they were skiing in Switzerland."

"Oh, so you do know it then," Hunter said as though she was unconvinced.

"Of course I know it," Owen retorted indignantly.

"Then stop fidgeting," she snapped, glancing at him sternly over her book, "you're freaking me out. All you have to do is get in the car and go home to get ready for tonight."

"I don't like flying," Owen mumbled, sitting back in his seat again.

"Yeah, well Hawk does, he's been flying in these things for as long as he's been alive. Get it together." Owen grimaced at her. It wasn't like he was about to get on a plane with a bunch of other people who would question him about it, so why did it matter? A part of him suspected that she simply liked being able to boss him around. The second that they had left The Farm she had officially become his handler and backup. Though, they didn't have long before they were to be separated for the first time in a year, so Owen supposed she had to get her bossing in now. The plane shuddered slightly and Owen closed his eyes for a moment before pulling out the brand new phone he'd been given.

It had a handful of numbers programmed into it already, including the car and concierge services he was supposed to use. It may have been a giveaway to have a number for Hunter in the phone so they'd worked out a little hack for him. As they did not want him out of touch with her if he needed her, the emergency call function of the phone called her instead of 911. Owen skimmed through the photos on the phone. All of them were of him in a dozen locations he had never been in his life. He had long since stopped questioning the capabilities of the folks at The Farm. The intercom of the plane crackled for a moment and their pilot informed them that they were ready to descend into New Jersey. Owen instinctively smoothed his pristine vest and took a deep breath.

"Hey," Hunter said, closing her book and leaning towards him, "you got this, trust me. I just hope you'll be able to survive without me."

Owen snorted and adjusted the purple tie beneath his vest. "Yeah, what will I ever do when I'm not dragging you out of your bed in the morning?"

"Not every morning," Hunter snapped, "like today, I was up before you."

"Only because you never went to sleep," Owen countered at once.

"How the hell would you know that?"

"You never sleep before the big days. Not before the advanced marksman tests, or before the survival training, or before..."

"Alright," Hunter said, throwing up her hands.

"Like it or not, I know you probably better than anyone now. I know that today you're going to drive into the city, report to your new captain, then, after a long day of settling in, you're going to go and get the one thing you've been missing more than your job or your family or your home. You're going to head to Chinatown for steam rice rolls from Joe's, sweet mini cakes from Ling's, then stop at the bakery on your way home for hot chocolate with that stupid marshmallow flower in it. Then, and only then, will you head back to your apartment and enjoy the meal you've dreamed about for a year."

Hunter stared at him for a moment before calmly setting her book down and clasping her hands together as though praying for patience. "*Stupid* marshmallow flower?" she snapped. "That flower holds a chocolate truffle which melts into the hot chocolate, making it the single greatest thing in the world. How do you even know that?"

"Because you lament about it every time we ate in the commissary, or in the field, or at the house, or basically any time food was presented to you in any form."

"You're a dick," Hunter mumbled.

"Am I wrong?"

Hunter frowned at him for a minute, evidently trying to find something witty to say, then finally settled on bursting out, "It's really good, ok?" Owen smiled at her and she continued to pout until they had touched down in Teterboro. By all accounts it was a perfect landing, only a slight bump as wheels hit tarmac. In spite of this, Owen was still gripping the arms of his seat with indecent force, leaving impressions of his fingers in the soft leather. The jet taxied away from the main terminals of the airport towards a row of hangars and a much smaller building for private plane arrivals and departures. Two cars were waiting for them in front of one of the hangars. One a sleek town car that would deliver Owen to his new home, the other an expertly restored 1970 Chevelle painted cobalt blue.

"You had to go muscle car, huh?" Owen asked, peering out the window as they drew level with the vehicles.

"Wouldn't you?" Hunter replied with a grin, "Besides, it feels more like a detective's car."

"Whatever you say," Owen said, shaking his head as he pulled on the overcoat. Autumn was descending early on the city, cutting through the gray and brown with splashes of red and yellow. The door of the jet popped open and unfolded into a set of steps.

"You ready?" Hunter asked, slinging a canvas bag over her shoulder.

"Yeah, I'm ready," Owen said, retrieving his own leather carryon from the seat next to him and stepping towards the door. Hunter left first, heading for the Chevelle without a backwards glance. Owen paused on the threshold of the plane, staring at the ground in front of him. Then there was the roar of an engine and Hunter floored it away from the plane. Owen thought he heard a whoop of laughter come from an open window over the engine and he smiled. Feeling the bullet in his pocket, he stepped off the plane and the driver of the town car hurried forward to take his bag. In that instant, between plane and ground, Owen Reid died and Andrew Hawkins was born.

CHAPTER 5

"HOW LONG HAVE YOU been away, Mr. Hawkins?" asked the man driving the town car. Without a single question at the airport, the man had loaded Andrew's bag into the trunk of the black car and opened the door for him to slide in. The interior was well maintained and spotless, not even smelling of the cleaning agents they used. There was also a small stock of alcohol and other drinks complete with crystal glasses. The driver himself was perhaps mid-thirties, clean cut, and with a slight Indian accent.

"It's been a long time," Andrew replied as they pulled out of the small tunnel that led to the lower deck of the George Washington Bridge. He gazed out upon the city he had left as a different person a year earlier. He had left as his world was falling apart, but the city looked just as it always had. It seemed wrong that he had lost so much and yet the world was ultimately unchanged by it. Andrew took a deep breath and poured himself a glass of scotch. If there was any sort of judgment in the driver's eyes, after all it was only 10:30, Andrew couldn't spot it. Then again, the rich seemed to drink whenever they wanted, so who cared?

"Well, my name's Ram and I'll be at your disposal whenever you need. I can pick you up within half an hour of a call, any time at all, or book a time for a planned trip. That lawyer of yours set up an account with the service for you."

"Appreciate it," Andrew said. There was no lawyer, not really. Some agent had set up all his accommodations in the weeks leading up to Andrew's arrival. This included the condo they were headed to now. The rest of the ride passed in silence as the driver slid smoothly between traffic, following the Hudson until they entered Tribeca. When Ram slowed to a stop in front of one of the buildings, Andrew had to try hard not to gape up at it. It wasn't that it was particularly tall, especially for New York, but the place just oozed money. The facade of white stone and glass looked brand new and loomed with a certain elegance that older buildings lacked. Ram quickly hopped out of the car and rounded it to open Andrew's door.

"There you are, Mr. Hawkins, I'll just get your bag for you. Will there be anything else?"

"No, thank you," Andrew said. As Ram handed over the bag, Andrew slipped a bill from his pocket and passed it over to the driver.

"Thank you very much, sir," Ram said happily, pocketing the hundred dollars, "do let me know if you have need of me."

"Will do," Andrew replied, hefting his bag and walking up to the entry of the building. A man in a pristine uniform opened one of the glass doors with a swishing sound and waved Andrew inside before tipping his hat. With a nod of thanks, Andrew passed into the lobby of black marble and glass decorations. An intricate stained-glass sculpture hung from the high ceiling, sending motes of coloured light dancing across the floor. His footsteps echoed off the walls as he made his way towards the small desk where two security guards in suits sat. As he got closer, one of the guards stood and Andrew clocked the Sig Sauer half concealed by his jacket.

"Can we help you, sir?" the guard asked.

"I'm supposed to be meeting a Miss Evie Collingwood," Andrew said. No sooner had the sentence left his mouth than a door, indistinguishable from the wall behind the desk, opened and a woman emerged in a smart skirt and blouse.

"I suppose that makes you Mr. Andrew Hawkins?" she asked, extending a hand as she rounded the desk.

"I suppose so," Andrew said with a small smile.

"I'm very pleased to meet you," she said sincerely, guiding him away from the desk with a hand on his shoulder. "I think you'll find this building very much to your liking. Completed four years ago, we pride ourselves on having only the most discerning tenants." They arrived at a bank of four elevators and Evie pressed the button to call one. "Of course, you have access to all our world class facilities including an Olympic sized swimming pool, billiards room, café, and even a private squash court. All located on the seventh floor for your leisure. Our security is all ex-military and is on duty twenty-four seven so rest assured you'll be safe at all hours."

"Very reassuring," Andrew said idly, and Evie beamed at him as though he had been giving the most enthusiastic review. The silver doors of the elevator opened and the pair stepped inside, Evie pressing the number eleven. He looked at this woman more closely and decided that she was clearly who they sent to make the hard sell. Her perfume was not overdone though very noticeable, and the blouse was perhaps a little more low cut than was professional. Coupled with her long, dark hair and subtle makeup, it gave the impression of a promiscuous secretary. She certainly looked at him like she was ready to do whatever it took to make a sale.

"I take it everything is taken care of financially?" Andrew asked, if only to stop her staring so avidly.

"Oh yes," she said at once, her face falling slightly, "your attorney, Mr. Graves, explained your situation and we're so pleased you've chosen to come live here in these troubled times. Oh no need to worry," she added at Andrew's raised eyebrow, "I'm very discreet. Your secrets are safe with me." Andrew barely had time to decide if this meant something about losing his parents or if she was offering sex when the doors slid open with a ding. Evie led him down the hall, brightly lit with large windows at either end, to a door marked 1101.

There were three other units on this floor and each was clearly very large given the space between the doors. Evie held out a gold keychain that held a pair of keys and nodded encouragingly towards the door. Andrew took the keys, inserted one into the lock, and opened the door to his new home. Some sort of automated system chimed in welcome and the blinds covering twelve-foot windows all rose to reveal a panoramic view of the river beyond. Past the entryway was a very large open floor plan housing a sitting room, kitchen, and dining room. Andrew wandered in slowly, taking in the details. The kitchen was somewhere between something from the future and the set of a cooking show. Every appliance imaginable was laid out across gleaming countertops and hanging above the kitchen island with built in gas range was a full twenty piece set of copper pots and pans. The marble tiling transitioned into rich hardwood leading into the sitting room which was laid out with comfortable seating, heavily ladened bookshelves, and a fireplace in one wall whose mantle held an impressive dry bar. The dining room area, which was as large as the kitchen, held a twelve seat mahogany table with cushy leather chairs. The entire house at The Farm could have fit inside this one massive room. Art pieces, both paintings and sculptures, were dotting the walls and pedestals. Just enough to be tasteful rather than tacky. Andrew thought he recognized a Monet that he suspected was real.

"There are two bedrooms through there," Evie said as she pointed towards a pair of doors on one wall, "and a cinema room over there," she pointed to a sliding door that led beyond the dining room. "Finally, the master bedroom is up those stairs there," she pointed to a staircase set almost invisibly into the wall by the other bedrooms. "The shades, lights, and most of the appliances can be programmed and scheduled using your phone. You'll find instructions on the counter there. Your furniture was all moved in for you when your attorney finished the paperwork so you should feel right at home. Is there anything else I can do for you?"

"No," Andrew said in a slight daze, dropping his bag and stepping forward slowly, "thank you, Miss Collingwood."

"Evie is fine, Mr. Hawkins," she said with a radiant smile.

"Call me Hawk," Andrew said without thinking. Hunter had had a point; the new name was still odd to him and the nickname felt more natural.

"Well, Hawk," Evie said, stepping forward and slipping a business card into his hand, "give me a call whenever you need. I live here myself so day or night, I'll be here with bells on." She winked at him and strode back to the door, closing it softly behind her. Andrew stared at the door for a minute, realizing as he did that she had actually been flirting with him. Maybe it was part of her job, but really, he just hadn't been expecting it. They had had him grow his hair over the year and given him contacts to replace his glasses, but deep down he still felt like the nerdy guy he'd always been.

How was it that they could teach him so much about getting people to like him but fail to explain what being flirted with was like? Thankfully he did not have to dwell on this for long. The lavish condo beckoned, and he made his way slowly through each room, seeing what was now his, or at least being loaned to him. One of the spare bedrooms had been turned into what looked like an office with a top-of-the-line gaming setup. He knew, of course, that the regular looking casing on the products hid the undoubtedly drastic upgrades that came with a seemingly unlimited budget.

The master bedroom at the top of the stairs held a massive California king sized bed and a huge walk-in closet filled with more of the tailored clothes like those he wore now. The bedroom had a similar window setup whose shades opened as he entered the room, revealing the same dazzling panorama as below. Exhaling slowly, Andrew fell onto the bed, still reeling slightly. It was hard to believe there were people who actually lived like this. A painting, Van Gogh's Apricot Trees in Blossom, hung near the bed and Andrew pulled on it on a hunch. Sure enough, the painting swung open to reveal a wall mounted safe with a glowing blue display. He punched in the code, a combination of his deceased parents' birthdays, and a soft thunk sounded. Inside were several stacks of cash, a couple of passports, and a loaded pistol with a suppressor. There would be more of these caches throughout the condo, the others mostly containing additional weaponry in the event of an attack.

Andrew walked through the condo for an hour, learning it and taking it in and could have stayed for hours more. Or, for that matter, planted himself in front of the 120-inch screen in the theater room. Unfortunately, if he did not hurry, he would be late for afternoon cocktails before dinner. As anticipated, he discovered a set of keys in a little dish by the door, scooped them up, and left the condo. The elevator took him quickly down to the lobby where he found his way out the back to the private parking lot nestled between his building and the next. A third guard, also armed, stood at the arched porte-cochere to check the vehicles coming in. Andrew clicked the remote on the keys and a beeping chime indicated the car he'd been given. Sitting in a spot marked with his name was a dark red, top of the line BMW M4. Grinning to himself, Andrew climbed into the car and started the engine which purred smoothly to life. No dramatic roar like Hunter's Chevelle, just quiet power. He nodded to the guard who opened the gate and Andrew pulled out of the lot to join the flow of traffic towards the Brooklyn Bridge.

CHAPTER 6

ANDREW COULDN'T HELP HIMSELF as he drove deeper into the Hamptons. As the traffic from the city slowly faded, the other cars splitting off to their destinations, he found the highway nearly deserted. His speed crept up until finally he was screaming along at two hundred miles an hour. The car had definitely been modified and Andrew was not sorry about it. His somewhat suicidal run down the Sunrise Highway meant that he ended up pulling into the beach house's driveway right on time.

The driveway led through a copse of trees that provided privacy to the expansive property. The crown jewel of the place was the three storied Victorian inspired beach house, all white and light gray. A handful of cars were already parked at the end of the driveway, each of them a luxury model built for both comfort and style. Andrew pulled up next to a beautiful Rolls-Royce and got out. A fresh breeze tugged at the leaves too stubborn to fall and tousled Andrew's hair as he climbed the steps.

He pressed the button beside the door and a set of regal sounding bells chimed inside. A rippling figure appeared on the other side of the frosted glass, drawing closer. The door opened to reveal a woman in her late fifties in a fairly spectacular dress.

"Good afternoon," she said, somehow showing off all her perfect teeth as she smiled, "you must be Andrew."

"Yes ma'am," Andrew replied with a smile.

"Christ, boy," she exclaimed, "I already feel old enough without you calling me ma'am. Call me Margaret. George has told me all about you, please, come in."

"Thank you, though I feel somewhat underdressed," he added as he stepped in past her.

"Nonsense," Margaret said with a little twirl, "I just like reminding George of how much I make him spend on me, especially when Ms. Pedroso comes around for a visit. You'll see," she added in response to Andrew's questioning look before leading him deeper into the house. The whole place was painted with light tones of gray and blue, complimenting the wood of the floors. Margaret led Andrew into an airy sitting room where half a dozen people sat with cocktails. A man in a white shirt and bowtie stood at the side of the room behind a small bar.

"George, darling," Margaret said as she approached one of the men in a salmon blazer and tan pants. Even as he was laughing at something, Andrew thought this man had a cold, almost dead look in his eyes. When he looked around at his wife and Andrew entering the room, the eyes seemed to analyze every inch of him in half a second. He expected no less from the former director of the CIA.

"Well, if it isn't little Andy Hawkins," George said jovially as he got, somewhat laboriously, to his feet, retrieving a cane that had been leaning against his chair. "Come on in, son, have a drink and we'll introduce everyone."

"A Negroni, please," Andrew said to the bartender before shaking hands with George. "It's good to see you, Mr. Randal."

"And you, my boy," George said before clamping an arm around Andrew's shoulder and wheeling him around to face the others in the room. "Everyone," he said, gesturing with his martini, "this is Andrew Hawkins. I met his family years back in Paris and had more than a few adventures after sampling the local wine selections." His suggestive tone got him a few snickers from around the room.

"Dean Warpole," a short black man said as he got to his feet and held out a hand. He had a slight southern accent that somewhat explained the bolo tie he wore with his suit. Warpole enclosed Andrew's hand in his own massive one and shook vigorously. "And this is my wife, Violet," he added, gesturing to a woman in a pale blue dress sipping a mojito, "we own about seventy restaurants this side of the Rockies."

"A pleasure to meet you," Andrew said, nodding politely to Violet who was examining him critically over her glass.

"These two," George said, indicating a pair of handsome men in their forties standing close together by the bar, "are the Samson-Wallers, Patrick and Harold." The men both smiled in a knowing sort of way at Andrew before stepping forward to shake hands. "They each come from money dating back to the civil war."

"Suffice to say our families were not thrilled when we got together," Patrick said, "but when everyone else dies and you inherit the money, it doesn't seem to bother anyone anymore." Harold slapped Patrick playfully on the arm.

"Come now, Patty, you make it sound like we murdered them for the money." Andrew smiled ingratiatingly, deciding it was better not to comment.

"And finally," George said, leaning heavily on his cane as he nodded to a woman who was entering the room. She was tall, with black hair and caramel colored skin that made Andrew suspect Brazilian. Her figure was certainly that of a model who had simply aged out of the profession the moment a single wrinkle appeared.

"Marcia Pedroso," the woman said with a thick accent, skipping a handshake and opting for a tight hug that was just shy of mounting him. Andrew looked at Margaret who had an 'I-told-you-so' sort of expression on her face. "It is always good to meet new blood," she said as she broke away from him, sizing him up, "the people around here like their routines."

Andrew had misjudged her. The accent was definitely leaning towards Spanish rather than Portuguese. So when Andrew replied, *"I'm delighted to entertain,"* with a little smile, it was in perfect

Spanish. His guess proved fruitful as Marcia's face split into a radiant grin.

"You speak impressive Spanish," Marcia said, *"where did you learn it?"*

"My nanny for many years was a delightful woman from Spain," Andrew explained, *"whenever we visited her home she insisted I spoke only Spanish."*

"How charming," Marcia said, switching back to English smoothly, "where have you been hiding all this time?" Everyone else in the room had been keenly listening to the exchange, apparently fascinated by Andrew. Though, as Marcia had said, perhaps it was simply that he was new blood for a community that tended to be very close.

"I attended Oxford for a time," Andrew explained, taking his drink from the bartender, "but I've decided to return home after my parents' deaths. Keep an eye on things, so to speak." Andrew could tell that this freshest gossip would soon make its steady way around everyone these people knew. Exactly as it had been planned. Filter a story through enough people and it turns from rumor to fact more effectively than one person telling the same story. They all adopted looks of deep sympathy and Marcia grabbed Andrew's free hand.

"Well, you are among friends here, we all look out for one another. I think you will fit in wonderfully with the children, don't you think?" she added, looking around the room. They all nodded enthusiastically.

"I believe they're all upstairs," Margaret said, making to get to her feet again, "why don't I show you?"

"I'll take him," George said, holding up a hand to stop his wife, "my leg could do with a stretch anyway. You enjoy yourself, darling." Margaret beamed at him and he waved for Andrew to follow him from the room. They climbed the stairs that led up from the foyer and Andrew noticed that George's limp was far less pronounced away from the guests. A CIA man through and through, never letting the full truth slip out.

"In here a minute," George grunted, his welcoming tone evaporating as well. He took Andrew by the elbow and steered him into a lavish, wood paneled office overlooking the water. After closing the door and locking it, George turned on his heel to look at Andrew again. "You clean up nice," he said, "wasn't sure about all this when they showed me your picture, but this isn't half bad."

"Thank you, sir," Andrew replied curtly.

"Now listen up," George said, lowering his tone, "all I know is that they've spent a lot of money getting you here and that you've got some special assignment. I did what they asked. Those kids up there have grown up together, they know each other extremely well and moreover they know every other rich brat in the state. All I'm giving you is a chance to weasel your way in, nothing more. Don't you dare come crying to me if you haven't got the balls to see something through. I retired for a reason."

"Understood," Andrew said at once. Away from company, George spoke a lot like the drill sergeants back at The Farm. "Is there anything I should know before heading up?"

"You expect me to do your job for you?" George demanded.

"No sir," Andrew replied, suppressing a slight grin, "but I figure a former company man like yourself has already done a lot of it anyway. Why swim when someone's got a boat?"

George's eyebrows shot up as he stared at Andrew for a moment, then he grinned. "I knew a man who used to say that an awful lot. What a shit saying. How is old Bakowski these days?"

"Still spewing that kind of shit to everyone who passes under his command," Andrew said, relaxing a bit, "and he sends his regards. Oh, and a reminder that you owe him a drink."

"Over my dead body," George mumbled.

"He also said if you said that, I had full permission to make it happen." George burst out laughing and smacked Andrew on the shoulder jovially.

"Alright, kid, listen up then. Those brats have had silver spoons up their asses from the day they were born, including my own. They're all in their twenties and think they're invincible because they're rich. Marcia's kid, Diego, is also the son of Colombia's President, Luis Juarez. Real friendly with the Colombian representative to the UN. The Warpole brat is a typical party kid. If there is a building with loud music, booze, and drugs, he's been there. Patrick and Harold adopted a baby, a little girl they named Eliza. She has a real talent for sleeping her way through the city, but it does mean she's got an awful lot of people who would do her a favor at a moment's notice."

"And what about your daughter, sir?" Andrew asked when George fell silent.

"My daughter is a good girl," George growled, the protective father beating out the agent for a moment. Then he sighed and added, "She has a weakness for art. Spends all her allowance on private tours of museums, fundraisers for inner city art programs, and buying pieces she likes. Drop an opinion of some famous painting and she's putty in your hands. For business purposes only," George snapped, putting a finger in Andrew's face who raised his hands in mock surrender.

"Wouldn't dream of anything else, sir. Thank you for doing this. If you need anything, please feel free to reach out to Detective Caitlin Hunter at the 5th precinct." George nodded simply, understanding the role Hunter played in this.

"Head up the stairs, double doors on the landing. You'll find them there." Andrew thanked him again and slipped out of the office, heading for the second flight of stairs that would take him to the top floor. Elegantly carved doors stood waiting for him at the top of the house, muffling the voices and laughter inside. Andrew took a breath to steady himself, then pushed open the door to start the first step in the operation. Or as Morris had called it, 'meet the brats.'

CHAPTER 7

THE DOOR SWUNG OPEN to reveal four people strewn about lazily around a billiards table. They all looked up as the door opened and there was a moment where everyone simply took each other in. One of them, a man with caramel coloured skin and features he no doubt inherited from his mother, stood bent over the table, having just made a shot. He wore simple black pants and a blue shirt with several buttons undone. Standing behind him, leaning against the wall with a pool cue, was a man in a slightly crumpled maroon suit and sunglasses who looked to be nursing a slight hangover. Two women sat on the leather sofa behind the billiards table. One was dressed in a smart pantsuit that accentuated her hourglass figure and was playing idly with her curly brown hair. The other was the only one who had not spared Andrew more than a glance and had instead returned to applying lipstick in a small compact. The short red dress and four-inch heels made her look a little like a stripper, though the kind that clearly had a selective clientele.

"Can I help you?" the woman in the pantsuit asked, getting to her feet and rounding the pool table.

"My name's Andrew Hawkins, your father invited me," Andrew said to her, for this simply had to be George's daughter.

"Oh right," she said, looking him up and down again, "he mentioned someone else was coming. How do you even know him?"

She sounded somewhat defensive and perhaps a little more hostile than someone welcoming a guest might have usually been. Andrew had been warned that this was the attitude amongst this crowd. They were protective of their friends and were always on the lookout for people who might be trying to weasel their way closer to their money.

"I don't, at least not well. I met him when I was a kid, years ago. He knew my parents better though." The two boys looked a little more interested now having assessed that Andrew did in fact come from money.

"Oh, are they here as well?" George's daughter asked.

"No, they're dead," Andrew said in a forced harshness that he knew would only make it look like he was faking it to cover his true emotions. Nothing better than creating a mystery and sympathy at the same time. "I just moved back to New York and when your father heard what happened, he invited me out here to meet some new folks."

"How did they die?" asked the girl who looked like a stripper, though her tone was almost sarcastic.

"Come on, Liza," said the man on the wall, pushing himself forward towards Andrew, "you don't ask shit like that until you've at least introduced yourself. Dirk Warpole," he added, extending a dark hand towards Andrew who shook it.

"Caralynne Randal," said the girl in the pantsuit, shaking hands next and looking slightly embarrassed.

"Diego Pedroso," the model-looking man said as he swept a hand through his dark hair, "and that little ray of sunshine is Eliza Samson-Waller." Eliza flipped Diego the bird before bestowing Andrew with a radiant smile that likely could have blinded a satellite.

"Well," Dirk said, "we know you, you know us, you've got a drink, what more is there? You play pool?"

"Once or twice," Andrew said, "I'm shit at it though."

"Excellent," Dirk said, throwing an arm around Andrew's shoulders, "we'll give you a few games to settle into it before the real fun starts." The four of them started taking it in turns to play a game with Andrew and he made sure to lose each one. Caralynne somewhat surprised him when she slipped off her jacket, racked the balls, and swept the table without hardly a chance for him to respond. All the while they poked him with questions. When did you get back? Where were you before? Where are you living in the city? What kind of car does he drive? And so on. As Eliza sank the 8-ball, her cleavage threatening to spill out of the dress with every movement, there was only one question left hanging.

"So where did your family get its money?" Diego asked in his lightly accented English.

"My father was a trader for a long time. Made some good buys and banked his money. Then when Bitcoin came around he thought it had potential. When it crashed, he thought there was no harm in hanging onto it and buying up what he could. When it started doing really well again a few years back, we went from doing well for ourselves to having more money than we knew what to do with."

A couple of them looked impressed by this. Indeed, if they ever somehow got a look at Andrew's financials, they would find a practically limitless supply of wealth.

"Then you won't mind if we make things a bit more interesting," Dirk said, smirking from his spot on the wall as he sipped a glass of champagne.

"What's life unless we add a little spice?" Andrew replied, "How much are we talking?"

"Not money," Eliza said from the sofa where she had dropped next to Caralynne, "we've all got money, who needs more? No, we bet things. Something the other person wants or would like. Diego and Dirk have been trading a car back and forth for a year."

"So, what do you say?" Diego asked, "You ready to lose some shit?"

"Nah," Andrew said, chalking his cue, "but I'll be happy to take yours."

"Awfully cocky there Hawkins, especially as you've not won a single game," Caralynne put in over the rim of her red wine. Andrew shrugged and the four friends grinned at each other. Andrew got the impression that this was a regular event with new people they met. Had to have their fun somehow, Andrew supposed. Diego snatched the pool cue off the end of the table and started racking the balls.

"I get first crack," he said, "because I'm leaving with that M4 I happened to notice you roll up in."

"Oh, I see how it is," Andrew said, "I get to sit here and get robbed of five things you'd all like as what? Initiation into your gang?"

"Yep," Dirk said with a sly grin, "now shut up and take it." Andrew rolled his eyes and turned back to Diego.

"So, what are you putting up for this?"

"*If* you win," Diego said mockingly, "you can have my car, that oh-so-sexy '65 Corvette sitting down there."

"Alright, deal," Andrew said, and Diego rolled the cue ball down the length of the table. Andrew caught it and positioned it before leaning low over the table. The cue slid smoothly as he wound up. Diego exchanged smug looks with Eliza and Dirk, but Andrew noticed that Caralynne was watching him carefully. She, unlike the others, had clocked that Andrew was no longer acting clumsy like he had been so far. The rack had barely lifted off the balls when Andrew fired off his first shot, making Diego jump slightly as the balls exploded in front of him. No fewer than three solids fell into pockets with dull thuds. Diego looked between the table and Andrew several times, his mouth working without any sound coming out.

Andrew shrugged as he moved to take his next shot, "Just lucky I guess." The game was over in a matter of minutes, Andrew forcing himself not to win outright. Diego, wanting to show he was better, sank ball after ball, but choked on the last, giving Andrew a window to win. Which he did, very quickly. With an air of a father having to give up his own child, Diego passed over the keys to his Corvette and fell onto the sofa.

"Who's next then?" Andrew asked, racking the balls again. Dirk got to his feet now, patting Diego on the shoulder.

"So, you were playing us?"

"Of course, how else was I supposed to make it interesting for me?"

"Well, you've tipped your hand now. What have you got? I enjoy good bottles."

"How about a 60-year McCallan? Unopened, of course."

Dirk raised his eyebrows and said, "That would certainly be a prize to behold. I'll put up a bottle of Shackleton then, straight from the ice." Andrew nodded and they were off. Despite his warning that Andrew had tipped his hand, Dirk went down in only ten minutes. He, at one point, had looked rather smug as he cut off Andrew's only shot, but looked like he might cry when Andrew turned it around on him, forcing him to scratch and ultimately lose. Without a word, Dirk slumped against the wall and downed the rest of his drink, ambling over to a sideboard to pour himself another.

Eliza was next and Andrew made short work of her as she was far and away the worst of the group, winning himself a date with any one of her friends. An offer that was apparently on par with the use of his condo for twenty-four hours. The details of which she had failed to elaborate on. Finally, only Caralynne remained. She got to her feet slowly, depositing her jacket once more over the back of the sofa with care before turning to him and rolling up her sleeves.

"Well?" Andrew asked, "What is it *you* want from me?"

"I don't know, what have you got? Cars and expensive alcohol won't win me over so easily, nor will using your condo for an orgy."

"Why don't you offer something up then and I'll try to match it?"

"Very well," she said, suddenly businesslike as she clasped her hands behind her back and began pacing the length of the table. "I've got a set of sketches, drawn and signed by Edgar Degas." Andrew resisted the urge to smile. Of course it was art, exactly like George had said.

"Seems fair," Andrew said, "I'll put up a Van Gogh then."

"There are only a handful of Van Gogh paintings in private collections," she said skeptically, and Andrew merely nodded in agreement. "Fine, but if you're lying I will personally crush your balls in a vice." More than a little unsettled by this image, Andrew racked the balls again. He allowed Caralynne the break and she moved the cue ball all the way to the side of the table before bending low over it and looking up at Andrew. Her eyes never left him as she fired the ball down the table. It struck the other balls with the signature clack and the perfect triangle erupted to the side. For a heart stopping moment, it seemed that the 8-ball teetered on the edge of one of the pockets, attempting to secure victory in one swift motion. But it stopped, only a fraction of an inch away.

"Don't breathe too hard, Caralynne," Andrew teased and she grimaced up at him before standing up straight again.

"Don't call me that," she said, "only my father calls me that. Just call me Cara." Her grip on her cue tightened and Andrew thought for a moment that she was going to run him through with it.

"Ok," he said, holding his hands up, "Cara it is." She narrowed her eyes at him and prepped her next shot, carefully threading the cue ball between two others and sinking a solid. Four others followed suit before Cara backed herself into a corner, unable to make another clean shot.

"Do your worst then, Hawkins."

"Hawk," Andrew said with a slight grin, and she rolled her eyes. Andrew bent down and fired off shot after shot, sinking all but one of the stripes. With each ball hitting the fine leather of the pockets, he could see Cara become slightly less composed. Dangling the possibility of the Van Gogh in front of her had clearly gotten her more excited than the others put together. A small part of him felt bad for taking that from her. A part that would in no way feel better when she had to hand over the sketches.

"You're awfully good at this, Hawk," Dirk commented, a slight bitterness in his voice.

"Well," Andrew said as he examined the angle of his next shot, "I imagine it's much the same reason as Cara. I grew up playing my father. He wasn't exactly one to let me win. Then in boarding school it was a good way to make some extra money. Everyone thought they could get the better of me. They were wrong." He bent over the table again, took one final glance at the flicker of fear in Cara's eyes, then took his shot. The cue ball struck the last striped one dead centre, which was the exact wrong thing to do. The ball hit the corner of the bumper and bounced straight away from the pocket. Andrew made a good show of slumping against the table as everyone snickered and Cara's eyes lit up.

"Apparently all of that just wasn't enough," Cara said, bumping him out of the way with her shoulder. She finished him off in three swift, precise shots that ended with the cue ball spinning in a little pirouette before stopping right in the centre of the table. "Now then," Cara said, leaning against the table, "were you telling the truth or do I have to find a vice?"

"You'll get what you want," Andrew promised, "whenever you want to come retrieve it."

"Good," Cara said in satisfaction, retaking her seat beside Eliza, "I'll be there Friday morning." There was a knock at the door and the bartender from downstairs poked his head inside.

"Pardon me," he said to the room, "but dinner is ready." The group left the room and Andrew followed them down into the lavishly decorated dining room. It was built as an addition on the back of the house with windows on all sides, giving the impression of dining outdoors. Andrew was directed to a seat at one end of the table with the others from the billiards room. All of the parents immediately continued with their gossipy conversation they had been having before. This left the opposite end of the table shrouded in the gloom of recent loss. Save, of course, for Cara who braved the silence with a few more probing questions directed towards Andrew. The others slowly came around again and by the time dessert was served, they were all laughing at a story Dirk was telling them. Andrew got the impression that none of them disliked him, not really, just that he was still new and unknown to them. But it was the first step anyway.

Everyone retired back to the sitting room for coffee, giving the parents the chance to brag about their children to a fresh set of ears. Andrew learned that Cara was a chess prodigy and a champion fencer. Diego had done a number of high-profile modeling jobs in both Colombia and the States. Eliza, despite her appearance, was apparently quite the businesswoman, having taken over a handful of the various family-owned companies. Dirk, meanwhile, was a star athlete, having competed internationally in both soccer and cricket. Andrew merely listened to this boasting, filing all of it away in the mental files he was developing on these people. When the party began breaking apart, Andrew made sure to thank George and Margaret again before stepping out into the chilly September night.

Dirk, Diego, and Eliza were huddled together near the bank of cars, waiting for their parents to stop saying goodbye. Diego was looking forlornly at the Corvette parked next to him like he was visiting the grave of a loved one. Andrew examined the car for a moment. He didn't have the same appreciation for classic cars that he knew Hunter had, but he had to admit it was nice. Diego met his eyes for a moment and was about to look away when he flinched and caught the keys Andrew had just tossed him.

"But you won," Diego said, a little stupidly.

"Yeah," Andrew said, "but I can still only drive one car at a time. Besides, I hate to be the one to make you look like a kicked puppy." Dirk snorted and Diego hit him hard on the arm.

"Thanks, Hawk," Diego said bashfully, "you're a good guy."

"I do what I can. Dirk, I also don't need that whiskey, but I'll take a dram while I remind you how badly you lost."

Dirk smiled, "Sounds like a deal."

"Eliza," Andrew began, but she interrupted him, not looking up from her phone.

"Yeah, yeah I get it," she said, "you're a big man who doesn't want to look like a dick to a bunch of people he just met. Congrats. I'll still set you up if you want, but," she glanced at him, "you look like you don't need the help. Anyway, I'll text you." With that she turned on the spot and walked to a large Land Rover, climbing into the back.

"She knows she never got your number, right?" Cara asked, emerging from the house behind them.

Andrew shrugged, "I assumed it was just a standard goodbye for her."

"Yeah, well here," she said, snatching his phone right out of his jacket pocket and unlocking it, "no passcode?"

"I got nothing to hide," Andrew shrugged.

"I don't believe that for a second. Here, all of our numbers in case you need to get a hold of us. But I'm sure we'll see you around."

Andrew nodded his thanks and waved to the others before climbing back into his car, starting it up, and pulling away from the massive beach house.

CHAPTER 8

ANDREW SPENT THE NEXT few days reacquainting himself with the city and ensuring he was familiar with the streets immediately around his condo. Morning runs were the perfect excuse. Even with the designer track clothes and thousand dollar running shoes, Andrew was invisible as soon as he joined the stream of runners who passed up and down the waterfront trails. It only took a few days to learn the people who ran regularly. A woman with a stroller. A man always wearing the same bright orange hat. A couple jogging together, the man clearly doing it to impress the woman. These people became part of Andrew's routine, seeing them meant, on some level, everything was normal. Of course there were others, but mostly those who went on spur of the moment runs when they felt particularly energetic. The Friday after the dinner party, Andrew had gotten a text from Cara saying she would be there to pick up the Van Gogh at noon.

So, Andrew ran in the morning, establishing his cover through these regular runners. It reminded him slightly of the drills that he'd run daily at The Farm, but he relished in the normalcy of it. This was not trying to fit in with high society, nor was it learning how to field strip a weapon. This was something simple. Andrew slowed to a walk as he came back up the Greenway, his breath misting slightly in the air. He approached a coffee cart and bought himself a muffin and a black coffee before strolling down Pier 26. The rising sun was cresting over the buildings, making the Hudson look far more attractive in the golden light. Andrew sat on a bench towards the end of the pier and was only mildly surprised when Hunter sat next to him.

She looked much as she had the day they had landed in Teterboro. Jeans and leather jacket over a soft cotton sweater. "You're getting awfully predictable, Hawk," she said casually, taking the muffin and breaking a piece off.

"I know," Andrew said, "that's the point. Can you spot the difference though?"

"You haven't bought a muffin before," Hunter said, shrugging as she popped the piece into her mouth.

"Very good, but that's only because you've never joined me on this bench."

"What are you talking about?"

"Your Chevelle isn't exactly subtle," Andrew said as he sipped his coffee. "I saw you the last couple days. It was really sad if I'm being honest."

"No way you saw me, I wasn't even driving the Chevelle!"

Andrew grinned at her and she smacked him on the arm. "Alright, alright, you did very well. I only spotted you yesterday on the corner a couple blocks south of here. Figured you would make contact sooner or later."

"You were going to buy a muffin everyday until I showed up, weren't you?"

"I don't know what you're talking about," Andrew said in a dignified voice. "Anyway, I'm surprised you're up this early."

Hunter was quiet for a moment, chewing the muffin as she stared out at the river. Andrew finally looked over at her. Her red hair was tied back again, like it had been when she'd found him in that alley. "I haven't been sleeping well, actually."

"Problems at work?"

"Problems with you, idiot."

"What do you mean? I haven't even done anything but go to a party."

"I know," Hunter said, slumping against the bench, "but what if you get hurt? I'm responsible for you now."

"I'm responsible for myself, you're just here to keep an eye on me. You were right there with me for training, you know I can handle myself just fine."

"I know," she said again, "first week jitters I guess. How was the party?"

"It was fine," Andrew said, clocking the change in subject and allowing it. "George did well, bringing together a group that's well connected. Though I suppose we have his daughter to thank as well. I think they like me enough that a few more run-ins should get me into their group properly. Cara Randal is coming by today; it'll give me an idea of how they feel about me. What about you? Any friction at the precinct?"

"Not yet," Hunter replied, "everyone in homicide is pretty alright. The captain isn't too thrilled about the strings that were pulled to get me there but as long as I pull my weight and follow orders then he's fine with it. They're all still trying to gauge whether I'm an idiot who got lucky or if I actually am smart enough to be there."

"So how long until you let them know you're smarter than the rest of them?"

"I figure I'll let them wonder for a bit. Captain has me going over a couple of unsolved cases until I get settled, fresh eyes might help."

"Anything fun?"

"You'd be surprised at some of the shit that goes unnoticed in this city. There are two unsolved cases right now. One looks like a pretty standard mugging gone wrong in the park. They're canvassing for possible witnesses until they dig something up, nothing special. The other one, though, is messed up. The guy took seven shots at the victim before they finally went down and wasn't finished there. Mutilated the body pretty good. Bashed his face badly, flayed the skin on parts of his hands and feet, and even found semen on the clothes."

"Teeth missing from the beating?"

"Yep."

"Sounds like someone trying to cover up the identity of the victim while making it look like they're just crazy."

"Exactly what I thought," Hunter said, nodding, "but I think it really is just a psycho. There were broken bones that just made no sense for covering evidence. Even someone meticulous can't replicate the random choice of a lunatic."

"Where'd they find the body?" Andrew didn't really care; the finer points of a dead body wasn't exactly his go-to for a chat over breakfast. But Hunter lived for this sort of thing, it was just a puzzle for her, and he could tell she was more upset than she let on.

"Alley behind his building. Probably jumped on his way home. Low velocity rounds were all still in the body and techs figured they were from a Glock because of the polygonal rifling, not exactly narrowing it down. It was also raining when they found him, so blood splatter was being washed away."

"Where in the alley?" Andrew asked.

"What do you mean?"

"In the middle? Leaning on a wall? Where?"

"Right at the base of the wall."

"What did they do with his apartment?"

"It's still locked down until the case is solved, but it's not a crime scene. The vic was single, no roommates, no nothing so no one has been in there since the preliminary sweep which turned up nothing relevant. It's a low rent building, guy barely had a bed."

"Who did the sweep of his apartment?"

"Uniformed officer who responded to the 911 call, super let him in, he saw no blood or anything, then left. What are you getting at, Hawk?"

Andrew stood up and crossed to the railing of the pier. It was still early so there was hardly anyone around. Perfect for an early morning chat about murder. "What I'm getting at is not every beat cop is as keen as you were. What if the broken bones weren't all from a beating? What if the beating was used to cover up perimortem damage with postmortem evidence?"

"So what?" Hunter said, her brow furrowing, "The guy jumps him, breaks an arm and a leg, shoots him seven times, bashes his skull in, then rapes the body?"

"What floor was the apartment?"

"Fourth," Hunter said without thinking and Andrew smiled as he looked to watch the gears turning in her head. "You think he was dropped out the window?"

Andrew shrugged, "Who doesn't love a good defenestration? As long as the scene is preserved, no harm in going back and looking with a slightly more trained eye. Might find something where the killer slipped up." Hunter sprang to her feet, clearly pleased, and whacked him on the arm apparently to let off her feelings.

"This could be big in securing me a spot in their good books. The detective assigned to the case is pulling his hair out trying to figure it all out. You're the best."

"I do what I can. But Hunter?" She stopped bouncing on the balls of her feet to look at him inquiringly. "Please sleep. I'm ok. I will be ok. You can't hold my hand through this. I promise that I'll reach out if I'm in trouble." Her face fell slightly but she nodded solemnly.

"Ok, I'm sorry. It's just...Morris made it very clear that whatever happens to you is on me. I'm supposed to have your back no matter what." Andrew grinned at her. "What?" she demanded, immediately throwing up her defenses after having opened up to him.

"Nothing, he just had the same talk with me. I'm here for you too, you know."

She blushed slightly, like she always did when he said something nice. For a cop, Hunter blushed very easily, it was sort of cute. "I can't exactly waltz into your condo on a regular basis. Looks fishy."

"Fishy?" Andrew asked incredulously, "Are we in a Hardy Boys novel now?"

"I'm clearly Frank," Hunter said very seriously.

"Regardless," Andrew said, suppressing a smile, "I've been thinking about how you could visit if you needed. I came up with a couple options."

"Alright, shoot."

"Well, I figure someone of my status would surprise no one by hiring a high-class escort. I figure all you'd need is a trench coat and...well that's it."

Hunter wound up and punched him hard in the chest. "Not happening. Wanna try again?"

Andrew danced out of her reach as he rubbed the spot where she'd punched him. "Alright, I was just joking, I swear. No, I was thinking about my parents' death."

"The helicopter crash?"

"Yeah, what if it wasn't an accident?"

"But it was," Hunter made a show of looking around before adding, in a stage whisper, "also it never actually happened."

"Well, the death certificates, insurance investigation, funeral, and subsequent pair of urns would beg to differ. Why not talk to...whoever you're supposed to talk to and open an investigation into a couple 'associates' of my parents who might have liked them out of the way. God knows there are enough people out there like us who you could investigate. Then you can come ask me questions for the investigation as needed."

"That's actually not bad," Hunter admitted, "but I don't see the higher ups being ok with prolonged regular contact."

"Tell them it's my fault. Tell them I'm having a hard time adjusting and that you'd like to be able to keep a closer eye on me for at least the next few weeks."

"You'd be ok with that? They could pull you from this."

"Nah," Andrew said, "they've spent millions of dollars training me, outfitting me, and getting my identity in place. Plus they wanted me for existing skills and a personal motive that's pretty hard to replicate. They'll bend over backwards to keep me in this."

Hunter stared at him for a moment, slowly turning red again before throwing herself at him. Expecting another attack, he was slightly surprised when she crushed him with a hug.

"Thanks, Hawk, I appreciate it. Really."

"Of course," Andrew mumbled into her shoulder, "but you're insane. I'm clearly Frank." Hunter laughed, let him go, and picked up her half a muffin from the bench where she'd left it. With a little wink and a far more chipper demeanor, she strode past him.

"See ya around, Hawk. Have fun with the pretty rich girl."

"I never said she was pretty," he called after her and she spun around, taking a few steps backwards.

"Tell that to the little smile you had when you said her name."

CHAPTER 9

ANDREW'S PHONE RANG AT twelve o'clock on the dot. He pulled it from his pocket as he descended the stairs into the sitting room. The screen simply read 'Security' and Andrew held it up to his ear, answering.

"Mr. Hawkins, sir," said the voice on the other end, "it's Ryan from the front desk. There is a Miss Cara Randal here to see you. Shall I let her up?"

"Yes, Cara is a friend of mine. No need to bust out the enhanced interrogation." There was a laugh on the other end of the line and Ryan promised to send Cara up unharmed. A few minutes later there was a knock at the door. Andrew crossed over to it and opened it to reveal Cara in a violet shirt and black knee-length skirt. She held a large portfolio style case and a somewhat shocked look on her face.

"That's some security you've got down there," she said lightly before stepping into the condo.

"Yeah, I was promised that they're all ex-military. Bit of a step down from patrolling the Middle East to this."

"Oh, I don't know," Cara said, "paparazzi and crazed stalkers can certainly give terrorists a run for their money." Andrew laughed, though Cara seemed quite serious. "Well? Have you brought me here for nothing?"

"Right this way," Andrew replied, leading her over to the stairs. He had already swapped the Van Gogh with one of the other paintings in the bedroom which now hid the wall safe.

"What the hell is this?" Cara asked the moment she saw the bed, "Some convoluted hookup tactic? You think I'm really so shallow as to-" she was cut off abruptly as Andrew grabbed her shoulder and spun her around to see the painting. "Holy shit," she whispered, approaching the wall, "you actually weren't lying."

"Had no reason to," Andrew said, sitting on the bed. "Tell me though, you just walked past a Klimt, a Monet, and a Pollock downstairs. Why did none of them grab you like this one has?"

"When I was a little girl, four years old, my father pulled me out of my preschool because he had the day off. It was maybe the best thing I could come up with in my tiny imagination. We went to the park, got ice cream, and finished the day with a trip to MoMA. I remember seeing Starry Night for the first time. After all the weird modern art installations, it was this total breath of fresh air. I couldn't stop staring at it."

"So that was the start of an obsession?" Cara shook her head and slowly backed away from the painting until she hit the bed, falling onto it next to Andrew.

"The obsession came the next day. I woke up, still feeling like I was dreaming in the swirls of color that Van Gogh used as I drew with crayons in my room. No one had come to wake me or get me ready for school. I could hear my parents arguing but didn't really care. Turns out those swirls were real when I looked out the window. I could see the fire and the smoke after the first plane hit the tower. I watched as the second hit. Then, an eternity later, the tower fell. Everyone was so scared and angry, everything felt and looked gray. Except for art. Art still had its color. Van Gogh was still magic on a canvas."

Cara fell silent, almost in a trance as she stared at the painting on the wall. Andrew, meanwhile, was staring at her. The brusk, businesslike woman he had met days before was gone. Replaced by a much younger, much more innocent girl staring at something she couldn't believe. A tear fell onto her shirt, staining the fabric a deeper shade of purple. Cara blinked rapidly and wiped away another tear.

"I can't take this from you," she whispered, and Andrew shook his head.

"This was something my father bought years ago; I've seen it all of three times in my life. It deserves to be hung somewhere it'll be appreciated. I think that's with you. It means far more to you than it ever could to me."

Cara took a shuddering breath and nodded. "Thank you, Hawk...I think," she looked at him through red eyes, "I think I need a drink." Andrew smiled and nodded before leading her back down the stairs. Cara fell into a chair by the window and Andrew poured two measures of scotch for them.

"Are you alright?" Andrew asked, handing her one of the glasses and sitting on the edge of the chair opposite her. "I didn't mean to upset you."

"No," Cara said, shaking her head, "you didn't, I'm just not in the habit of telling people that story. Still one of the hardest days of my life, even as a little girl who didn't know what evil was yet."

"So why tell me?" Andrew asked after a pause. "You don't even know me."

"Maybe that's why," Cara said before a long swig of the scotch. "Maybe it's easier to admit to a stranger for some reason. Or maybe it's simply because I wasn't actually expecting for you to have that painting. But honestly, Hawk, I just sort of trust you. I love the others, but none of them get why art is such a big deal to me. They see it as just another thing to prove how rich they are and fail to see how it can enrich your life in a different way."

Andrew placed a hand gently on her knee and she looked up at him, meeting his eyes. "If you ever want to talk about it, or just want to get away from the others for a bit, you know where to find me."

Cara smiled at him. It was the first time he'd seen her smile genuinely. It was not because it was polite or because she had beaten him or because it was hiding something more sinister. This was a real smile that seemed to brighten her features, making blue eyes sparkle with warmth.

"What?" she asked, the smile fading slightly as Andrew stared at her.

"Nothing," he said quickly, dropping his hand from her knee and feeling his face grow hot. He tried to cover the moment by taking a drink, but Cara still looked a little suspicious. They chatted idly about the other pieces in the condo. Cara was pleasantly surprised to find that Andrew was well versed in art beyond the usual vapid comments about its beauty. Cara was just telling him all about some of the inner-city programs that she had been a part of, helping kids learn all kinds of art, when her phone buzzed. She pulled it from where it had been wedged in the waist of her skirt and her eyes widened. They had been talking for at least two hours.

"Shit," she said as she sprang to her feet, "I was supposed to meet my mother ten minutes ago." Cara looked up from her phone, looking very sorry but Andrew waved away her concern.

"It's alright, let's go get your painting and we can continue this another time, yeah?" She nodded with a tight smile and dashed for the stairs. By the time he caught up, she was already putting the painting into her folio case and zipping it up, but then paused to look up at him.

"Are you sure? Really? I didn't mean to come across as just trying to use you for your stuff."

"Cara, stop," Andrew said, "it's yours. Really."

She smiled again and lifted the case. Andrew walked her to the door and opened it for her. She was across the threshold when she stopped again and turned to look at him. "Listen, Diego invited all of us to this event at the Turner on Sunday. Apparently his father is donating a couple of perfectly preserved manuscripts they discovered. Diego is supposed to be there on his father's behalf with a couple others from the consulate. Anyway, the whole fancy gala thing isn't really my cup of tea, but it might be more fun with someone. Wanna be my date?"

"How fancy are we talking?"

"Oh, you'll need to bring your A-game, black tie mandatory."

"Oh, I dunno. I'm not sure you can handle my A-game."

"Wanna bet?" Cara asked, her eyes suddenly blazing.

Andrew laughed, "Alright I'm in. Text me where and when and I'll pick you up." Cara grinned at him before swooping in and kissing him on the cheek. She dashed away before he could even say good-bye. He closed the door and fell into one of the chairs in the theater room. This was good. A chance to see them all again and maybe even forge some new connections, guided, and helped by Cara. Andrew checked his watch and cursed himself. He was going to be late too if he didn't hurry. Pulling on a jacket as he locked the door, his phone was already pressed to his ear.

"Ram, it's Andrew, I need to be at 72nd and Central Park West in half an hour. Think you can get me there? I'm just heading down to the street."

"Absolutely, I'll be there in just a minute, sir. Don't you worry." Andrew hung up the phone and jammed the first-floor button on the elevator. By the time he was stepping out of the front door, the doorman giving him a little salute, the sleek car was pulling to a stop and Ram leapt out barely as the shifter hit park. Andrew waved him back and opened his own door before sliding inside.

"That was quick," he commented as Ram pulled away from the curb again, "do you just sit nearby and wait for me?"

"Trade secrets, Mr. Hawkins," Ram said with a wink in the rearview mirror.

"Just Hawk is fine, Ram" Andrew said, "Mr. Hawkins makes me feel like I'm ready to have a coronary on the golf course."

Ram grinned, "Yes sir, Mr. Hawk, whatever you say. I take it your previous meeting went well? With a young woman perhaps?"

Andrew frowned at the back of the man's head, suddenly on alert. "How the hell do you know that?"

"Trade secrets," Ram said mysteriously again, but then snort-ed and jerked a thumb over his shoulder, "that and the lipstick." Andrew pulled out his phone and flipped the camera to examine himself. Sure enough there was a distinct purplish lip mark where

Cara had kissed him. Ram held a handkerchief through the open partition and Andrew took it, wiping his face.

"She's just a friend, Ram."

"Of course, sir." The rest of the ride passed in silence until Ram pulled up smoothly to one of the entrances to Central Park. "72nd and Central Park West, sir. Shall I wait for you?"

"Please," Andrew said, "I shouldn't be more than a half hour or so. Grab a coffee or something and I'll meet you back here." Ram nodded and Andrew slid out of the car, pulling up his collar as he entered the park.

The bench he was looking for wasn't too hard to find. It was slightly off the main paths that were busy with people, hidden by a small copse of trees. Andrew sat down and waited, watching the few people that passed him. He wasn't sure who exactly he was looking for, only that it was to be the analyst assigned to him. They would monitor communications, chatter within the city, and be on call for support as needed. Supposedly they were a savant with all things electronic and could hack just about anything. A woman walked by holding a little girl's hand and Andrew found himself thinking back to Cara's story. It had stirred something in him that he was not entirely prepared to feel. He ended up so lost in thought that he didn't notice the man who had sat down on the bench beside him. The man was at least seventy, with wiry gray hair that seemed to stick out in every direction, and extremely thick glasses. With his wool suit and trembling hands, he looked rather like a deranged professor. The man breathed into his hands before rubbing them together and jamming them in his pockets.

There was protocol for this. If the meet was compromised then Andrew was simply supposed to walk away and try again the following day. He'd made it a few paces when his phone buzzed in his pocket and he withdrew it. It was a text, though the ID showed 6H0UL instead of a name or number. Frowning, Andrew opened the text.

Come back here, dolt.

Andrew froze, turned on the spot, and stared at the old man who seemed engrossed by the leaves on the tree above him. The phone buzzed again and Andrew looked back down.

Perhaps sometime before I die, if you can manage it.

Still confused, Andrew returned to the bench and sat down again, glancing sideways at the man. Finally, the man looked around at him, the glasses magnifying his brown eyes to twice their normal size.

"So, you're the kid?" he asked. He had a slight southern accent, Georgia maybe.

"I guess so, you're the computer expert?" Andrew sounded a fair bit more skeptical.

"Got a problem?"

"No, no, not at all. I just didn't think that meant you were there when they invented them."

"Hilarious. My name is Duncan."

"Andrew."

"Well, as you so delicately indicated, I've been in this game since your daddy was still shitting his pants. You need it, I can do it. Believe me."

"Alright, if you say so," Andrew said, and Duncan narrowed his eyes at him.

"Give me your phone." Hesitating for just a moment, Andrew held out his phone and Duncan snatched it from him. With a dexterity that frankly shocked Andrew, his phone was disassembled in a matter of seconds and Duncan was fiddling with something on one of the chips.

"What the hell are you doing?"

"These company issued phones are barely more than what you could buy at a pawn shop in the Bronx. I'm boosting your reception so that you can use it anywhere. Underground, middle of nowhere, wherever you want."

"Really?" Andrew asked, surprised in spite of himself.

"Yes, really," Duncan replied in exasperation, "I assure you that I'm perfectly capable of whatever you need. Believe me or not, I don't really care. I'll be keeping an eye on things regardless and you'll be able to reach me with this. Just dial 0." He handed the reassembled phone back to Andrew and stood up.

"Alright hang on," Andrew said, grabbing his arm, "I'm sorry."

"And here I thought your generation forgot the meaning of the word. You're alright kid. I've been taking shit my whole career. First because I saw the wave of the future that was computers. They all told me it was a fad. Then they laughed when I said we could make computers better, faster, and even portable. Now I'm the cooky old bastard who thinks he's a hacker. Each time people have been proven wrong, I suggest you think carefully if you believe me or not. Might save your life one day. Be seeing you, Andy."

CHAPTER 10

SUNDAY AFTERNOON FOUND ANDREW standing before the huge mirror in the cavernous closet attached to his room. It reminded him powerfully of standing in front of the mirror in his room at The Farm. Had it really only been a week since then? He adjusted the bowtie of his tuxedo, feeling decidedly awkward but doing his best not to show it. Cara had texted him the day before saying that he could pick her up from her apartment at around four o'clock. He'd been somewhat surprised to learn that she lived in a fairly plain building in Greenwich Village. He'd gotten the impression that Diego, Dirk, Eliza, and Cara had simply lived with their parents as did many of the wealthy who lived in the same city as their families. More often than not the family would have some house or condo or similar that was simply the family home. Cara, however, seemed to be different. This fact only made Andrew more curious about her.

Andrew found Ram waiting for him outside again, door opening the moment he approached the car. "Afternoon, Mr. Hawk, looking good."

"Thank you, Ram." It was only a ten-minute drive to the address Cara had given him which turned out to be a corner building on Waverly Place that held a bookstore and apartments above. Andrew got out of the car once Ram had parked in a miraculously empty spot and looked up at the building. A handful of teenagers were standing on scaffolding, painting a large mural over the bookstore. Andrew watched them for a few moments, it looked to be some sort of reading themed pride display, then crossed the street. A girl, maybe twelve or thirteen, with paint smudges on her cheeks and dirty blonde hair in a ponytail made a show of jumping off the scaffolding from where she was perched. She landed right in front of Andrew who quickly swerved out of the way, only to find she sidestepped to block him.

"Closed site during painting," she said, holding up a hand like a crossing guard, "don't need any rich dicks trying to mess with us, thanks."

Andrew blinked a couple of times then took a step back with his hands raised. "I'm sorry ma'am, don't want any trouble. Think I can go around though? I'm trying to find a friend of mine."

The girl smiled in a smug sort of way at being called ma'am and crossed her arms importantly as she looked him up and down. "You sure you're in the right place?"

"Leave him alone Em," someone called from above on the scaffolding, "that's Hawk." Andrew looked up in surprise to find Cara leaning over the platform she was standing on, a brush covered in gold paint in her hand. Andrew barely recognised her without an outfit you'd see in a law office. She was dressed in denim overalls and a wool sweater, all of which was splattered with paint, as was her face and hair which was tied up in a messy bun.

"Oh, so this is the dork you won't shut up about?" the girl named Em asked and Andrew glanced back down at her before looking up at Cara.

"Oh yeah?" he asked, eyebrows raised.

"Shut up, Em," Cara said severely as she set her brush down and swung off the platform, sliding down one of the supports, and landing neatly next to them. "Hey, Hawk, glad you made it."

"Yeah," Andrew said, still taking in this casual look, "though it looks like I'm early. You look good."

"Nah, you're right on time," Cara said with a grin, "I thought you might wanna see what we've been working on. That's Diane," she added, pointing up to the only other adult who was painting, "she runs a group for kids in the village. Most of them are taggers or vandals who do community service with the group. She figured it was easier to get them doing authorized projects than trying to get them to quit art altogether."

Indeed, several of the teens were using spray paint rather than brushes as they added to the mural. "Smart idea," Andrew said appreciatively, and Cara beamed at him.

"You wanna help?"

"I'm no artist," Andrew replied at once.

"Aww come on, we've got hours before we actually have to leave and even an idiot like you can paint a big section of gold with me." She pointed up to the giant painted book that she'd been filling in with gold paint. The look she was giving him was certainly compromising his ability to refuse.

"Alright, I guess it couldn't hurt."

"Typical," Em muttered from her perch that she'd returned to.

"Shut it," Cara snapped before climbing back up herself. Andrew took off his jacket and tie, slung them over one of the bars, then rolled up his sleeves. He climbed up easily until he was on the platform with Cara. She handed him a brush and nudged the bucket of gold paint towards him before dipping her own brush in. Andrew got to work and after an hour they were looking up at a finished book of gold.

"Perfect," Diane said, pushing her glasses up her nose as she made her way over to them, "we'll just let it dry and then the kids can fill it with what they want. Thanks for the help."

"No problem," Cara said cheerfully.

"Though I see it wasn't without its casualties," Diane added, nodding towards Andrew.

"Damn," Cara said at once, grabbing Andrew's arm and pulling it towards her. There were a couple smears of the gold paint on his sleeve. "Oh, Andrew I'm sorry."

"Don't even worry about it," he said, waving her away, "no one will see it under the jacket anyway."

"It's not hopeless," Cara said, ignoring him, "come on, I've gotten my fair share of paint off clothes before. I have to get ready anyway."

"You mean you're not going as a hipster farmer to this thing?" Cara laughed and shook her head before making her way down to the street again. Andrew followed, dropping and grabbing the edge of the platform to swing off onto the ground.

"That was shockingly badass of you," Cara commented, retrieving Andrew's jacket and tie from where he'd left them.

"Rock climbing," Andrew said, "makes anyone a shocking badass." Cara snorted and grabbed his arm, pulling him towards the door that led to the apartments above the shop. They climbed to the third floor and Cara let them into a fairly roomy one-bedroom apartment.

"Here we are," she said, "my own little escape from high society." It was cozy, with a little couch surrounded by bookshelves. If it weren't for the occasional priceless piece of art, Andrew would have thought this was any old apartment. The Van Gogh was already hanging in pride of place where a TV would normally have been.

"It's cute," Andrew said, "but why not something bigger?"

"Don't really need anything bigger. I like having something that makes me feel normal sometimes. Besides, I'd get lonely in a bigger place. Now, shirt off."

"What?"

"Give me the shirt, I'll let it soak a bit while I get ready."

"Oh right," Andrew said. He undid the buttons and pulled the shirt off, slightly thankful for the sleeveless undershirt he was wearing beneath.

"You're pretty strong for a rich brat," Cara commented idly as she examined the paint smears, "now sit. I won't be long." She disappeared into the little bedroom and shut the door. The sound of a running shower filled the apartment and Andrew settled in. Cara turned out to not be one of those women who need hours to get ready. She was only gone ten minutes before she emerged from the bedroom in a towel, drying her hair with another. Andrew tried to look away out of some sense of decency but there wasn't much room to look anywhere else. He could feel her staring at him, so he finally met her gaze. Strands of wet hair clung to her face, and she was frowning at him slightly.

"Quite the scar," she said, nodding to one of his arms. He'd gotten it when he'd failed to get a knife away from his attacker during training.

"I fell while I was climbing Half Dome. My line got caught around my arm and ripped straight through the skin."

Cara winced, "That's why I like painting. Less mutilation."

Andrew laughed and shrugged. Cara retrieved a garment bag from the back of the door and disappeared again for another ten minutes. This time she came back with dry hair and wearing a floor length, backless red dress, she was carrying his shirt and handed it back before spreading her arms and spinning once.

"Thoughts?" she asked. Andrew opened and closed his mouth several times and she smiled again, blushing slightly. "Yeah, that's sort of what I was going for."

The dress stopped swirling around her ankles and Andrew finally managed to say, "Uh, yeah, wow." Andrew realized he was still holding his shirt and quickly got up to put it on. There was only a slightly damp spot where the paint had been. He put his jacket on and started to tie his tie while Cara applied crimson lipstick and mascara in a small mirror on one of the bookshelves. The other shelves held a variety of things beyond the books, including several pictures in gold frames of Cara as a little girl with her parents. Part of him still couldn't reconcile the paint splattered girl in overalls with the gorgeous woman who was standing before him now.

"You're not like the others, are you?" Andrew asked eventually.

"How do you mean?"

"I mean, Eliza would probably throw a fit if she had paint on her that she hadn't applied to her own nails. You're just as rich as the rest of us, but you don't seem to care about always looking like it."

"That a problem?" Cara demanded, wielding a mascara wand like a sword that she pointed at his chest.

"No," Andrew said genuinely, "it's intriguing, and kind of refreshing. I always feel like every time I leave the house I need to look just so. I sometimes miss being able to wear whatever I wanted. I miss being a kid. But you still act like one when you want to. I guess I'm sort of jealous you can pull it off." This had been a legitimate problem for him so far. There seemed to be such an expectation to flaunt the wealth he supposedly had. It was strange to him.

"Well, I realized a while back that there was no point in being wealthy enough to do whatever I wanted if I wasn't doing whatever I wanted. I bought this place two years ago and it's been so freeing for me to just be me. You should try it sometime; I wouldn't mind knowing the real you as well as this version." She handed him a spectacular necklace of diamonds and rubies before turning around and pulling her hair over one shoulder.

"I don't even know if there is a real me under all this anymore," Andrew said honestly as he draped the necklace over her and fastened it.

"Well," she said, turning to face him. He could feel her breath on his cheek as she looked up at him with those crystal blue eyes, "maybe we can find part of him tonight. Ready?" He nodded mutely and she stepped around him to exit the apartment. Ram met them at the car, a wide smile on his face as he gave a little bow to Cara.

"Good evening, Miss, please allow me," he said as he opened the door and Andrew crossed to the other side to get in. Two glasses of champagne were waiting for them and Andrew glared at Ram as he got in the car with a knowing smile.

"You certainly know how to treat a lady, Mr. Hawkins," Cara said with a smile as she took one of the glasses and held it up. "To unexpected sides of the same coin," she said. Andrew lifted his own glass and tapped it against hers with a sharp clink.

CHAPTER 11

"THE TURNER," RAM SAID cheerfully, pulling to a stop in front of the glass entryway to the museum. A plush red carpet had been set out on the pavement and held a steady trickle of guests in their finest outfits. Andrew got out first and rounded the car to open the door for Cara. She got out and he offered his arm to her.

"Of course," Cara muttered as a handful of reporters and paparazzi started taking pictures and yelling questions on the off chance they were someone famous.

"Do they know you?" Andrew asked, holding her a little closer as they were surrounded.

"They like to keep tabs on the elite of New York. Regular folks always like to hear what people like us are up to. Last year I made the front of Celeb Hype with Eliza because they thought we were dating. It's a little pathetic. I don't suppose you've had to deal with it yet."

"Not like this," Andrew said as he shouldered past a woman holding out a mic towards him. "It's not like I'm famous or anything. Not an actor or singer or something fun."

"Doesn't matter to them. Think about it. In this city you hear about every rich old bastard who dies and leaves all the money to his kids. You donate money to charity, people care, you buy some fancy new purse, people care. It's just the way it is for us."

Andrew looked away as several cameras flashed in his face and saw something out of the corner of his eye that made him do a double take. A cobalt blue Chevelle was parked a half a block down Madison Avenue. The streetlight above the car glared off the windshield but he was sure Hunter was inside. A regular police cruiser was parked behind it, two hefty uniformed officers leaning against it with coffee.

"What is it?" Cara asked, trying to look past Andrew's shoulder.

"Nothing," he said, pushing aside one of the reporters who tried to squeeze between them. "Back off," he said warningly, and the reporter took a hasty step away.

"Hey," a voice roared ahead of them, "I told you to clear out of here." A rather large Hispanic man was shoving two paparazzi out of the way and they all scattered before him. His accent and the pin of yellow, blue, and red stripes made Andrew sure he was security for the consulate. He opened the door for Andrew and Cara and nodded politely as they passed. Light instrumental music echoed faintly around the marble rotunda of the museum entrance. Doors on either side of them led to carpeted rooms crammed with books behind caged doors. Beyond the rotunda Andrew could see men in tuxedos escorting women in fine dresses around a dance floor. A pair of tables had been set up in the rotunda where the people ahead of them were checking in. Each of them were also being scanned by security with handheld metal detectors. Andrew and Cara stepped up to one of the tables and a woman smiled up at them with a tablet computer in her hands.

"Names?" the woman asked.

"Caralynne Randal and Andrew Hawkins," Cara said, and the woman looked down to scan the list of names.

"Ah yes, here we are. Go on ahead and enjoy your evening." Cara nodded her thanks and stepped towards one of the security guards. Like the man outside, this one appeared to be an employee of the consulate. He gestured Cara to step forward, then stop before he passed the scanning wand up and down her body. It beeped in reaction to the necklace and the guard grabbed it roughly to examine it.

"*Gently,*" Andrew hissed in Spanish, "*if you value having both hands.*" The guard raised his eyebrows at him but dropped the necklace and waved Cara through. He was eyeing Andrew suspiciously but made the sweep, checked the phone in his pocket, and waved him through without comment.

"What was that?" Cara asked as they left the security behind.

"Just saying hello," Andrew said as she took his arm again, "so what's the deal with all this? All I know is that Diego invited you."

"The Nazis had ties to Colombia during the second world war. What a lot of people don't realize is that, like Argentina, Colombia ended up the final resting place for some of the Nazis who fled when Hitler died. Diego's father has spent years rooting out these people, arresting those they can, but mostly trying to collect artwork and antiquities that were smuggled out of Germany. A big source of pride for his government. Every once in a while they throw a party like this when they return items to where they belong. Tonight they are displaying a handful of manuscripts and compositions looted during the war. The Turner acts as a museum and library so it made the most sense."

"Quite the gesture," Andrew commented. He supposed that it was something of an effort to quell the tension between the US and Colombia. The States felt that the Colombians were not doing enough to crack down on the cartels. This had led to some recent hostility between the nations. They entered the main gallery where the party was taking place. The marble floor was dotted with glass cases that held the donated pieces around the perimeter of the dance floor. A string quartet was situated in one of the corners, playing a slow tune. Waiters were weaving between the people standing around the outside of the room with trays of hors d'oeuvres and glasses of champagne. Andrew fiddled with his tie a bit and Cara looked up at him.

"You ok?"

"It's been a while since I attended something like this," he said.

"Don't worry, it's easy. Everyone is focused on the new donations and the people representing the Colombian government. All we have to do is eat, drink, and dance. Think you can handle that?"

Andrew met her eyes and felt some of his concern melt away. "Yeah, I can handle that." He snatched two glasses of champagne from a passing tray and handed one to Cara. They started to make their way slowly around the room, Cara stopping a few times to greet people that she knew and introduce them to Andrew. He did his very best to make a good impression. Like the guests at George's dinner party, these people seemed fascinated to meet someone in their circle that they knew so little about. It amused him slightly that a couple people offered condolences for the passing of his parents. He suspected that Marcia, if no one else, had been spreading that story like wildfire. Eventually, on the opposite side of the room from the entrance, at the spot where more doors led to further smaller gallery rooms, Andrew spotted someone he actually recognised.

"Eliza," he said in greeting as Cara moved to greet a couple old friends of her father's.

Eliza looked up from her phone just long enough to confirm who was there before returning to her text. "So she actually brought you."

"Why shouldn't she?" Andrew asked, a little taken aback by her somewhat hostile tone.

"No reason at all. You look cute together."

"I don't think it's like that," Andrew said awkwardly, and Eliza shrugged. Cara joined them and bumped her shoulder into Andrew.

"Don't think what is like what?" she asked at once.

"Nothing," Andrew and Eliza said together, making Cara narrow her eyes slightly. Thankfully, a distraction arrived in the form of a slightly drunk Diego.

"Hey," he said excitedly, putting an arm around Eliza, "you guys made it."

"Yeah, of course," Cara said.

"Hawk," Diego said happily as his eyes focused on Andrew, "what're you doing here?"

"Cara brought me along, hope that's alright."

"Absolutely," Diego said, scooping someone out of the crowd and turning them to face Andrew. The man was in his early sixties with tanned skin, a graying beard cut short, and slightly beady eyes. "Hawk, this is my uncle, Luca. My father hired him as deputy minister of culture. He's overseeing the donation to the museum."

"A pleasure to meet you," Luca said through a thick accent, shaking Andrew's hand. "I've heard about you from Marcia, my sister. I do hope you might be a good influence on these kids." He nodded towards Diego and Eliza.

"I'll do my best sir," Andrew said, and Cara opened her mouth to say something, but Luca held up a hand.

"I mean no offense, Miss Cara, I know you have been a good influence yourself. I dare say Diego might not have turned out as well as he did if it wasn't for you." Cara smiled in a slightly smug way. Andrew found it interesting that this man knew them so well. Though, he supposed, he may have just been close with Diego.

As though reading his thoughts, Cara said, "Luca has known us pretty much our whole lives. He was stationed in the consulate when we were all kids and even used to keep an eye on us sometimes." Luca turned to greet someone else and Cara leaned in close to whisper in Andrew's ear. "He also really enjoys rubbing elbows with us and our parents. So, prepare yourself for a new best friend, he'll try to be just that." Andrew smiled his thanks as Luca turned back. They discussed the gala and the donations being made to the museum which included a few handwritten compositions done by Beethoven and one of the only surviving Gutenberg bibles. Luca subtly steered the conversation towards Andrew and his parents, trying to learn more about him.

"I was terribly sorry to hear about your parents," he said, and Andrew merely nodded gravely as Cara squeezed his arm gently. "I met them once, you know."

"Did you?" Andrew asked with genuine surprise. He knew that the lives of Richard and Melissa Hawkins had been meticulously crafted, but this was something else.

"Yes, your father had made a rather significant contribution to a children's charity in Bogotá. They invited him and your mother to visit, to see his money at work. I was volunteering for the charity at the time and I must say it was a true privilege to meet such wonderful people. If their son is even a fraction as decent, then I'm very pleased indeed."

"Thank you, sir," Andrew said, a little stunned. Records had been made, tons of them, documenting the accumulated wealth of the Hawkins family, including several donations to charities around the world. This story was still lacking one crucial detail. Actual people. Before Andrew could ponder this further, one of the burly security guards approached Luca and leaned in to speak in a whisper that nevertheless carried across their small group. Perhaps he didn't care as he addressed Luca in Spanish and thought the outsiders would have no idea what was being said.

"Señor Pedroso, there is a problem with one of the pieces being donated, could you please come with me?"

Luca nodded and Andrew clocked the slightly sobered expression he now wore. He excused himself and Andrew watched him go, escorted by the security guard. Something bothered him about the interaction. Something bothered him about Luca too. Then it dawned on him. The guard had been speaking Spanish, certainly, but the accent was wrong. To anyone else it would have sounded fine, even the intoxicated Diego had not noticed, but Andrew had been trained for things like this. The guard had definitely been speaking in a Western Mexican accent rather than that of a native Colombian.

He dithered on the spot for a moment, trying to decide if he was overthinking things. He knew he was right about the accent, but what did that matter? Perhaps the guard had simply lived in Mexico where he picked up the accent before working for the consulate in New York. There were a hundred reasons Andrew should simply ignore the interaction. He probably would have if Luca hadn't just lied to his face.

"Will you excuse me for just a moment?" Andrew asked Cara and she nodded.

"Hurry back though, I'd say you owe me at least one dance."

"Of course," Andrew said, lifting her hand to his lips before stepping away from the group. Luca and the guard had been heading for a hallway off the main gallery and Andrew followed. There were a couple of people leaving the hallway, apparently coming back from the bathroom. At the far end of the hall, though, was a door that led to a stairwell. Andrew knew, having looked up a floorplan of the museum before attending, that there was another large gallery space above them and a sort of lecture theater on the floor below. Knowing the layout had been a habit drilled into him by Bakowski at The Farm. Always enter a building knowing as much as you can. One of the Sarge's many, many phrases he liked to throw around.

The door to the stairs was still swinging shut as Andrew hurried towards it, trying not to draw attention to himself. He pushed it open silently and stepped into the concrete stairwell. He heard footsteps bouncing off the tight walls like gunfire and he peeked over the railing. Three people were headed down towards the theater. He waited until he heard the door at the bottom of the stairs close before racing after them. His hand instinctively moved to his pocket where his phone was in case he needed to call for Hunter. The door at the bottom opened onto a narrow hallway that ran the length of the building. An entrance to the theater was here, but so was access to another staircase that led up to the loading bay. If they had been going for the loading bay, they could have simply gone out the back of the gallery upstairs. The washrooms in the basement also seemed a less than ideal place for a clandestine meeting. This left only one likely option. Andrew peeked through the window in the door to the theater and when he saw three men walking down towards the stage, he pushed it open and crept inside.

CHAPTER 12

ANDREW CROUCHED LOW, HIS heart pounding in his ears as he carefully closed the door to the theater and ducked behind the back row of seats. Thanks to the sloped floor, he could just see the stage between two of the seats. There were only a few lights on behind the curtain on the stage, casting a reddish glow over the three men in the otherwise dark room. Luca was there, along with the guard who had pulled him out of the party. The third was a wiry man who kept wringing his hands as they approached the stage.

"Sit," the guard ordered, and Luca fell into one of the front row seats. When the thinner man tried to sit as well, the guard grabbed him by the arm and dragged him up onto the stage. There was a spot in the middle of the pine boards that was oddly shiny, and Andrew realized it was a plastic sheet laid out. The wiry man tried to shift away from the sheet as though that would spare him whatever fate was in store for him. The guard countered this by grabbing his shoulder and shoving him to his knees, then turned to face Luca.

"Señor Pedroso, I believe we had a deal, did we not?" Andrew watched the back of Luca's head nod slowly. *"Then why is it that this man,"* the guard pointed at the man on his knees, *"not only knows who I am, but is looking for his own payoff."*

"I...I assure you," Luca said in a quavering voice, *"this man is fully willing to keep your secret. I have known him for thirty years and trust him with my life."*

"If only that were enough. No one alters the deal. Not even you." The curtains parted and Andrew was temporarily dazzled by the light that now spilled from behind the stage. A fourth man stepped in front of the light, only a menacing silhouette visible through the glare until he stepped out onto the stage properly. Andrew couldn't make out the specific features of his face, but he was dressed in jeans and a black jacket and seemed to be wearing gloves.

"Please," Luca said desperately, *"I'm sure we can work this out. I can pay him from my own pocket if necessary. Please, you don't need to do this."* The guard merely shook his head and Andrew had to watch helplessly as the fourth man drew a pistol from his jacket and fixed a silencer to the barrel. The wiry man on the floor began trembling and tried to crawl away, only to be dragged back by the man with the gun. He struck him on the head with the butt of his gun and the wiry man fell to the floor dazed. The barrel of the gun drew level with the man's head and the gun popped seven times. Andrew flinched with each shot as if he was the one being fired at. Deafening silence fell over the theater and Luca slumped forward in his seat, his face in his hands.

"I trust you understand what will happen if anything like this happens again in the future," the guard said to Luca who nodded into his hands. The guard straightened his tie, nodded to the executioner, and began to make his way out of the theater. Andrew was frozen, staring at the body, until finally the year of training kicked in. He scrambled silently backwards, deeper into the shadows and the guard passed right by him and out into the hall. The man with the gun began bundling the body in the plastic sheet while Luca simply sat there, apparently praying now. When the man left with the body and Luca made no move to leave, Andrew crept back out into the hall and made a break for the stairs, pulling out his phone as he forced his heart to slow down. He jammed his thumb into

the emergency call button and it rang only once before there was an answer.

"Hawk, what's wrong?" Hunter asked, cutting right to the chase.

"Hunter, listen, I don't know the specifics of why yet, but a man has been shot and killed in the theater below the gallery. Luca Pedroso is caught up in something and it's gotten another man killed."

"I'm on my way," she said, and he heard her car door open.

"No," Andrew hissed into the phone, "it's too late. The man who shot him is already gone with the body. Head around to the loading dock, I bet he's leaving through there to dispose of it. Try and track him down if you can. I don't want to cause a panic here if we don't need to."

There was a long pause then the slam of a car door that made Andrew jump again. "Alright I'll see what I can do. Are you hurt?"

"No, I'm fine, no one saw me. The guy you're looking for is tall, in jeans and a black jacket, wearing gloves too."

"Alright, get back to the party before anyone notices you down there. I'll handle this and call you later. I'll also let the company know what you saw, but I'll need a proper report too."

"Just be careful."

"Don't worry, Hawk, everything will be fine." The line went dead and Andrew stared at his phone for a moment. He felt a little like he had done the night Eddie had been killed. The same sort of helplessness and regret. He should have intervened, maybe he could have saved the man. 'And gotten yourself killed instead,' said a voice in his head that sounded an awful lot like Hunter. It was right. It was not Andrew's job to go in guns blazing to save anyone and everyone. If things had even been slightly different, if the guard had waited until Luca was alone before getting him or if Luca had said nothing about Andrew's parents, he probably wouldn't have even known someone had been killed that night. This way at least he knew something was wrong and it would be investigated. Andrew was just climbing the stairs again when he heard a voice calling his name from above.

"Hey Hawk? You in here?" He picked up the pace slightly and found Cara poking her head through the door into the stairwell.

"There you are, we thought you'd run...what's the matter? You look pale."

He cursed himself. He should have gotten it together way more before heading back up. "Uh, no it's nothing, don't worry about it."

"You're a terrible liar," Cara said, stepping through the doors properly to allow it to shut, giving them a moment of privacy. This made Andrew almost want to laugh. His whole life was a lie, everything he'd told her about himself was a lie. She had no idea how good a liar he was.

"I, uh, I was just on the phone with the NYPD, a detective."

"Is everything ok?"

"They think that my parents' accident might not have been an accident after all. I was supposed to be with them on the trip. I should have died too and that would have left a lot of money going a lot of places other than me. They think they were murdered."

"Oh, Andrew," Cara said, her face stricken as she wrapped her arms around his neck, "are you alright? Do they think you're still in danger?"

"There's no evidence of that yet, but I'll be meeting with the detective to talk about it. I'm alright, really." He still returned the hug, despite what he was saying. He wrapped his own arms around her, his hands resting on the soft skin of her back. It felt beyond comforting to have someone there, even if she didn't know everything.

"We should go," Cara said, "you don't need to be here."

"It's alright, really. We're here for Diego. Besides, I still owe you a dance, right?"

Cara pulled away, her hands still resting on his shoulders as she looked into his face intently. A little crease formed between her eyebrows. "Hawk, you don't need to do this."

"I assure you, stewing in my condo by myself won't help me. A party with you sounds far more enjoyable. So long as you're alright to stay then so am I."

"Ok," Cara said a little tentatively, still searching his face, "let's get you a drink and I believe they just laid out some fresh caviar. Want some overpriced fish eggs?"

"Always," Andrew said with a smile, opening the door for her. He did his best to keep his composure for the rest of the evening. By all accounts he did a good job. The training he'd received was doing its job better than he could have hoped for. He ate and drank with Cara and the others, met several more new people, and generally pushed the murder he'd witnessed from his mind. He trusted Hunter to follow up and start the investigation. It was not his place.

Andrew had just placed an empty glass down on one of the waiters' trays when a soft hand grabbed his own. "Come on," Cara said, "I requested a song." She dragged him out onto the dance floor just as the quartet was winding down their previous song. Cara stepped close to him and he placed a hand on her waist. As the music started and they began to sway slowly, Andrew listened.

"Unforgettable," he said, "Nat King Cole." Cara's head was resting on his shoulder, but he could feel the smile.

"Not bad," she replied, "wouldn't have pegged you for a classic music buff."

"My mother made sure I had a proper education in all the classics. Whenever there was a lazy Sunday or rainy afternoon, she would play vinyls. Everything from classic jazz acts to the 1812 overture. We'd just sit and listen, drinking hot chocolate and my father would tell stories about all the old shows he used to take my mother to when they were first dating." This was actually true. Something from his real childhood growing up in Brooklyn.

"That sounds wonderful," Cara said before pausing and asking, "do you miss them?"

"Every day," Andrew said, "but I realized that I can't just wallow in it forever. To quote my mother from her weekly dissertations, there is no point trying to relive what was when there is new music to be heard. She'd kill me if she ever found out I locked myself away and stopped living just because they had."

"I've never been especially close with my parents," Cara said quietly. "Don't get me wrong, I love them, and I know they love me. It just never really felt like we were the same after I stopped being a little girl. I think it's why I bought my apartment in the first place. I always felt like I had to hide who I really was at home because it didn't fit with the perfect image my mother wanted to portray." Andrew let silence fall after this and Cara didn't seem especially keen to break it either. They simply swayed together on the dance floor, ignoring everything else. When the song ended, there was the sound of someone tapping a microphone to test it. Cara broke away from him but kept a hold on his hand as they turned to face the small, raised platform where the band was situated.

Luca Pedroso, apparently over the earlier incident, was standing there with a radiant smile. Andrew narrowed his eyes slightly, searching for the terrified, shaking man he'd seen only an hour before. "Ladies and gentlemen," he said, "I'm so glad you could all join us tonight. I know I speak for my brother-in-law when I say that causes like this are an enormous point of pride for our people. These treasures," he indicated the display cases around them, "are finally being given back to the people. Borders may divide us and conflict is rampant, but we are still one people in the eyes of history. A history that should never be forgotten. This is why I, and my colleagues from the Republic of Colombia are so pleased to make this donation to the Turner Library and Museum. I thank you again for joining us and I will now get off the stage so you may stop listening to an old man ramble on."

The crowd tittered with laughter and applauded as Luca waved and stepped off the little stage. He was immediately reabsorbed into the crowd to shake hands. "Want to look around a bit?" Cara asked, "I could use some time away from the crowd." Andrew nodded and she led him out into one of the smaller rooms. It was lined with antique bookshelves and glass cases, muffled by soft carpeting and velvet curtains. Cara walked over to one of the glass cases before turning to face Andrew again.

"I don't get you, Hawk."

"What do you mean?"

"I know so little about you, I met you less than a week ago, and yet I've told you things that I've never told anyone."

"I'm sorry," Andrew said, unable to think of what else to say.

Cara laughed, "No it's ok. I'm actually sort of happy about it. I just can't figure out why. Regardless, I'm glad we met and I'm glad you came out tonight."

"Me too, thanks for bringing me, and thanks for opening up. You're not nearly as much of a bitch as you seemed at first." Andrew grinned at the shocked look on her face and after a moment she cracked a smile as well. Looking back, Andrew had to admit that the rest of the evening was fun. He and Cara spent most of the time talking and eating. He escorted her back to her apartment in the village and left with a smile when she kissed him on the cheek again.

CHAPTER 13

"WHAT THE ACTUAL FUCK were you thinking, Hawk?" Hunter demanded as she burst into his condo. She looked exhausted, with dark circles under her eyes and messy hair. She had clearly been up all night before coming over to see him. "You could have gotten yourself killed by following those guys."

"I was doing my job, Hunter," Andrew replied, firing up at once as he slammed the door behind her. He hadn't slept much better. Most of the night had been spent waiting to hear from her.

"What if they'd seen you? What if you'd been caught? You're here to observe and report."

"Which is what I did. One of the Colombians, the guard who brought Luca down to the execution, wasn't Colombian. He had a Mexican accent. When they left, I followed. I observed. Then I called you as soon as it was done. Like it or not, Hunter, this is exactly what I'm supposed to be doing." Hunter glared at him, then stalked away, falling onto the couch.

"I know," she said into a pillow, "sorry. It was a long night."

"Tell me," Andrew said, barely able to contain his impatience with not knowing.

"I saw the guy, just like you said, jeans and a black jacket. He was definitely a pro. Ducked all the cameras, loaded something into a black van with no plates and took off."

"Did you follow him?"

"Of course I followed him. But he slipped me somehow. I don't think he knew I was there, but he was trained to avoid a tail, just like we were. I searched for hours in the likely spots based on where he was heading. Nothing. I went to the museum after the party broke up. Nothing. You said it was in the theater?"

"Yeah," Andrew said, sitting down across from her, "I followed them down there. The Mexican accused Luca and another man of trying to change the deal. Apparently Luca was a little too liberal with the details of a certain deal they made. Then the gunman entered, shot the other guy seven times, and wrapped him up in the plastic sheet they'd put on the ground."

"Seven times?" Hunter asked, turning her head on the pillow to look at him.

"Yeah, trust me, I counted. Why?"

"I didn't find a single shell casing, a drop of blood, or even a scuff mark from a shoe. I can't even try to open an investigation because there is no evidence beyond what you saw. The van disappeared, there is no missing persons report yet, nothing. I don't know what you stumbled into, Hawk, but there's no evidence of it at all."

"Let's dig a little deeper then." Andrew pulled his phone from his pocket and dialed zero before putting it on speaker and setting it on the table between them. It rang twice before a series of clicks sounded and a voice answered.

"About time, kid," Duncan said, "I've been waiting for your call."

"Is the line secure?" Hunter asked into her pillow.

"Of course it's secure," Duncan snapped, "what do you take me for?"

"Had to be sure," Hunter mumbled.

"So, I take it you're calling about the drama last night with Mister Pedroso and his friends?"

"How would you know that?" Andrew asked and rolled his eyes at the sound of impatience Duncan made.

"You called Hunter, I was listening. You make a secure call to your handler; I get to know. It's just how things go. No, I won't listen to every call you make. Yes, I keep a record of them. Any other questions or can we get on with this?" There was the sound of Duncan loudly sipping a drink as though to emphasize his annoyance.

"Alright," Andrew said, "what have you got for us?"

"Luca Pedroso is squeaky clean. There is no indication in his financials or anything to suggest a payoff, or illegal activity, or embezzling, or any of the other fun activities his kind gets up to. I checked into him, his three ex-wives, four illegitimate children, and even his dog. Nothing. They all came up completely clean beyond a few citations in Bogotá for public intoxication."

"How about the others? There were four people down there including Pedroso."

"Well, if you'd let me know when it happened, I might have had more time to put something together. I was working with a forty-five second call that was mostly you two telling each other to not die."

"Alright, well-" Andrew began but Duncan cut him off.

"That being said, *Hunter* seems to know how to do this. She called and let me know more details, so I ran everyone we know who works in the consulate. I believe your dead man is Alejandro Lopez. He's an aide in the consulate, no criminal record, and a close friend of Luca's. There were three phones that went downstairs with you according to tower data. One was Luca's, one was Alejandro's, and the other was an unregistered number bought and paid for by the consulate. They keep their phone records private, though I don't know why. I busted through their firewall in about three seconds and it just lists the number as one of theirs."

"No fourth phone? There was the gunman as well."

"I'm aware of that, kid. If there was a fourth phone then I would have told you. I pinged Alejandro's phone leaving out the back of the museum before someone pulled the battery. I compiled data from every traffic cam in a ten-block radius, but your boy knows what he's doing. Disappears after leaving the alley behind the museum. I've sent a package to your home terminal with everything I have on Luca and Alejandro. Anything else?"

"Dig deeper into the consulate security," Hunter said, finally sitting up again, "see if you can get a list of the ones assigned to the party. One of them knows what happened. I want him."

"Yes ma'am," Duncan said, "I'm on it and I'll reach out if I find anything." The line cut out and Andrew grabbed his phone.

"Calls you ma'am, calls me kid," Andrew mumbled, pocketing his phone.

"Clearly he's a smart man. Coffee?" Andrew glared at her for a minute before getting up and heading for the kitchen. He hit a couple buttons on the chrome coffee maker, and it started grinding beans and heating the water. When he turned back to Hunter, she was vanishing into his office area. Andrew followed a few minutes later with coffee for her and found her scrolling through the files Duncan had downloaded to his computer.

"Duncan's right," she said, taking the coffee, "Pedroso is clean. Very clean."

"Too clean?" Andrew asked, "His brother-in-law is the president, that comes with a lot of sway and a lot of incentive to make his family look perfect."

"Tough to say, but I'll keep looking into it. By the way, good call on the fake case about your parents. Morris agreed that you might need a bit more support than we set you up with."

"Good, how are you though? Really?"

"Better, actually. Our talk definitely didn't hurt. You were right about the case, also. I went to the apartment that the vic was renting. Nothing was obviously out of place, but I found trace amounts of blood on the back edge of the bedroom door. It's definitely the crime scene. I was hoping to find a fingerprint, but the whole place was wiped down. We're dealing with someone who knows how to cover their tracks without making it look like it."

"Any leads on the identity of the victim?"

"Not yet. The apartment was absolutely not a permanent residence. Canvassing turned up a generic description of the guy but nothing specific. I can't believe that some random guy living in a place like that could possibly warrant a pro like this. I think you were right about the beating being a cover for the drop from the apartment. What's more, the medical examiner confirms that the fall happened before the shots that killed him. Looks like torture."

"Hell of a first case," Andrew said as he leaned on the desk.

"Tell me about it, but it gives me a solid excuse to keep an eye on you while making it look like I'm chasing down leads. The captain already thinks I'm a godsend for finding the actual crime scene. So, thanks for that."

"Sure, no worries." Hunter asked for more details concerning the shooting and what he heard. Andrew reported every detail he could remember and by the time Hunter left, she knew as much as he did. Neither of them, however, were satisfied by what they knew. There were too many unanswered questions.

Andrew spent the next several weeks working his way deeper into the elite. This meant a lot of time spent with Cara, Diego, Dirk, and Eliza. After the gala, Diego seemed ready to accept Andrew as an official member of their inner circle. Eliza seemed to not care either way and even Dirk eventually softened towards him. Soon Andrew was going out to clubs with them, attending expensive dinners, and hardly two days went by without seeing at least one of them. Diego was well connected with the other children of diplomats and would often invite a few of them to the clubs. As he anticipated, Andrew saw a fair amount of drug use. Everything from weed to cocaine. While he did not partake, nor did Cara, the others all became far more talkative while they were high.

Reports to Hunter now included random details about what the French, Chinese, Japanese, Russian, and Italian officials were up to. Nothing quite so dramatic as the murder of Alejandro Lopez, but it still painted a picture of how the various nations were feeling and acting. Hunter had so far been unable to find Lopez's body or any sign of the killer. Luca had been hanging around with Andrew and the others which, according to Cara, was nothing out of the ordinary. He seemed to simply enjoy the feeling of living a taste of the high life with them and Diego seemed to respect him more than his own father. Something still bothered Andrew about it, but he couldn't find anything remotely suspicious about the man. It was driving him insane.

Before he knew it, Andrew was a completely different person all over again. He was a member of an upscale squash club where he played with Dirk. He spent a ton of time with Cara, helping her with the different youth art groups she supported. Eliza liked using him as some sort of wingman to identify her next victims. Diego, meanwhile, enjoyed having someone he could bring to events with the UN kids who could translate if needed. Much like his old friends, all of them seemed fascinated by Andrew's gift with languages. All in all, Andrew was doing better than anyone could have hoped while Hunter started closing case after case. Even while her first was still unsolved, no one could expect better.

CHAPTER 14

CHRISTMAS LOOMED OVER THE city like a cloud. Snow began dusting the ground as decorations went up on every available surface. With permission from the company and in an attempt to maintain appearances, Hunter would be spending the holiday with her family in Florida. She had spent three hours the day before she left making sure Andrew wasn't going to get himself killed when she was gone. Cara was heading to Bali with her parents and the others had similar plans with their families. This left Andrew on his own for the holiday and feeling odd about it. The previous Christmas had been spent at The Farm which turned out to be surprisingly more festive than he'd have guessed. Before that he'd either spent the holiday with his family or Eddie's.

Andrew went for a run in the morning on Christmas Eve, like he always did. The dark and the cold kept him focused as he ran. Determined to do something productive with the time, he was stewing on the absence of leads concerning Luca Pedroso. With each step he took the details of that night flashed through his mind's eye. The fake security guard. The gunman. The terrified Alejandro. From what he had heard, the guard had paid off Luca to hide who he really was, but there was still no evidence of that. Short of breaking into Luca's home, there wasn't much more he could do. Andrew stumbled to a stop, breathing hard with clouds of vapor in the cold. His eyes were wide as he stared at nothing in particular. Luca Pedroso was back in Colombia with Diego for the holidays. Andrew had his address from Duncan's file. Could he really do this?

Andrew nodded politely to the two guards in the lobby as he sped through to the elevators. This was a stupid plan. Truly stupid. But he couldn't think of anything else to do. Not knowing was going to eat him alive. It wasn't that he didn't trust Hunter to do her job, she simply had no authority to launch an in-depth investigation into a Colombian official with no evidence. The elevator came smoothly to a stop with a dull ding and Andrew stepped out onto the muffling carpet of the hallway. He tried to shake himself off this train of thought, knowing that Hunter would kill him herself if she ever found out. He simply had to resign himself to the fact that for the next couple of weeks he was on his own and to do nothing.

Then he saw the picture. He'd gotten it framed along with a few others, partly because he wanted to break up the sterile feeling of a home he had no say in designing, but also because he simply liked it. It showed him and Cara, both splattered with paint and with the girl Em on Andrew's shoulders. It had been taken after a public library in the Bronx had wanted to do a mural on one of their walls. In an effort to educate the kids as well, Diane's group had done a massive Pollock style piece on the wall. The result was Andrew, Cara, and half a dozen kids spraying paint at the wall in every way they could. It had been one of the best days of his life, if only to see the smile on Cara's face. A smile that was now immortalized in his condo. A smile he would not see for a month until she got back.

Andrew shot to his feet, unable to sit and do nothing, and ran up the stairs to his bedroom. He opened the wall safe and pulled out a small bag of tools they'd given him in case he ever needed to, with permission, do something illegal. He hesitated as he was about to close the safe and grabbed the Glock 19 on a whim. He figured that he would rather have it and not need it than the opposite. He unscrewed the suppressor and slipped it into a pocket, checked the clip and the safety, and stuffed the gun into a special pocket on the inside of his coat before tossing it onto the bed. He changed quickly into comfortable jeans and a gray t-shirt before donning the coat again and heading back downstairs. He would want to be able to move easily if necessary. Suits and ties were all well and good until you needed to scale a building.

The elevator delivered him back down in the lobby and within a minute he was pulling out onto the soaked street in his BMW. The magical, delicate snowfall had given way to a dreary sort of drizzling rain as though to reflect Andrew's mood. Thankfully, this meant he would not be doing this in broad daylight. He'd been up so early for his run that by the time he was pulling up to the handsome brownstone in the Upper West Side, it was still dark. He scanned the line of houses, cruising by slowly to not draw too much attention by parking right in front. Once he'd spotted Luca's, he continued a couple blocks away before parking and getting out of his car. Turning his collar up against the chilly rain, Andrew hurried back along the street and up the stairs. No one was around this early on Christmas Eve, so Andrew pulled out the little pouch of tools and opened it.

The lock was top of the line, the sort that they would use in buildings like the White House, but of course that meant he'd been trained on them. He was just inserting a pick into the lock when a little flashing red light caught his attention through the window. He swore to himself. Of course there was an alarm, why wouldn't there be? Andrew left the picks in the lock and pulled out his phone to discover a text from Duncan.

Call me when you figure it out.

Andrew took a deep breath and dialed zero again. Duncan picked up right away and Andrew heard the clicks that meant the signal was being encrypted. "Good morning, kid," Duncan said cheerfully, "out for a bit of breaking and entering to spice up your day?"

Duncan had tracked him. Of course he had; it was his job. "I need to know more about Luca, Duncan. Official channels aren't going to tell us shit."

"I know, kid, Hunter was contemplating the same thing. She, however, has a certain sense of duty to that badge of hers. She'll do what needs to be done to protect you and the mission, but breaking into a foreign government official's house without evidence? That's a little much for her ethics just now. I just didn't think it would be day one of you being on your own that you'd grow too restless to sit on your hands. Congrats, kid, you've surprised me."

"I need the alarm deactivated," Andrew said, pulling a Bluetooth earpiece from his pocket and switching it on before stashing his phone back in his pocket.

"Already done," Duncan replied into his ear, "you're welcome. Just remember, he's got a Medeco lock so you're going to want to-"

"Bump it, I know," Andrew cut him off, "but this is newer than the standard Medeco. Bumping won't fly. Gotta go old school unless you want to hack the lock." Andrew's tone was derisive as he grabbed the picks again, but there was silence on the line. "Sorry," he muttered, "I appreciate your help, Duncan."

"That's more like it," Duncan said in his usual surly voice, "but ask and you shall receive." There was a soft beep from inside the house and the lock spun open on its own. Andrew stared at it for a moment, then tried the door. It opened.

"How the hell," Andrew began as he stepped inside, but stopped when he saw the mechanism on the back of the door as he closed it and it locked again. It was the sort of thing you could buy at a hardware store to let you open your door from your phone. "Seriously? Top of the line locks and a twenty-dollar Bluetooth device that opens it? I figured he was smarter than this."

"The rich always think they are. Now listen up, we found nothing to indicate that he's gotten a wire transfer for whatever he's involved with, so you're looking for something else. Cash, jewels, art, whatever. Something he shouldn't have. He's rich, but not that rich."

"I got it," Andrew said quietly. The instinct to whisper, even in an empty house, was not an easy thing to overcome while breaking the law. The house was decorated like an eighteenth-century castle. Gilded wood paneling covered the walls and accented with truly gaudy gold fixtures. The furniture all looked antique, but it was too new and sterile to be authentic.

"I'm tapping into his local network, just to take a peek around...damn, he's got some next level encryption on his laptop. If you find it, hardwire your phone in, makes it easier on me."

"Duncan," Andrew said as he felt along the edges of a few gold frames with replicas of famous works, "can I ask you a personal question?"

"Go for it, kid."

"Why are you still doing this? Surely you could retire pretty comfortably if you've spent so much time as the best. Why not give this up and spend your days on a beach or something?"

"I tried that for a while. Got myself a boat down in the Caribbean and a shitload of rum. Didn't have a care in the world for a good two years. Then it got boring. So I came back and they let me pick and choose missions to be on."

"Wait, so you chose to be the support for me and Hunter?"

"Yep. Two of the youngest operatives I've ever seen going in to infiltrate high society. Couldn't pass that up."

"Ok," Andrew said slowly, sensing something in Duncan's voice, "what's the real reason." There was a sigh on the other end of the line and a very pregnant pause before the answer came.

"My oldest kid joined up when he was a little older than you are. Trained up at The Farm and was posted in Europe somewhere, they never told me where. He was in the field for a week before they found his body nailed to a wall with a note addressed to the company, telling them to back off. You sorta remind me of him."

"Oh Christ, Duncan, I'm sorry. What was his name?"

"Theodore," Duncan said in a quiet mumble.

"Well, I'm honored you chose to help us, really."

"Yeah alright, kid, just get on with it. You see anything?"

Andrew passed through an open doorway into an office. The room was dominated by an ornate desk complete with gold desk lamp and antique books, not unlike those that had been donated to the Turner. The effect was somewhat ruined by the clunky laptop sitting on top.

"I've got a laptop, hooking you in now." He pulled a small cable from the pouch of tools and connected one end to his phone and the other to the laptop.

"On it," Duncan said as the screen flared to life, "keep looking, if the alarm cycles, then I lose control and you're going to prison...probably in Colombia...where you will probably die."

"What?" Andrew hissed, "Why would you not tell me this?"

"The odds of it happening are pretty slim, but not zero, I also don't know when it'll happen so there was no point telling you. I've stopped the signal from broadcasting to the alarm company, but the pricey ones tend to reset the systems to stop lowlife scum from bypassing them and rummaging through the owner's stuff. Anyhow, keep rummaging through his stuff, but maybe quicker."

Andrew stifled his reply as he scanned the office for anything of note. He was about to move on from the room when he spotted something out of the ordinary. The bottom two shelves of one of the bookcases had been converted into a small cabinet. It might have gone completely unnoticed by Andrew if it hadn't been for the fact that the cabinet panels were a slightly lighter color of wood. If the room, like the rest of the house, had not been so clearly designed with a single style then it wouldn't have stood out. Andrew knelt in front of the cabinet and opened the doors. Behind them was a fairly sophisticated safe with both a key and combination lock.

"I've got a safe here," Andrew said, "looks like a Brown, key and dial combo."

"Pulling up specs now. The key is nothing special, you can pick it no problem. The combination is a different story. You either have to crack it manually or guess the combination."

"I don't think so," Andrew said, standing up straight and looking around, "this is a man who installed a device making it child's play to rob him on his front door. I can see him not being the type to remember his combination off the top of his head."

He grabbed the lamp and checked underneath it. Nothing. He opened each of the drawers and felt along the bottom of them. Still nothing. Then he examined the books. It would take hours to check each one individually, but maybe it was easier than that. Luca was a stupid man who thought he was smart, probably had a sense of humor that amused himself more than anyone else. Andrew scanned the titles of the books, most were in Spanish, but then one jumped out at him, Treasure Island.

The book appeared to be bound in black leather, but on a whim, Andrew tapped the spine with his knuckle. It was hollow, sounded like nothing more than an empty box so he slid it from the shelf. The cover was magnetically sealed but with no kind of lock, so Andrew popped it open easily. The inside was a simple wooden box with a handful of important looking, but probably not critical, documents. At the bottom of this little stack was a scrap of paper with three numbers. 46 83 17. Smiling, Andrew replaced the book and fell to his knees at the safe again. It only took him a minute to slide the pins of the lock into place with a satisfying click. Then he took a deep breath, cracked his knuckles, and tried the combination. The moment the dial spun the last few ticks to the seventeen, there was another, louder click.

With a slight fluttering of his heart, Andrew twisted the handle of the safe and it clunked open. The door swung on well-oiled hinges without a sound and revealed only two things. A Colombian Consulate ID card that was missing its photo and a black USB stick. He reported his findings to Duncan who made a satisfied sort of noise.

"Not bad kid, sounds like Luca might be selling positions in the consulate. By the way, the front door just unlocked."

"Yeah thanks, but I'm not done looking around yet."

"No, idiot, someone just unlocked it. You aren't alone. Move."

CHAPTER 15

ANDREW'S SENSES SLAMMED INTO overdrive as pure adrenaline coursed through him. He closed the door of the safe as quietly as he could and locked it again, making sure to grab his picks. He closed the cabinet just as he heard the door open and the shrill beeping of the alarm indicating it had started a countdown. Duncan must have reactivated it a moment sooner. A few beeps indicated that whoever was there punched in the code and everything fell silent again. Andrew yanked his phone and the cable from the laptop and crept towards the door to peek out into the hall. Two large men were lumbering towards him, and he wondered silently if the alarm had reset without Duncan telling him.

As slowly and calmly as he could manage, Andrew moved behind the cracked door so that it would open on top of him. He felt sort of stupid by doing it. It was the sort of thing you'd see in a cartoon. That feeling diminished slightly as he drew his weapon and silencer. Slowly, painfully slow, he screwed the silencer into place as the footsteps grew closer.

"In here," one of the men said and Andrew recognised the Mexican accented Spanish of the fake guard at the gala. The door was pushed open and fell short of hitting Andrew by an inch. One of the men moved into the room while the other stood in the doorway.

If he so much as glanced to his right, he would see Andrew standing there in the gap between door and wall. He didn't even dare to move to aim the gun, instead he just stood frozen, watching the man paw at a tablet computer with huge hands. The stench of cheap tobacco oozed from the man like a fog, driving its way into Andrew's nose and making him want to gag.

"Hurry up, I don't want to hang around here long," said the man standing next to Andrew. This was definitely the same man as that night. So, then who was the other? The safe clunked again as the other man unlocked it and Andrew saw the closer man catch something and plug it into the tablet. It was the USB drive from the safe. He could not see the screen, but the man started poking at it again, waited, then unplugged it to toss it back to the one by the safe.

"You're sure this will work?" asked the second man.

"Mine did, just grab it and let's go, the boss isn't exactly patient. Unless you want to end up rotting in a drainage tunnel too." The other man apparently had no response to this and simply locked the safe again and exited the room. Andrew finally let out a breath he had not realized he was holding and crept around the door again just as the men left out the front.

"Freeze," Duncan said in his ear and Andrew nearly shit himself before doing as he was told. There was a beep from down the hall. "Ok go, alarm is disabled again. Motion sensors missed you by about a second. Nice job, kid."

"How do you know I was moving?"

"I turned on your phone's camera, dumbass. Now grab that USB, I want to see what's on it. What did they do?"

Andrew recounted the brief events as he unlocked the safe again, setting his gun on the floor next to him. When he'd opened the small metal box, it now only held the drive, no ID card. He grabbed it carefully by the sides and moved back to the laptop on the desk. With his phone reconnected and the USB plugged in as well, Duncan made another satisfied sound in his ear.

"Figured as much. The USB has only one thing on it. An encrypted file with the details of a Cayman Islands bank account. Gimme a second here...yeah, it's got a couple million sitting in it. There's your payoff. I'd bet my left nut that the card was already keyed to open every door in the consulate, just needs a photo."

Andrew was half listening as he rummaged through the drawers until he found what he was looking for. He grabbed a roll of clear tape and tore off a small strip. Very carefully, he pressed the tape against the flat surface of the USB, then peeled it off and held it up to the light. A perfect thumbprint was now held on the tape and Andrew smiled to himself. He placed the tape on a clear credit card sized piece of plastic from his kit for safekeeping and stuck it back in the pouch.

"I've got a clear print from the drive," he said into his earpiece, "I'll scan it and send it to you later."

"Great job, kid," Duncan said, sounding impressed, "I've just finished cloning the hard drive so put everything back and get out of there before someone else decides to come knocking."

Andrew replaced the USB in the safe, locked it, and made sure everything he had touched was back where it should be. Duncan unlocked the door for him, and he slipped out onto the stoop. The street was still deserted, and Andrew was able to walk calmly back to his car through the rain. He was still shaking slightly from the adrenaline as it faded, something that no amount of training could prevent. It was just a function of the body. His sense of satisfaction lasted about four blocks before a new need for answers started pushing in on him. Then he realized he was still on the line with Duncan.

"Any idea what's going on? Big picture I mean."

"My best guess is that someone is planning something to do with our friends in Colombia. Something big if they want to infiltrate the consulate directly. There are secure lines there direct to their government back home that I admit are easier to access than if they were there. The biggest hurdle is consulate security, but that's who these guys are pretending to be."

"Do you figure they're just hired help? They've got some pretty advanced skills, the way they dealt with Alejandro."

"That one is definitely a pro. No government beyond us and a few allies regularly employ folks like that. So yes, I'd say they're just a hired crew."

"But what does the consulate have that's worth taking?"

"No clue, but I'll start parsing through Luca's hard drive and see if I can't find us some answers. For now, take it easy, you're on vacation, kid."

"Yeah alright, thanks for your help Duncan, and thanks for telling me about your son. I think you're doing his memory proud by helping idiots like me."

"Skip the therapy session, kid, I've made my peace with it all. Just stay out of trouble." His voice was softer than Andrew had heard it thus far. The line went dead and Andrew pulled the earpiece off and tossed it onto the seat next to him. The idea of going back to the empty condo was not exactly desirable so he blew an hour or two grabbing coffee and wandering around the city. He'd always loved how quiet things were in the days before Christmas. The usually chaotic city tended to hunker down in their homes, enjoying time off work and school. The rain persisted, but he didn't really care, it helped him to stop dwelling on Cara.

Andrew knew that this was all part of the assignment, he had to look like he was living a regular life. But he hated having to lie to her. For the most part he didn't, but not telling her what he was really doing felt just as bad. The other part of him simply didn't care. He just wanted to be with her regardless. And why should it matter? For all intents and purposes he was this person now and would be for a very long time. Who was to say he couldn't maintain a relationship during it all?

He sighed and tossed his empty coffee cup into a garbage can next to where he'd parked and climbed back into his car. The sky was growing darker and he might as well get something done. He would go home, send Duncan the print, and keep stewing on what Luca was up to. He didn't seem the type to betray his country, but people did strange things for money. How had he gotten mixed up in this though? Why him? And what had happened to Alejandro's body?

There was still no report filed for a missing person and no one had found a dumped body that would match his description.

Thunder cracked the air as Andrew pulled back through the gate into the private lot behind his building. The guard stationed there, bundled in waterproof gear, nodded politely to him as he got out and hurried across to the door. Aware that he was dripping all over the floor, Andrew tried to hurry through the lobby to the elevators, but a voice halted him.

"Hawk," a woman called from behind the security desk. It was Evie, still dressed in an outfit designed to show off more than might have been professional. She flashed him a dazzling smile as she rounded the desk and sauntered over to him. "Good lord, you're soaked. You must be freezing."

"I'm alright," Andrew said simply.

"Well, I just thought I'd let you know someone came by to drop off an early Christmas present for you, let them in to deliver it." Her tone was light and playful, but Andrew's brain seemed to freeze. Someone had come to see him and Evie had just let them in? He was ready to scream, to pull his gun and demand what the hell she'd been thinking. The whole point of this gaudy place was to keep shit like this from happening.

Evidently one of the regular guards saw his distress and called over, "No need to worry, Mr. Hawkins, we saw this, uh, gift arrive as well."

"Just trust me," Evie said, taking his arm and leading him over to the elevator, "I'm sure you're going to like it." Andrew took a deep breath and allowed himself to be steered through the golden doors of the elevator. Evie pushed the button for his floor, winked at him, and left.

The moment the doors closed, Andrew pulled the Glock from his jacket and checked the clip and safety before clutching it in his pocket. Every single person he knew that might have thought to get him a present was already outside of the city. Unless they'd had it couriered or something, but he didn't know that he meant that much to any of them yet. Hunter could have gotten him something, but surely she'd have found a better way than having a stranger enter his condo. Cara had promised she would have something for him when she returned from her trip, but other than that there was no one. The elevator reached his floor and he peeked out cautiously before stepping into the hall. Everything was quiet and much how it always was. Several of his neighbors, whom he had met over the last couple months, had left for holidays of their own. His door was closed and locked, like always, but he tightened his grip on the gun as he inserted his own key.

Evie had failed to say if the person had simply dropped off a package and left. If they had, then surely it could have been left at the front desk. No, if she had let someone in, it was the opportunity for something far more sinister. But who? Had someone figured out who he was? Unable to come up with an answer, Andrew turned the key and pushed open his door. The lights were off in the condo. A sign in and of itself. He left the door open and made his way slowly into the condo. Lightning flashed across the sky, illuminating the huge windows and revealing a figure standing there. A woman. Andrew blinked a couple of times to make sure he was seeing right. He definitely recognised her, which meant he should really, really not shoot her. He dropped the gun in his pocket and quickly shunted his jacket off before tossing it haphazardly into the closet and closing the front door.

"Cara?" he asked cautiously, and she turned to face him. A dazzling array of multicolored lights flicked on next to her, revealing the massive tree that now stood in the corner.

"Merry Christmas, Hawk," she said, smiling broadly at his stunned expression. She was dressed in flannel pajama pants and a tank top with her hair tied back in a messy ponytail.

"What are you doing here?" he asked. His heart rate steadied again and he walked over to her and the huge tree. "What the hell is this?"

"I couldn't stand the idea of you being on your own for Christmas. No family, all of us gone. So I skipped the usual trip South this year. I'm here for a pajama Christmas movie double feature," she gestured to her outfit. "How the Grinch stole Christmas, original animated version, obviously, and Die Hard. Only way to go." She held up a pair of Blu-ray disks.

Andrew blinked at her several times, trying to process his thoughts. Then he just stopped thinking. Closing the distance between them, Andrew grabbed Cara by the waist with one hand and lifted her chin slightly with the other to kiss her. The movies tumbled from her hands and after a slightly stunned moment she wrapped her arms around his neck and pulled herself deeper into the kiss.

CHAPTER 16

ANDREW'S DAMP CLOTHES WERE scattered over the floor of his bedroom, mingled with the hastily stripped off pajamas Cara had been wearing. The storm had finally blown itself out and a weak afternoon sun was trying to break through the clouds. It cast a few solitary beams of light across the bed where Andrew and Cara were lying on top of each other, still breathing hard. Cara twisted around, the sheets clinging to her skin as she looked down at Andrew's face.

"Well," she said as Andrew's hand slid up her back, "that was fun."

"Fun? That's all I get? It was fun?"

"Alright," Cara said, kissing him softly on the neck, "that was spectacular. Better?"

"Much better," Andrew replied with a coy sort of smile.

Cara made a satisfied sort of noise, stretching luxuriously over him and wrapping herself around him more completely. They stayed like that for quite a while, dozing occasionally until darkness fell around them and Andrew woke to an empty place beside him. He sat up in bed just as Cara emerged from his expansive closet wearing only a soft blue sweater of his like a dress.

"I think you have more clothes than I do," she said teasingly before crawling back into the bed to sit in his lap.

"Pays to be prepared," he said, "you never know when a girl might start stealing them."

"I wouldn't have to steal if you hadn't literally torn my shirt off."

"A price I am more than willing to pay. You still want to watch your movies?"

"Of course," Cara said at once, "I'm not going to let sex with you ruin a fifteen-year tradition." Andrew smiled at her. He always smiled more easily whenever she was around.

"Alright then, let's go."

"I'll make popcorn, you put something on," Cara said before kissing him again and sliding out of the bed. Apparently with no thought to her pajama pants, she disappeared down the stairs. Andrew, meanwhile, walked into the closet and pulled on a pair of gray track pants and a white t-shirt before heading down to join her. She was sitting on the counter, swinging her feet happily as she waited for the popping bag in the microwave to stop. The colorful lights from the tree she had brought for him were shining across the condo, making her hair glow softly with rainbow light. Andrew stopped at the bottom of the stairs and simply watched her for a few moments until she noticed him there.

"What?" she asked defensively, her legs falling still again.

"Nothing, I just don't tell you nearly often enough how beautiful you are."

"Shut up," Cara said, looking away from him with embarrassment, "my hair is a mess, I've got no makeup, nothing special at all."

Andrew walked over to her, taking her hands in his. "Beautiful," he said earnestly, and she grinned in spite of herself before leaning forward to kiss him. By the time the first movie was starting on Andrew's massive screen, Cara was curled up on his lap in one of the spacious leather recliners. Her head rested on his shoulder as one of his hands traced patterns over her bare legs. It was the first time since arriving back in New York that Andrew had felt no sense of worry. The unanswered questions which had promised to create a hellish couple of weeks were now out of his mind completely. He could deal with those things later. The world could wait.

The next few days were spent in a sort of haze, mostly leaving bed only to retrieve food from the kitchen or delivery drivers who usually looked shocked at whatever state of undress one or both of them were in. The exception to this, however, was Cara insisting they go to see the tree in Rockefeller Centre on Christmas Day, another one of her traditions apparently. Cara seemed unwilling to leave Andrew's side for the first week, making it impossible for him to sneak away long enough to send the print he'd retrieved to Duncan. But that all seemed so unimportant too.

On New Year's Eve, Cara had suggested that they abscond to her family's beach house for a few days, which proved to be just as wonderful. The utter silence away from the city made it seem as though the snow, falling steadily since Christmas Day, had muffled all else. It was perhaps the best nights of sleep Andrew had gotten in a long time. As they settled into a sort of comfortable cohabitation, Cara began opening up more than ever before. She shared her own art with Andrew, something she said she had never shown to anyone. Meanwhile, Andrew felt that this time had truly solidified his identity. He truly was Andrew Hawkins with Cara and had no reason to think of who he had ever been before.

The ventures from their little dens grew more adventurous in the days after the New Year. They attended the symphony, took in shows, and Cara took Andrew to her favorite exhibits in the MET. The day before both Eliza and Diego were due to return to the city, which would more or less mark the end of the solitude, they went for a walk through Central Park. It was the sort of walk you saw old married couples taking together. Walking arm in arm, bundled against the cold, and chatting about nothing in particular. Their footsteps crunched in the snow of the path they were on which only made it so much more obvious when another set of footsteps sounded over their own.

Andrew had spotted the man about five minutes earlier, lurking between two trees. He'd been dressed in all black and kept one hand constantly in his pocket. He knew what was coming and while it did not frighten him in the slightest, he wanted to keep Cara safe.

As soon as he heard the accompanying footsteps, Andrew lagged slightly, sliding his arm out from Cara's. She hardly noticed as she walked on, now a little ahead as Andrew moved half a step behind her to keep himself between her and the obvious assailant. A hand suddenly grabbed his arm and whirled him around and the barrel of a short revolver was pressed into his chest.

"Give me your wallet," the man growled, "nice and easy." Cara had frozen midstep and turned as well, her eyes wide with terror. "And you," the mugger added to Cara, "drop that purse unless you want your boyfriend's brains staining the ground."

With a slightly shaking hand, Cara reached up to grab the strap of her purse. She was moving slowly and deliberately, clearly making sure the man did not suspect her of trying anything.

"Cara, it's alright," Andrew said with absolute calm, "just stay there, keep your things."

"Shut up," the mugger spat, pushing the gun a little harder into Andrew, "I'm the one with the gun here. Maybe I'll just kill you anyway and take her for myself, show her what a real man can make her feel."

This was too far. Andrew's blood ran cold as Cara took a little step back in fright and the man turned the gun on her to keep her still. It was over in two seconds. Andrew grabbed the man's wrist, digging hard into the soft part of the joint and twisting hard. The gun fell from his hand in surprise and Andrew caught it with his free one. The man fell to the ground with the slightest push from Andrew before receiving a swift kick that undeniably cracked a rib. Andrew popped the cylinder open, removed the bullets, and pocketed them before tossing the gun as hard as he could towards the pond nearby. The revolver broke through a thin film of ice and sank out of sight before the man had even caught his breath enough to cough. Cara was staring between Andrew and their would-be attacker, more than a little stunned.

"Apologize," Andrew said, looking down at the man as he placed a reassuring hand on Cara's waist.

"I'm sorry," the man wheezed, trying to scoot away from Andrew while clutching his side, "I'm sorry."

"Are you alright?" Andrew said to Cara now. She'd fallen into him slightly, still somewhat stunned by his response. Without warning she stepped forward and stomped down as hard as she could on the man's crotch. He curled up in silent agony and Andrew almost laughed.

"I am now," Cara said, taking Andrew's arm and pulling him away. He could still feel her shaking so thought it best to cut their walk short. He put her in the passenger seat of his car only a few minutes later and took off back towards his condo. They made it five minutes, Andrew guessed it was as Cara's adrenaline cooled off, before she asked the question.

"How did you do that, Hawk?"

He knew the question was coming, he knew it would always come at some point, so he had an answer. "I wasn't exactly the best kid growing up," he said, changing lanes smoothly to make the next turn. "When that attitude didn't shift as I was supposed to be maturing, my father thought a couple years in a military academy might straighten me out. He wasn't entirely wrong. They beat some discipline and respect into me along with a whole bunch of skills I don't exactly have a use for."

"What else do you know how to do?"

"I'm a half-decent shot, I know some hand-to-hand combat, stuff like that. Also, if we're ever stranded in the forest, I've got survival training too."

"Useful," Cara said, a tiny note of sarcasm in her voice, which Andrew took as a good sign, "what with all the forests in the city."

"Exactly," Andrew said. Silence fell between them and he took Cara's hand, threading his fingers through hers. "I'm sorry he threatened you. I should have taken him down faster."

"It's not my first mugging, Hawk, I've lived here forever." Her voice was determinedly hard, but he still sensed the lingering fear.

"I promise to keep you safe," he said, "no matter what happens, I'll make sure you're alright." Cara smiled at him and squeezed his hand a little tighter. They spent the rest of the evening with a quiet dinner and more cuddling up in the theater room. As they sat together, Cara nodding off in his arms, he realized how much he meant what he'd said. Mission aside, she was quickly becoming his top priority. Something he found he was perfectly ok with.

CHAPTER 17

IT FELT STRANGE TO be away from Cara the next day. They'd spent every moment together since Christmas and Andrew would have been perfectly ok with that arrangement continuing a while longer. Sadly, Cara had already agreed to have brunch with Eliza when she'd returned from her vacation. So, after a long shower and procrastinating in bed, Cara had kissed Andrew goodbye and promised to come right back. This, while irksome to his newly filled heart, allowed him to finally follow up on his new leads. The jacket with his gun and the little pouch of tools was still stuffed into the bottom of the closet beside the door. He retrieved it and, after replacing the gun in his safe, pulled out the little plastic card with the fingerprint on it.

It took only a few minutes to peel it off, apply a tiny amount of fine fingerprint powder, and scan an image of it. He sent the image to Duncan and received a text almost at once.

About damn time. Hunter is back too. We all need to have a little chat about what you found. Call me when you get together.

Andrew picked up his phone and thought for a moment. He and Hunter were supposed to have limited contact in person and trying to sneak away now that Cara would be with him most of the time made it all the more difficult. But she was already gone now. He dialed her number and she answered on the second ring.

"Hawk," she said in her familiar teasing voice, "you're going to have to get used to the idea of me being away sometimes. I know you're just a lost little puppy but don't make me put you in a crate when I leave."

"Hilarious," Andrew said, "no I just thought I would let you know that I may not be here when you get back. I got a call from that detective right after you left and I'm going down to talk to her. I'll leave a key for you at the front desk though, ok?"

"Sure," Cara said, a little morosely, "everything alright?"

"Yeah, she just wants to update me on the case. I'll be alright. You have fun."

"Ok Hawk, I'll see you later."

He was off the phone less than a minute before he called Hunter and she agreed for him to come over. Hunter's apartment was only a ten-minute walk from the condo, so he opted to leave his car behind. His breath steamed in the air before him as he walked and took in the feeling of the city ramping up after the holidays. He was buzzed into Hunter's building and he made his way up to the third floor. The door opened to reveal Hunter blinking sleepily at him in a robe.

"You look dead," Andrew said by way of greeting, stepping past her into the open loft apartment, "why aren't you at work?"

"It's my last day of vacation," she said, "and I was still asleep when you called. What do you want, Hawk?" It was slightly funny to him how different the nickname sounded coming from her versus Cara.

"Duncan has something for us. I, uh, sort of found a lead on Luca while you were away."

"Oh yeah? I thought he was in Colombia."

"He was, but his house wasn't." This took a moment to penetrate the layer of sleep that still muddled her brain. When it did sink in, though, her eyes widened and she whacked him on the arm.

"What the hell are you talking about? I told you to play it safe while I was gone."

"I did, I was very safe, I swear. I needed answers and I couldn't stand just sitting there." Andrew filled her in on everything that had happened while she was gone. Both about Luca and the men who were bribing him, and Cara. Naturally, he skipped over the finer details of their time together, but she got the picture. Hunter demanded coffee before responding, so Andrew hustled over to her little kitchen at once.

"I'm happy about you and Cara," she said finally after a long sip, "you two seem cute together."

"Thanks," Andrew said, blushing slightly.

"I'll be sure to send her flowers when I kill you. You almost got caught, Hawk. I swear to God you're going to give me an aneurysm."

"Well I wasn't caught. I know you couldn't have done it, not as a cop. I just needed something to go on. I'm sorry."

"I know," Hunter said, sighing heavily, "at least we have more solid ties between Luca and these men who killed Alejandro. It's more than just threats or extortion, he's actually doing this voluntarily."

"I dunno about that. The two who showed up for the blank ID seemed pretty afraid of pissing off their boss. They might be paying Luca, but I wouldn't be surprised to find out there is still a threat involved. They said they could end up in a drainage tunnel too."

"Drainage tunnel? That seems oddly specific."

"That's why I'm telling you. I suspect that's where Alejandro ended up. Although that was months ago now, there's probably not much to find. Anyway, Duncan said we needed to have a chat." Hunter nodded and Andrew set his phone on her kitchen island before dialing Duncan on speaker.

"How up to speed is she?" he asked as soon as the call was secure.

"I told her what happened and what we found, she hit me and accused me of having a death wish. So what have you got?"

"Honestly, a lot less than you'd expect from a guy's personal computer. All the usual boring crap, some consulate stuff, and a disturbing amount of porn. But that's it. No banking info, no email accounts, nothing. Until you start digging into a nice little hidden section of the drive."

"In which you found?" Hunter prompted.

"A single email account with exactly two messages. The first seems to lay out the deal that was struck. Three IDs for the Colombian consulate security, all access, for a small fortune each. The second was sent from Luca about a month ago but he did something to it I've never seen before. His cyber-security was a joke, but this is some next level encryption on just this one email. I'll let you know when I crack it. Regardless, I think it's safe to say Luca is expecting one more payment. The bank account had only two IDs worth of money."

"I'll keep an eye on him," Hunter said, "what about the print Hawk sent you?"

"That is actually quite interesting. It belongs to a man named Mateo Diaz, registered with immigration and everything, native of Mexico. That is, until you dig a little deeper. It seems Mister Diaz didn't exist until about six months ago. On a whim I threw the printout for comparison to the Colombian criminal database. Turns out his real name is Dante Hernandez, a lieutenant in the Vargas cartel in Colombia."

"So, what? The accent is just an act to fit into his fake identity?" Andrew asked. "Seems like overkill, especially if you're trying to fit in with a bunch of people from your own country."

"The consulate employs a fair number of folks from other places," Duncan said, "easier to hire locals sometimes. Anyway, the Vargas cartel is brutal, one of the worst in the world and responsible for a hefty chunk of the drugs coming through the States. Doesn't surprise me he's using a couple different ways to distance himself from them while he's here."

"Any idea what they're after yet?" Hunter asked.

"I have a hunch that the encrypted email will tell us just that, but I can't say for sure. I'm not willing to speculate further until I have a better understanding of what I found. In the meantime, keep a watch for mystery man number three. Whoever is paying Luca will likely want their last ID. Until then things should stay reasonably calm. Hunter, I'll reach out if I find anything else or when I get through this encryption. Welcome back, ma'am."

"Thanks, Duncan," Hunter said before hitting the phone to end the call. She leaned a little heavier against the island countertop and breathed in the steam of her coffee.

"You ok? How were things at your parents'?"

"Oh fine," Hunter replied, "now that I'm back here *and* have a big promotion my dad is all proud of me again. My mom just kept saying she knew I'd be back in the thick of it."

"But?" Andrew asked.

"It just made me feel like I don't deserve it. A feeling that is in no way helped by the fact that the first case they assigned me is still unsolved."

"I take it you still haven't found anyone who might be able to ID the guy?" With no real leads after discovering the true crime scene, Hunter had been spending a lot of her time trying to track the guy's movements. The hope was to find someone, anyone, who had any clue as to who the victim was.

"Nope. We've got two sketches now though; both seem to agree on what he really looked like, but we still haven't found him. The sketches are too imprecise to run facial recognition or anything like that. He gave a name to the landlord when he rented that apartment, but it was definitely fake. Paid in cash for a month so nothing to trace. It's driving me nuts."

"Now you know how I felt just sitting around."

"I know, Hawk, I really understand. I just wish I'd been here for backup if you'd needed it." She seemed to realize that she was worrying perhaps a bit too much and went on quickly, "So what about the two guys you saw? Could one of them have been the guy who shot Alejandro?"

Andrew tried to remember the exact details of the men. The one who had stood near the door where Andrew could see him was unquestionably the guard from the party. The other, though, he'd just seen a quick glimpse as he entered and left the office.

"No," Andrew said eventually, "the one we got the print from, Dante or Mateo or whatever, he was definitely the guy who brought

Luca to the execution. The other guy was way too short to be our killer."

Hunter sighed and drank more of her coffee, apparently waking up more by the second. She fixed a bowl of fruit with an intense stare as she thought, processing everything she'd been told so far. Andrew's phone buzzed on the counter, sliding towards him a bit. Diego's name popped up on the screen and Hunter raised her eyebrows at him. She was asking what Diego was calling for, so Andrew simply shrugged and answered the call on speaker.

"Hey," Andrew said, "when did you get back?"

"About an hour ago. I swear I'll never get used to the cold up here."

Andrew laughed, "So what's up? Or did you just call to bitch about the cold?"

"Hey, I got on a plane feeling warm and got off in this frozen hellscape, I have a right to bitch. I'm calling, though, to tell you I got a table at the Traveller House next week."

"How the hell did you manage that? I thought they were booked for the next four months."

"Oh they are, but I know people who know people. So you want in? Cara too, obviously, since you two are, you know."

"How the hell did you find out about that so quick?"

"Eliza texted me about thirty seconds after she found out. It was important for the over/under."

"What?"

"We've had a pool going for weeks. Eliza won."

"Well fuck you guys." Hunter was smirking into her coffee, trying hard not to make a sound that Diego might hear.

"Is that a no then?"

"Of course not, we'll see you then."

Just by the tone of his voice when he responded, Andrew knew that Diego was smirking. "Sounds good, I'll text you the details." The line cut out and ended the call which was the signal for Hunter to start laughing properly.

"What?" Andrew demanded.

"I'm just glad to know that I'm not the only one who finds you predictable." Andrew grimaced at her and steered the conversation back to the details of his findings.

CHAPTER 18

WITH CARA NOT DUE back home for a little while and Hunter's coffee already wearing off, Andrew was banished back out onto the street. He started heading home anyway, figuring that he had little better to do when a slight shift in the breeze made him look around. A shawarma cart two blocks up was emanating succulent steam from the little foggy windows. Of the things he actively missed from his old life, street food was up there. Not that the wealthy didn't eat street food, because much of his generation did, but it all felt so preppy and hipster to him. Old school street meat where you're questioning what it is you're even eating was a staple of New York that just didn't seem to exist in his new world.

Figuring that if Wall Street guys in three-thousand-dollar suits could do it, why shouldn't he be able to? That, at least, was his justification when he was already halfway to the cart. He stepped into the small line to wait and he sensed rather than saw someone join behind him. The person cleared their throat softly and Andrew frowned, he recognised the sound because he had heard it a thousand times at The Farm whenever his attention was slacking. The line moved forward and the smiling middle eastern man running the cart nodded in greeting.

"Good day to you, sir, what can I get for you?"

"I will have a lamb wrap with falafel, extra spicy sauce too." It took the man a moment to understand that Andrew had replied in Arabic. It wasn't one of his most fluent languages, but he could get by for something like this. It seemed for a moment that Andrew had guessed wrong, it was tough to tell middle east accents apart sometimes, but then a huge grin appeared on his face.

"I cannot believe you speak Arabic," the man gushed, *"that is truly wonderful. I will throw in some extra lamb for you, sir!"*

"Thank you," Andrew said, slipping back to English, "and I'll be paying for whatever he would like as well." He jerked a thumb over his shoulder to the man who had entered the line behind him.

"Of course, of course," said the cart owner, "what can I get you?"

"Whatever he's having," came the reply from Tom Bakowski as he stepped up next to Andrew. The man bowed in acknowledgement and put together the two wraps with lightning precision and did indeed pile extra lamb onto Andrew's. Bakowski looked much like he had at The Farm, crew cut and rigid posture. He did note, though, that he wasn't in any sort of uniform or fatigues, a true rarity that he had never seen before. Andrew paid for them both and a couple of sodas, handing them to Bakowski before the two of them strolled up the street in silence until they found a bench that was free of snow and sat down.

"How ya doing Sarge?" Andrew asked as he unwrapped his shawarma. This, though seemingly mundane, earned him a painful punch on the arm which almost made him drop his food. "What the hell was that for?"

"You shouldn't be calling me Sarge," he replied, "you aren't even supposed to know me."

"There's no one around to hear us, hardly anyone on the planet who could connect us, and I'm just the stranger who bought you lunch, I think we'll be ok."

"Oh," Bakowski grunted, "alright then."

"For someone in your line of work, you aren't exactly subtle."

"Yeah ok I get it," he said, unwrapping his own food now and taking a huge bite.

"So what brings you to New York?" Andrew asked.

"My daughter and three grandkids live here," Bakowski said, "came here to spend a bit more time with them."

"Why now?" Andrew asked, figuring there was more to this than a friendly visit.

"Because they finally found a reason to kick me out," he said with a heavy sigh, "I'm officially retired. Cancer," he added when Andrew looked confused.

"Jesus, Sarge, I'm sorry."

"Save the pity party," Bakowski snapped, "it ain't too bad yet, just enough to get me a medical discharge. I still got plenty of years before I shuffle off, just thinking I'd catch up on time I missed when my girl was growing up."

"Good of you, but I don't imagine you broke all protocol and probably a couple laws just to tell me you're dying, so what's up?"

"They read me in on your little assignment here now that I have no affiliation to the armed forces. Apparently even knowing about it would have been committing some kind of treason since you aren't supposed to be here. Anyway, they knew I was headed up here so asked me just to look in on you. Morris was supposed to do it himself, but he's tied up in Europe somewhere."

"Hunter makes regular contact with the company," Andrew said suspiciously, "they know exactly how we're doing."

Bakowski sighed and ran a hand over his face, "You know I'm no good at this. Fine, I'm here because Morris asked me for a favor, off the books."

"Alright," Andrew said, "go on then."

"I may not know about all...this," he gestured vaguely towards Andrew, "but I've seen my fair share of company men roll through my camp. A lot of them rotate around and lots come by for a drink now and then. A lot of them fall into the same trap when they're new, one you're getting really close to yourself."

"What kind of trap?"

"You're falling in love, Andrew, with someone who should probably be viewed as a target or an asset. Look," he went on as Andrew opened his mouth to argue, "I don't know the details, I don't want to know the details, I'm just passing on a message. You aren't the first to let this happen and you won't be the last, but you're in a line of work where everything could change tomorrow, just be careful." Andrew knew that this much conversation with anyone was a lot for Bakowski, let alone about something like this, but he seemed to really mean it.

"I'll be careful," Andrew promised, unsure how to feel about what he was saying, "but I can't just cut off ties with this person now."

"I get that," Bakowski said, "just be ready, that's all. I'd throw you one of my lines about being ready, but I think you know them all by now and I'm not your commanding officer, I'm just a friend doing a favor for another friend."

"Morris really asked you to say all this?"

"Surprised to find out some of us actually like you and want to look out for you?" Bakowski asked sarcastically. "Yeah, he really did. He went through this exact same thing himself."

Andrew nearly choked on his shawarma, "You're joking," he spluttered, "the guy who is basically a robot? Who people say actually doesn't have the muscles to let him smile? He fell in love with a target?"

"People don't start out as robots, Andrew," Bakowski said darkly, "something turns them into one, usually something terrible. Just keep in mind what I said, try to be careful, and don't tell Hunter you saw me, I'd hate for her to have to report that I know you're both here."

Bakowski stood and Andrew stood with him, promising again to be careful before shaking hands and telling him to take care of himself. Now alone at the bench, Andrew abandoned his half-eaten wrap and started walking, he needed to move, needed to think. Was he getting too close to Cara? Well, he thought, yeah he was, but why was that a bad thing? It wasn't like he was running around getting shot at every other day, and it's not like she was someone he had to take down. She was just a normal girl who he had met by chance, that was it.

When Andrew returned home, it was to find Cara dismantling the tree she had surprised him with. When he'd asked her about it she had simply said that it had taken both the delivery man and a couple of the building's security to bring it up. That and a few bribes. Looking at her, he decided on the spot that Bakowski's warning had been unnecessary, nothing was wrong with this. She stood on one of the dining room chairs, reaching to the top in order to reach the highest ornaments.

"You know, you didn't have to do any of this," Andrew said, taking an armful of ornaments from her to return to their box. "Just you being here would have been plenty.

"I know," she said with a smile, "but it was worth it just to see your face."

A few minutes passed in relative silence as they took down more of the ornaments. When finally the massive star came off the top, Cara hopped down and sidled up to Andrew, putting her hands on his chest.

"How did it go with the cops? Is there anything new?"

"Not really," Andrew said, a slight twisting feeling in his gut for having to perpetuate the lie. "There is a new person of interest, but the pieces of the puzzle still just aren't lining up. How was brunch?"

"Oh good, Eliza seems to have spent all her time on vacation making 'friends' with the locals."

"Of course she did. So, you told her about us?"

Cara frowned up at him. "How did you know that?"

"Easy really. The slight twitch of your nose, the size of your pupils, and also she texted Diego about two seconds after you told her." She snorted with laughter and smacked him on the chest.

"Well done, excellent deductive reasoning. Holmes would be proud."

"Does that make you Doctor Watson?"

"Doctor Watson wasn't sleeping with Holmes. Clearly, I'm Irene Adler."

"Of course, how silly of me."

Cara looked up at him for a long moment before speaking again, apparently struggling with something. "Hawk, I've been thinking a lot about what happened in the park."

"Ok..." Andrew said, unsure where she was going with this.

"I just can't help but picture what might have happened if you weren't there. What that guy might have done to me."

"Don't worry about that," Andrew said, pulling her more tightly against himself, "I'm not going to let anything happen to you."

"But you aren't always going to be there with me. I need to be ready."

"Ready how?"

"I want you to teach me how to fight. Or at least," she went on quickly, seeing his look of surprise, "how to fight someone off long enough to get away. Please, Hawk? My father was always very adamant that owning something like a gun was simply asking for trouble, but what if I didn't need one?"

Andrew let out a long sigh, "I don't want you to go looking for trouble."

"I won't, I swear, I just want to be able to stay safe."

"Alright," Andrew said after a moment, "but only enough to get away. I don't need you picking fights with the other women on Fifth Avenue because they took a purse you wanted." Cara grinned up at him radiantly and he felt his heart melt slightly.

CHAPTER 19

THEY MOVED THE FURNITURE to the edge of the room and Cara ran off to put on something more sporty. She had brought a large bag of clothes over with her on Christmas, apparently intent on sticking around.

"First off," Andrew said as she stood before him eagerly in sweats and a baggy t-shirt, "do you carry anything for self-defense? Mace, pepper spray, that sort of thing?"

Cara shook her head and shrugged. "I've never really thought about it much before now. I guess I never really felt like I was in a whole lot of danger growing up."

"I thought you said you'd been mugged before," Andrew prompted.

"Yeah, but that was more of a purse snatch kind of thing. The guy was gone before I could even look up."

"We'll get you something, that's an easy place to start. If your goal is to simply incapacitate and run, then your targets are pretty easy. Eyes, fingers, and balls. Break or damage any of them and you're guaranteed to shock the hell out of them."

"Fingers? I don't see them standing still while I try to break a finger."

"Sure they will because they'll be standing still to try and kill you. A lot of people, especially amateurs, make a fatal flaw when it comes to strangling. Ideally they stand behind you so you can't see them or hit them easily, but that's where the problem comes in."

Andrew walked around behind Cara and placed his hands gently around her neck, applying just a small amount of pressure. "Ok so what's the problem?" Cara asked. Andrew could feel the vibrations of her words in his fingers.

"If I was a pro," he said, "I would do it like this." He curled his fingers so that he was squeezing with the knuckles rather than the pads before uncurling them again. "But most don't. Pinky fingers are the weakest because they are the smallest. All you have to do is stay calm, grab them, and pull down as hard as you can."

She reached up and grabbed his pinkies, clenching her fists around them and pulling. Not hard enough to cause damage but enough that Andrew let go out of instinct. "Good, depending on the bone and the person, it can take only a little force to break them. Pulling fingers like that can snap them or otherwise massively damage them. Just pull as hard as you can and work your way up the hands. At some point they will either let go or won't have enough grip strength left to keep it up."

"Ok, what next?" Cara asked, obviously enthused. Andrew walked her through a few more basic ways to deal a lot of damage quickly and by the end she was even slipping his grip on her and twisting away. An hour later, Cara fell onto the displaced sofa, panting slightly and rubbing her arms.

"You didn't have to squeeze so hard, Hawk."

"You're the one who literally asked for it. I believe you called me a pussy and said I could do better than that about half an hour ago. Don't blame me for you being right."

"Well, thank you anyway, can we keep going another time?"

"Sure," Andrew said, "totally up to you. But I'll still make sure nothing bad happens to you, I promise."

"You can't promise that," she said very seriously, looking up at him, "bad things happen. They always do."

"Good things too though," Andrew said, sitting down beside her.

"I know, but still." She scooted over to him and rested her head on his shoulder. They were silent for a while as Andrew was unsure what else to say.

"Oh I forgot to mention, Diego asked if we wanted to come out to dinner next week."

"Where?" Cara asked.

"Traveller House."

"What? Really? What did you say?"

"I told him we're in, I've only heard amazing things about the food. Mostly from you. Hope that's ok."

"Oh definitely," Cara said at once, "more than ok." She reached up and kissed him softly before laughing like a kid. She explained, again, that the food was supposed to be some of the best in the world while Andrew simply held her close.

Their week after that was a fairly relaxed one as well. They spent a couple of days with Diane and her art group painting wooden panels that were to be hung in a community centre. Dirk and Diego dragged them out of their little cocoon of new relationship bliss to go to a new club that had opened uptown. Cara eventually went back home to get a fresh bag of clothes and to check in with her parents when they got back from their own vacation. The weekend slipped by uneventfully and suddenly it was the day of their dinner with Diego and the others.

Cara, clearly more excited about it than Andrew was, nitpicked over his outfit for at least an hour, making sure it was good enough for the illustrious meal. Andrew simply let her have at it as it clearly made her happy. Ram was waiting for them in the sleek town car when they emerged from the building, bundled up against the cold. Andrew was feeling a little surly because he'd still not heard anything new from Hunter or Duncan. He figured that, regardless of the encryption, it wouldn't have taken Duncan this long to figure out what Luca was hiding. But, he reasoned, tonight would be a good opportunity to subtly press Diego for information about his uncle.

"I'm sorry, sir," Ram said as they approached the restaurant, "it looks like this is as far as I can get you until this clears up a bit."

Andrew peered up between the front seats and saw a scene of vehicular chaos. It looked like a garbage truck had overturned on the road ahead and was creating a total gridlock. Emergency vehicles were trying to negotiate their way closer through the throngs of cars. They were only about a block from the Traveller House, so he looked over at Cara who shrugged.

"No problem, Ram, we'll walk from here. I'll call you later for a ride back."

"Yes sir, I'll be around. Enjoy yourself, sir, ma'am."

Andrew hopped out of the car and jogged around to open Cara's door for her. She took his proffered hand and they slipped a little on the icy pavement before making it to the sidewalk. The accident up ahead had completely blocked off traffic going towards the restaurant from all sides. As they drew nearer, Andrew saw two cars pinned under the truck. It appeared, however, that no one had been killed and the paramedics were tending to several minor injuries now. They walked past the scene and were just coming to the door when Andrew felt his phone vibrate in the inside pocket of his coat. He pulled it out and saw an unknown number that he realized was Hunter's.

"I should probably take this," he said as Cara looked up at him questioningly, "I won't be long though, you go ahead, out of the cold." He leaned down to kiss her and she went on ahead while Andrew ducked into the alley beside the Traveller House. The only other people around were a couple of men unloading crates of produce from a van at the kitchen entrance father down the alley. He accepted the call and held the phone up to his ear.

"Hawk," Hunter said before he could even say hello, "where are you?"

"I'm about to go for dinner at the Traveller House, why?" Her voice was more panicked than he had ever heard it, even when he had been doing something potentially dangerous. This worried Andrew greatly. Hunter was not one to get jumpy easily.

"Duncan cracked the encryption on the other email. It was a list of four names and four pictures to go along with them."

"Whose names? The people buying the IDs?"

"No. Dirk Warpole, Eliza Samson-Waller, Caralynne Randal, and...and Andrew Hawkins. There are pictures of all of you, too. Clear shots of your faces."

Andrew's blood ran suddenly cold. Why had Luca been sending pictures of them with their names? There was only one real possibility and Andrew did not like thinking about it. He'd been wandering down the alley as he talked but froze as the sound of gunfire erupted in the building next to him.

CHAPTER 20

"SHOTS FIRED," ANDREW SAID urgently into the phone as he hurried back towards the mouth of the alley, "automatic weapons, at least two shooters."

"Hawk," Hunter said, trying to cut in but Andrew was not about to be stopped.

"I need police here now; I'm going to get a better look inside."

"Hawk, stop!" Her tone made him freeze on the spot at the end of the alley. People on the sidewalk were fleeing the scene as the gunfire continued in bursts.

"What?" Andrew demanded.

"You are not going in there. Stay put, wait for the police, do not enter a building with an active shooter. I've got dispatch sending units now."

"That's not good enough," Andrew shouted back, "the street is clogged from an accident. Cara is in there, Hunter, I'm not just going to stand here and-" he faltered as the side door of the restaurant banged open and he heard the unmistakable sound of someone screaming through a gag. Whipping around, he saw two men in black masks and guns slung over their backs hauling two people out of the restaurant. They had hoods over their heads and their hands were bound, but he recognised the cashmere suit of the man. It was Dirk.

"They're taking them, Hunter. Dirk and Eliza are being loaded into a van beside the restaurant."

"Give me details, Hawk. Make? Model? How many men?" Andrew heard her as though from very far away. Two more men had just emerged from the side door, both struggling to move a third person to the van. She was fighting back against them hard and one of the men had a limp. The phone fell from numb fingers and clattered to the ground. That dress, the coat, and the muffled screams. He watched with building terror as Cara was thrown violently into the van after one of the men hit her upside the head with the butt of his gun. One of the men slammed the door of the van shut before limping around to the driver's side.

"Hey!" Andrew shouted breaking into a run to charge back down the alley again.

The driver flinched and looked around, staring at Andrew with wide eyes beneath the mask. He reached for his gun, hesitated, and ran for the van again. The engine roared to life just as Andrew reached it and slammed his elbow into the driver's window. The glass shattered, showering the masked man with the shards.

"Go," someone yelled from the back of the van. Andrew managed to land a punch on the driver whose head jerked sideways. He slammed his foot on the gas and the van skidded into motion. Andrew hung onto the man, his feet skidding along the ground before he found footing on the small step at the bottom of the door.

"Let. Them. Go," Andrew grunted, emphasizing each word with a punch to the man's head. Bullets erupted from the back of the van, narrowly missing the driver but clipping Andrew in the shoulder. Pain blossomed along his arm and the hole left behind burned like someone had stabbed him with a hot knife. His grip on the driver slackened at the same moment that the van swerved slightly to pass close to a dumpster. It struck Andrew on the side and he was thrown off, tumbling several feet while the van peeled out into the street and disappeared. With traffic blocked by the nearby accident, it gave the kidnappers an unobstructed path straight out and away from the restaurant.

Andrew groaned as he rolled over onto his back, pushing himself with his uninjured arm. There was definitely a cracked rib or two and blood was trickling from his shoulder, but otherwise he was mostly dazed. He got up slowly, head spinning and his vision blurry, but determined to chase the van, no matter how pointless. He only made it a dozen steps, just to the mouth of the alley, when he fell to his knees as a wave of nausea flooded through him. Someone was standing in front of him, and he looked up to see an EMT setting down a kit and kneeling. They were speaking, but Andrew couldn't hear them for some reason. He reached up to scratch his head, it just felt so itchy, and his hand came away slick with blood.

"Oh," he said softly before slumping forward onto his hands. Fresh pain tore through him as the paramedic tried to maneuver him into a sitting position. With a sudden burst of strength, Andrew grabbed the sleeve of the man's jacket, smearing blood over the crest.

"Detective Caitlin Hunter," he said weakly, "call her. Get her down here now." Then everything went dark.

When he came to, it was in the back of one of the ambulances. Flashing lights danced across his face and he had to squint hard as his eyes fluttered open. His head felt strangely heavy, so he reached up to feel it, only to find his left arm was bound to him in a sling. His right hand instead found the bandage tightly wrapped around the wound on his head. Someone was sitting beside the stretcher, arguing with an EMT standing outside with his hands on the doors.

"Ma'am, we really need to get him to the hospital. He needs x-rays at the very least."

"I told you, not yet," the woman sitting beside Andrew snapped, "I need him here first. Unless you're able to provide a detailed account of what happened here before you all bothered to show up." This effectively silenced the EMT who threw up his hands and walked away.

That's right, Andrew thought, something had happened. He'd seen people with guns coming out of the restaurant, and then Cara had been taken. He shot bolt upright on the stretcher and immediately regretted this decision when dizziness threatened to knock him out all over again. Hunter jumped in alarm at the sudden move and put a hand on his leg.

"It's alright," she said gently, "you're alright. Hawk, how do you feel?"

"Dizzy," he said, closing his eyes. This only welcomed flashing images of the scene he had witnessed to pour through his mind. "Where are we?"

"Still outside the restaurant. I heard you go after the kidnappers and then your phone went completely dead. I thought you'd been killed too."

"Not yet," Andrew groaned.

"If you weren't so banged up I would beat the shit out of you myself. You've got a gunshot wound, at least one broken rib, they think you may have cracked your skull, and then about a thousand cuts and scrapes. What the hell happened, Hawk?"

Andrew took a deep breath, trying to reassemble the scattered thoughts in his mind's eye before answering.

"There were four of them," Andrew said, "black ski masks and automatic rifles. They opened fire in the restaurant, then came out the side with Cara and the others. There was a white delivery van there, they all got inside and that's when I ran at them. I got a few good hits in, but they shot me and I fell."

Hunter let out a long breath, then asked, "Did you see anything that could identify the men? Anything at all."

"No, but this must be why Luca sent pictures of us. I was supposed to be in there. I should have been taken too."

"Where's Diego?" Hunter asked, "Wasn't he meeting you guys too?"

"He was supposed to, I don't know. I should have just gone into the restaurant. I could have helped."

"Hawk, stop it. There was nothing you could have done in there to stop them. They would have just shot you and been done with it. Right now you're going to go to the hospital and get checked out. I need to report what happened to you, but we'll need a full statement later. Do not leave the hospital and do not try anything before I come see you. Got it?"

Andrew was about to argue, to say that he should be out here looking for Cara and the others, but whatever pain medication he'd been given was not keeping up, so he nodded. Hunter laid him back down and got out of the ambulance. She was about to close the doors when she paused to look at him.

"We'll find them, Hawk, I promise."

CHAPTER 21

"LET ME GO," ANDREW said, struggling to sit up in the hospital bed. It had been hours since the ambulance had carried him away from the scene. There had been no word from Hunter since and being forced to sit still was going to kill him.

"No," the uniformed officer standing at his bedside said shortly. A little golden badge on his chest read 'K. Nevins' and was pinned to a particularly crisp uniform shirt. "Detective Hunter made it very clear what she would do if we let you go. You're under police protection until we're told otherwise. So lay down, shut up, and try to get some rest or I will restrain you."

There came a knock at the door and the officer turned, one hand resting on his holstered weapon. Clearly Hunter had put the fear of God into him. The door opened and the second officer assigned to Andrew stepped in with a small gift bag.

"This was left for him," the new officer said, "Hunter called and said to deliver it."

Nevins frowned but walked over and took the little bag before peeking inside. He grunted a short laugh and brought the bag over to Andrew, holding it out to him.

"Fucking rich people," Nevins muttered under his breath, "got someone to do everything for you."

Andrew took the bag and saw a nest of tissue paper which held a brand new cell phone. Apparently his had been destroyed when the van had run over it in the alley. A tiny note was tucked into the tissue paper and Andrew pulled it out to read.

Usual number.

"You can leave now, officer," Andrew said, and Nevins raised his eyebrows.

"Excuse me?"

"Get out. I'm tired, I'm in pain, and I'd like to make a call in peace. It's not like I'll be able to sneak past you and I somehow don't see myself surviving a four story drop to the street out of the window."

"Whatever," Nevins grumbled. He struck Andrew as the sort of man who had been a cop for at least two decades and was stuck in his current position. He'd likely been passed over for promotions so often that he no longer even made it into consideration. Cops, being notoriously superstitious, the moment any of them is seen as cursed then they never exactly do well after that. Nevins shuffled from the room, clearly pissed off but Andrew simply didn't care. The moment that the door closed, he dialed zero on the new phone and put it on speaker before setting it down on the table across his legs. It rang only once before the series of clicks indicated the call was being secured.

"Hey kid," Duncan said in a much gentler voice than Andrew had heard from him thus far, "how ya feeling?"

"Like I was shot and run over," Andrew said.

"Yeah well I included something that should help. Check under the paper." Andrew reached for the little gift bag and pulled out the wads of tissue paper. Beneath them was a tiny plastic bag with three bright pink pills inside.

"Are you trying to get me high, Duncan?"

"The opposite," replied the voice on the phone, "I bet you've been feeling a little out of it since they pumped you full of drugs. This stuff is something a friend of mine developed back in the eighties. Give one of these to a tweaker on the biggest high of his life and it still cuts right through the brain fog. I want you alert for this conversation, kid. Rest later, talk now."

Andrew shrugged and opened the little bag. It was true that he'd gone from dizzy due to the head wound to loopy from the drugs and back several times. He swallowed the pills with a drink from a paper cup on his table and almost immediately felt a surge of energy.

"Jesus, Duncan," Andrew said as he felt like his eyes were vibrating, "what the hell did you just give me?"

"Some choice vitamins, a little caffeine, and a wildly illegal cocktail of designer narcotics. Nothing too harmful, just don't take them all the time. The doctors won't be able to tell you took anything so just don't run your mouth. It only lasts a few minutes."

Andrew felt like he could have run a marathon, broken rib and all. Colors in the hospital room sharpened and he could swear that he could hear every word of Nevins' conversation with the other officer outside.

"Ok so what have you got?" Andrew asked.

"Well," Duncan said, and Andrew could hear him typing on a keyboard, "Caitlin filled me in on what happened and what you saw. I pulled traffic camera stills and footage from every security camera in a three block radius. It shows the van pulling up to the restaurant about half an hour before you got there."

"Any shots of the men who took Cara?" Andrew asked at once.

"None that show faces. The alley itself is in a bit of a blind spot and the driver was wearing a baseball cap and sunglasses on his way there. The others were never even seen on camera, probably because they were in the back."

"What about cell phones?"

"Smart boy, I pulled up the tower data and ran through every number that pinged off the towers that would put them in the area. Most of them came back clean but there were four burner phones. Obviously they can only be traced back so far, but I was able to ping them a couple more times and got a general direction that they headed before the signals died. What was interesting, though, is that one of the phones got a call about thirty seconds before Hunter called you. Looks like someone was watching the restaurant for you all to show. If they had waited just a bit longer, they'd have seen you take a call and likely delayed the go signal. Hunter may have just saved your life, kid."

Andrew bit the inside of his cheek. On the one hand he was thankful for the situation, but on the other he still believed that he could have been more help to Cara and the others if he had been taken too.

"So where did they go? Were you able to track Cara's phone or any of the others?"

"Miss Randal's phone, along with two others, were left in the restaurant and like I said already, the burner phones went silent a couple blocks away."

"Is there any good news here, Duncan?"

"Honestly, not really," Duncan replied, and he sounded genuinely sorry. "I'm running a clip I pulled from the security camera through a gait recognition program, but a hit might take time. I was really just wanting to ask you something."

"Alright," Andrew said, closing his eyes and willing himself not to think about what might be happening to Cara at this very moment.

"Do you think it's at all possible that Diego had something to do with this?"

"What?" Andrew said, his eyes flying open again to stare at the phone. "Besides Cara, he's the closest friend I have in that group. He loves them like family."

"I need you to be objective here. Diego's uncle sent your names and pictures to someone, and Diego was not included in them. Three of you have been taken, should have been four, but Diego was never a target. He wasn't there in the restaurant at all even though he invited all of you, but his cell still pinged off the tower too. He was there, Andrew."

The use of his actual name struck Andrew, driving home just how serious Duncan was about this. He tried to imagine Diego as a conspirator in this plan but nothing about the man suggested he would be willing to do this to his friends.

"Where is he now?" Andrew asked finally.

"At a bar around the corner from his condo, been there since he left the scene in a hurry."

"What about Luca?"

"No clue. His phone is completely inaccessible, which means it's not just off, the battery has been removed or it's been destroyed."

"I just don't see Diego doing this," Andrew said, shaking his head as though it would make it untrue, then, "I'm going to go talk to him. Send me the address of the bar."

"No," Duncan said shortly as Andrew tried to get up again.

"What do you mean no?"

"You need to rest, kid. Hunter is already on her way to talk to him. Bringing him in would trigger about a dozen responses from the Colombian government so she's hoping that she can get through to him privately. Limping your way down there won't do any good and I can already tell you'd rip his head off if you didn't get answers."

"What are you talking about?" Andrew snapped viciously.

"I know you were close to the girl, Andrew. You're too close to this and it's too fresh. You'd blow your cover in half a second to get her back and the company isn't about to be ok with that. Stay. Rest. We'll keep you in the loop."

"Duncan," Andrew complained, "I can't just sit here and do nothing!" Tears were burning in the backs of his eyes now as the exhaustion and emotion started pushing back against the drugs.

"I'm not letting you end up like my kid," Duncan said in a voice of deadly calm before the line went dead and the phone's screen darkened. Andrew wanted to throw the phone. What right did Duncan have to stop him from doing his job? Cara was missing and he was just sitting here. Rage boiled in him for a long while, but it eventually faded as more tears came. He pressed the button on the bed's remote to call in a nurse and, after being checked by the officers outside, the door opened.

"Is everything alright, Mister Hawkins?" asked the nurse. He was about Andrew's age with sandy hair and a small scar on his lip that twitched as he frowned slightly. He wore a look of such pity that Andrew knew he must look like a mess.

"Have you got something that will help me sleep?"

The nurse walked to the end of his bed to check his chart before nodding and crossing to a drawer in a stainless steel cabinet. The moment that the drug had been added to the saline solution pumping into Andrew's arm his eyes grew heavy. The last thing he saw was the nurse turning off the lights and slipping back out of the door.

CHAPTER 22

WHEN ANDREW WOKE AGAIN the room was still dark. This turned out to be largely due to the heavy clouds that had rolled in over the city. The windows were obscured with heavy snow blowing violently in the wind. He stayed quite still for a while, assessing the pain he still felt. The worst of it was his head and the huge bruise that had no doubt formed over his ribs. The bullet wound was more of a dull ache than anything. None of it, though, compared to the sense of despair and dread he felt when his thoughts wandered back to Cara. A slight movement made him look around and he saw Hunter sitting in a chair at his bedside. Her feet were up next to him and her leather jacket was draped over her like a blanket.

He sat for a long while, watching her sleep. A small part of him knew that to wake her would be to rob her of the relative peace she'd found next to him. Undoubtedly she had been up all night and he felt a small pang of guilt for getting angry at her. Hunter just wanted to keep him safe and he knew she would do everything to bring the others back ok. Hunter stirred and opened her eyes blearily. When she caught sight of Andrew watching her, she sat bolt upright, the jacket sliding to the floor.

"Hawk," she said with relief, "how do you feel?"

"What did you find?" Andrew asked, ignoring the question. Hunter's face fell and she rubbed her eyes for a long moment before answering.

"Honestly, not a whole lot. A ton of AK-47 casings scattered all over the place. Three others are in the hospital and two are dead. Witnesses said that the kidnappers emerged from the kitchen, shot wildly around, and then took three people with them. They wore masks, so no one saw their faces, and gloves to not leave any prints behind. We found the van abandoned by the docks and...a huge amount of blood in it."

"Whose blood?" Andrew asked at once, panic gripping him.

"We don't know, only that it's definitely not Cara's or Eliza's. The blood was B-positive and neither of them are. They sent a sample to the lab and I have a request in with the FBI lab as well. Haven't heard back yet."

"The FBI won't help," Andrew said bitterly, "unless we know they've crossed state lines."

Hunter simply shook her head, running a hand through her hair, "We've received no word from anyone yet. The families of the victims have all been informed. I made the calls myself."

Her voice was so hollow as she said this and Andrew held out a hand. She took it silently and he squeezed it reassuringly. The discussion lapsed for a moment as Hunter wiped a tear from her eye and cleared her throat. Then Andrew had to ask the question that had been hounding him since his talk with Duncan.

"What did Diego say?"

Hunter laughed humorlessly, "He was barely able to get three words out before a small army of consulate personnel descended on the bar. Two different lawyers yelled at me for a while then they took him and left. They said I either had to charge him, with evidence presented, or wait until they agreed to a scheduled interview. It did a really good job making him look..." Hunter trailed away but Andrew finished the thought.

"Guilty," he said. "I still can't believe he would do this to us, but it also looks like Luca was directly responsible. Any sign of him yet?"

"No," Hunter said sadly, "and I can't exactly get a warrant, we're not supposed to have any of the evidence we do."

Andrew frowned and replied, "This seems like the sort of thing that our company friends would be good for, they don't need that sort of approval."

"You know we can't do that. You and I aren't even supposed to be doing what we're doing. We have to find a solid link between Luca and what happened. Something I can bring to the captain. I've convinced him to assign me to this full time since it involves someone from another case I have. He also just wants to see everyone brought back in one piece, it's all hands-on deck."

"I'll talk to Diego," Andrew said, his voice determined, "they can't have a problem with a friend visiting him after we've both suffered the same loss."

Hunter seemed to realize that she was not about to convince him to leave it alone so she nodded slowly. "Just be careful, I know that we've seen proof that Luca was the only one who made this deal, but we can't know for sure. Hawk, you should also know that we found the body of Alejandro Lopez last night. Not that anyone knows who it is yet."

"What do you mean?" Andrew asked, confused.

"Well, he was wearing the same clothes as the gala when he was killed so I knew who it was, but we can't make an ID. He's got no fingers or head; they were cut off."

"You mean they decayed away, right? He died months ago now."

"That's the thing," Hunter said slowly, "he's not decayed at all. They found him stuck in a drainage tunnel, frozen solid. He looks like he could have died yesterday."

"But even if they dumped his body, there was plenty of time for decay to start and even finish before it got cold enough to freeze him. So they must have brought him somewhere and kept the body on ice until any potential heat died down. But Hunter," Andrew added, pleased to have something else to focus on, "the no fingers or head sounds an awful lot like your cold case you got when you started."

"I know," Hunter said, nodding, "ballistics confirmed it was the same weapon. Somehow that case, Alejandro, and the kidnapping are all connected. We just don't know how."

Andrew finally let go of Hunter's hand as the door opened behind her and a new uniformed officer poked his head inside. "Ma'am," she said to Hunter, "Mister Hawkins has a visitor. Should I let them in?"

"Who is it?" Hunter asked defensively, getting to her feet.

"Uh, George Randal, ma'am. The father of one of the victims." The officer sounded extremely nervous and Andrew suspected that George had bullied her into letting him in.

"Let him in," Andrew said, and the officer looked at him quickly before her eyes flicked back to Hunter who nodded her approval. The woman vanished and George Randal pushed his way into the room. His face was white and his eyes bloodshot. He did not have his cane and any sign of the limp was gone now. His eyes scanned the entire room before landing on Hunter.

"Get out," he barked at her, and she raised her eyebrows at him.

"It's alright, sir," Andrew said, pushing the button to raise himself into a sitting position, "George Randal, meet Detective Caitlin Hunter."

"Oh," George said, the bravado deflating slightly, "good to meet you."

"And you, sir, we spoke on the phone last night."

George nodded as he squeezed his eyes shut and groped for Hunter's vacated seat which he fell into heavily. "Tell me what happened, all of it, I know you know more than you said on the phone."

Andrew and Hunter relayed what had happened while George listened intently, color slowly returning to his face as anger replaced the emptiness. Hunter assured him that the police were doing everything they could and that she and Andrew had other leads that they would be looking into.

"Where is the Pedroso brat?" George demanded when they were finished. "I'll beat the answers out of him myself."

"Sir," Hunter said weakly, but George held up a hand.

"Save it," he said, "my daughter is gone and if that little piece of shit is involved then he has to pay. Excuse me if I don't trust Cara's life in the hands of a newbie detective who has seen less action than my left nut!"

"That's enough," Andrew snapped at him and George looked for a moment like he was going to start yelling at him next. "You do not get to sit there and talk to her like that. I'll be dealing with Diego, not you. You're going to go home and wait with your wife until you hear something from the kidnappers. You don't take three wealthy targets unless you want something out of it. What's more, you're going to apologize to Detective Hunter because so far she's done more to find Cara than anyone in the entire fucking city. Don't you dare, for one second, think that you're the only person in this room who cares for Cara."

George blinked at him several times before looking back at Hunter. "I'm sorry," he mumbled, "I just want my little girl back."

"I understand, sir," Hunter said, a little stunned by Andrew's outburst, "I'll do everything in my power. But sir, there is something else you could do for us."

"Anything," he said at once.

"As former director of the CIA, I have to imagine you have a fair few contacts in the FBI. I know that we have no confirmation of the kidnappers crossing state lines, but the extra resources certainly wouldn't hurt."

"Of course," George said, nodding again, "Director Cransley owes me a favor or two from back in the day. I know he'll help. I'll put him in touch with your captain to coordinate."

"Thank you, sir," Hunter said as George got to his feet and headed for the door. He paused with his hand on the handle and looked back to meet Andrew's eyes.

"Bring her home," he said desperately, "no matter what it takes."

"I will," Andrew replied, and he truly meant it. George Randal left again, closing the door behind him. Hunter let out a breath and sat on the edge of Andrew's bed.

"Thank you," she said, "that was nice, what you said."

"It was true," Andrew said, shrugging and immediately regretting the action as his shoulder screamed with pain, "he was thinking like an agent, not like a father. He needs to be home right now. When can I get out of here?"

"The doctors have cleared you to leave but I'm not willing to call off the protective detail until you're well enough."

"I'll be fine," Andrew said sternly, "trust me. Have them escort me home if you want but after that I need to be left on my own."

"Why? What are you going to do?"

"Nothing illegal," Andrew said, not entirely truthfully, "I just don't need them babysitting."

"Alright, give me a day to call them off," Hunter said. "I need to find an excuse for it since we don't know that they won't make another run at you. Listen, though, if you're going to leave your condo, you have to report in more often. You aren't meant to be running field operations like this."

"I thought you were going to try to talk me out of it," Andrew said, a little surprised.

"No, I know that I would have to arrest you to get you to stop. Besides, there are things you can do and places you can go that I just can't. I'm trusting you to keep your cover and to keep yourself safe. No extreme action, no tactical operations, and for the love of God stay armed until this is over."

"Yes ma'am," Andrew said with a slight grin, grateful for her understanding. "As soon as your boys go home I'll go have a little chat with Diego. At the very least he might know where Luca is hiding."

CHAPTER 23

HUNTER LEFT THE HOSPITAL for a few hours after that. She said that she had to go check in with the precinct and see if there had been any updates. Meanwhile, Andrew was receiving a final check from the doctors before he left. The bandage on his head had been replaced by a much smaller one over the gash on his forehead and he still had a sling over his arm. The bullet had luckily not hit bone, instead it had torn through the muscle and exited through the back.

"How does that feel?" the doctor asked, prodding around the broken rib. He was young for a doctor, but definitely one of the better ones Andrew had seen in his life.

"Hurts like a bitch," Andrew said lightly, and the doctor smiled kindly.

"It'll get better. In the meantime though, take one of these whenever it's a bit much," he pulled a bottle of pills from his pocket and shook them, "only one, and give it a few hours between doses. By the way, is someone coming to give you a ride home? Family? Friends?"

"No family," Andrew said dryly, "and all my friends who would show up here have just been kidnapped."

"That would be where I come in," a voice said from the door, sparing the doctor from having to respond to this. Hunter was standing at the door with a leather bag Andrew recognised as the one from his own closet. She set it down on the foot of Andrew's bed and turned to the doctor.

"Final verdict?" she asked.

"He'll be alright. Lots of rest and no strenuous activity should do the trick."

"Thank you, doctor," Hunter said, "if you'll excuse us for a minute, I need a word about the case."

"Of course," he said at once, keen to get away from the glowering look Andrew was still throwing his way. He left promptly, closing the door behind him. Hunter opened the bag and pulled black pants and a blue button up shirt from it.

"Figured you'd need these, unless you want to go home in that," she nodded to the hospital gown Andrew was wearing.

"Thanks," Andrew said, undoing his sling to dress himself. Hunter had to help him with the shirt, maneuvering his arm through the sleeve.

"Your driver is downstairs to take you home and a patrol car is going with you. I managed to convince the captain that the kidnappers aren't likely to take another run at you, especially since we'll have you 'under surveillance' for the foreseeable future. They'll be gone later today."

"Thanks," Andrew said again, meaning it, "I need to ask Duncan to monitor Diego. We need to make sure he doesn't disappear on us too."

"Already done," Hunter replied, draping a new knee-length coat over his shoulders, "he's still at home. I'm asking you one more time not to do anything stupid, ok? I'll be busy with the investigation so I won't necessarily be able to drop what I'm doing to come save you."

"I'll be fine, I promise. I want to see the scene, too. I'm assuming it's still locked down?"

"Of course, CSU is processing it, but they'll be wrapped up this afternoon. They won't release the scene until I sign off so if you go tonight there will only be a patrol car out front to keep an eye on it. Nothing major since we don't expect anyone to return to it. We've taken everything relevant though, I don't know what you expect to find."

"I just need to see it." Hunter reached into the bag again and pulled out a gun, checked the clip, and held it out to him by the barrel.

"HK P30L," she said, "double action, rail mounted compensator, and fifteen round magazine. Flared mag well for easier loading which will help because of this," she poked his sling.

"Very nice," Andrew said, slipping the gun into the inside pocket of his coat while Hunter concealed a spare magazine in the sling. "Anything else fun that you've brought me?"

"Now you mention it," Hunter said, pulling a newspaper out of the bag.

"Oh my God, you brought me the nineties?"

"Just read it, dumbass, front page," she said as she smacked him in the chest with the paper. Andrew flicked it open with one hand and was greeted with a single, large picture splashed across the front page. It showed him hanging off the side of the van as it sped out of the alley under the headline 'Local Hero Attempts to Thwart Kidnapping.' He scanned the article, somewhat surprised to see himself there.

A highly regarded New York City restaurant was the scene of a brutal attack that resulted in the kidnapping of three people. Caralynne Randal, Dirk Warpole, and Eliza Samson-Waller, three of the city's elite, arrived at the restaurant only to be greeted by a hail of gunfire from four armed assailants. Witnesses report that while the attackers seemed to be firing indiscriminately, they were avoiding the three local socialites who were being surrounded. The attackers proceeded to force their victims to their feet and drag them towards the kitchen. Although Randal attempted to fight back, injuring one of the four masked men, the three were taken.

A ray of hope did appear, however, in the form of Andrew Hawkins, another socialite and friend of those taken. Hawkins, who was spotted outside when the attack began, valiantly ran to the aid of his captured friends. He shattered the drivers' side window of the van being used as a getaway vehicle and attempted to incapacitate the driver. His attempt, sadly, ultimately failed when he was shot at and wounded before being thrown from the van. Paramedics, responding to an accident nearby which is thought to be connected, rushed over to begin treating those injured in the attack, Hawkins among them. Sources in the NYPD report that two people lost their lives and three more are in hospital. I believe I speak for everyone when I say that our thoughts and prayers are with the families of the victims, and we wish Andrew and the others injured a swift recovery.

More details of Mr. Hawkins and his recent return to the city continued page 4.

"What utter shit," Andrew said, tossing the paper aside, "I'm no hero."

"Hawk," Hunter said gently, "you jumped onto the side of a van, hung on as it took off, and beat the shit out of the driver. There aren't exactly a lot of people lining up to do that. At any rate, the department has been protecting you from reporters for now, but just be prepared in case someone comes looking for an interview."

"Great," Andrew said bitterly, "people were hounding me before they knew who I was, can't wait to have them camping outside my building."

"Just don't cause a scene, alright?"

Andrew grunted his agreement and grabbed the bag before following Hunter out of the hospital room. The two officers who had been stationed there followed them down to the sliding front doors which opened onto a chilly day. The afternoon sun was still obscured by clouds, appearing only as a white disk in the gloom, and snow was still falling. Ram was there with his town car and practically fell over himself when he saw Andrew.

"Please, Mister Hawk, let me take your bag," he said as he stumbled over to Andrew and took the bag without waiting for a response. "When I heard what happened to you I rushed right over. The thought of you having to ride home in a police car was simply unacceptable. Now more than ever I am at your disposal for whatever you need."

"Thank you, Ram, but I'm alright, just a little sore."

"Of course, Mister Hawk, I will stay nearby regardless. Whenever you need me, just call." He put the bag in the trunk before hurrying to open the door. As Andrew stepped towards it, Ram reached to remove his coat, presumably since it would be awkward to maneuver with one arm. Andrew caught the man's wrist instinctively. He may not have been worried about being targeted, but he was not about to allow someone to take his weapon now that he had it.

"Ram," Andrew said with a gentle smile to cover the sudden move, "I'm really okay. No need to worry, I can still handle myself, I promise."

"Of course, Mister Hawk, my apologies." Ram gave an awkward little bow and moved around to the driver's side, getting in and waiting.

"These two will tail you home," Hunter said in a more business-like tone than earlier, jerking her thumb towards the officers. "As long as everything pans out this afternoon and we're sure you are not in any further danger then we should be able to call them off tonight. No earlier," she added in an undertone and Andrew nodded, taking it to mean that he was not to go and see Diego until the following day.

"Right, thank you detective. Please keep me updated about the case. Anything I can do, just let me know." They shook hands and Hunter turned to look at the two officers. They both nodded and moved to get into their cruiser. As they set off, the cops stayed close behind the town car, a position they maintained the entire way to Andrew's condo. As Andrew got out of the car, he found the officers hurrying over to him, scanning their surroundings. Andrew sighed, knowing that they were not about to back off. One of them stepped ahead of him to enter the lobby first, a move that nearly caused a shootout there and then.

Evie and two of the security guards were behind the desk, apparently watching something on a monitor there. Andrew could hear a news reporter recounting the details of the attack at the restaurant. They all looked up as the door opened and both guards shot to their feet in surprise when they saw him. One of the two, slightly unsure what else to do, rested his hand on the gun at his belt. Seeing this, both officers drew their weapons and aimed them straight at the guard's chest. More weapons were drawn, and Evie ducked down behind the desk.

"Put the guns down!" one of the officers shouted.

"Step away from Mister Hawkins," the guard called back. A tense moment followed before Andrew huffed in annoyance and stepped forward to put himself between both pairs.

"Jesus Christ, all of you just put them down. Donnie," he said to one of the guards, "these two have been ordered to escort me back for protection." He then rounded on the two officers, both of whom looked decidedly nervous about the possibility of a shoot out.

"Please, get out of the way," one of them said.

"Officer Capaletti," Andrew said in a tone of determined calm, quickly scanning the officer's name plate, "these men behind me are security for this building, ex-military, and could drop both of you before you even remembered to turn off your safety." Predictably, Capaletti immediately turned his gun to check the safety. He holstered it again as he flushed red with embarrassment and the guards snorted before holstering their own weapons.

"Mister Hawkins," Donnie said, "we heard all about what happened. If you're still in danger, we're more than up to the task of your protection."

"I know you are," Andrew said wearily, "which is part of the reason these two will be leaving tonight. I'm also convinced that I'm no longer in danger. I expect to be able to continue to come and go without hassle from any of you. I'm fine, I don't want to talk about what happened, and I'm really very tired, so if you'll all excuse me, I'm going upstairs."

Donnie and his partner nodded a little sheepishly as they returned to the desk. Evie looked over at Andrew as though she wanted to say something, but the look on his face was forbidding. Capaletti and the other officer piled into the elevator behind Andrew, staying silent until they had reached his condo and he'd opened the door.

"We'll be right out here should you need anything," Capaletti said weakly, but Andrew didn't even let him finish the sentence before he had slammed the door shut behind him.

The condo felt so empty to him now. He'd been all but living with Cara since Christmas and her absence seemed to hang over the place like an illness. It was like visiting the scene of some horrific battle in which the empty furniture and silent rooms took the place of bodies and craters blown into the ground. Andrew finally settled in his office, unable to look at the near continuous reminders of Cara in the other rooms. Photos of the two of them, a discarded sweater, or the art she had rearranged served only to stab him in the heart. The office was somewhere that she rarely went, somewhere that Andrew could focus on what came next.

CHAPTER 24

DESPITE HOW EXHAUSTED HE felt, Andrew failed to get much rest. Instead, he had been poring over case materials. Now that there seemed to be a connection between Hunter's John Doe and the murder of Alejandro, Andrew was determined to find something they had missed. He had a fair few things he really shouldn't have, like the composite sketch of the first victim, photos of the crime scene, and the autopsy report on Alejandro which Hunter had just sent him. She had likely sent him these things to keep him distracted and he was not about to ignore the effort. What Andrew couldn't figure out was why they had kept Alejandro's body on ice for so many months when they had left the first victim in a pool of his own blood in an alley.

What purpose had Alejandro served sitting in some freezer somewhere? Or had it simply been to distract the police, to make sure they never made the connection. If Andrew hadn't overheard the comment about a drainage tunnel, they likely wouldn't have found the body until it had started decomposing. That would have meant the missing head and fingers could have been more easily explained by the decomposition or some scavenging creature. Whoever this man was, he seemed to put a great deal of thought into his work.

On some gruesome level, Andrew had to admire him. Rarely did you hear about criminals that were so meticulous outside of spy novels. It wasn't the quality of the work that was puzzling Andrew, however. The real question he had was why were these two men both worth killing as part of the same scheme. It was safe to assume, based on the timing, that they were all tied up in the same plot. The plot that had apparently included his own failed kidnapping. But then why him?

That was easy, Andrew thought to himself, he could be held and made to pay his own ransom. Unlike the others, who would need the money from another source, Andrew was in control of his entire supposed fortune. Of all the targets, he actually made the most sense. At least in his mind.

A knock at the door broke through his ruminations and he looked up from the stacks of printouts scattered over his desk. He got up, resecuring his sling and checking that the pistol Hunter had given him was safely tucked in the back of his pants as he crossed through the kitchen to the door. Officer Capaletti was waiting outside, still looking afraid Andrew was going to yell at him.

"Just wanted to let you know we got our orders to stand down. The captain agrees that you're likely not in any danger but urges you to contact the precinct if you see anything suspicious."

"I'll do that," Andrew said, nodding once, "thanks."

The two officers shuffled off and Andrew waited until the elevator doors had closed before closing the door and ripping off his sling. The stitches in his shoulder still screamed in pain, as did the violently purple bruise over his ribs, but he didn't care. He had to see the scene. Had to know if there was something the cops had missed. Darkness had fallen hours ago and by now there must have only been the one patrol car keeping an eye on the restaurant, like Hunter said. Popping two of the pills the doctor had given him into his mouth, Andrew left the condo. It only took a few minutes to slip out of the lobby with hardly a glance from the security who had been so ready to gun down two cops earlier that day. He knew that they had spotted him, they always did, but they also respected the privacy of their tenants. Not wanting to draw too much attention to himself, Andrew hailed a cab outside the building and got inside.

"Where to?" the driver asked with a slight accent. Andrew gave an address that would put him a few blocks south of the restaurant, giving him a chance to approach without notice. He barely paid any attention to the cab driver until he realized the man was staring at him. Andrew caught his eye in the rearview mirror and the driver quickly looked back to the road. Silence persisted for a couple blocks before the man finally spoke.

"You're Andrew Hawkins, aren't you?" Andrew caught it this time, the slight Mexican accent. His mind slammed into gear as he took in the man, it was so similar to the accent of the fake consulate guards.

"That's right," Andrew said, figuring he would see how this played out, though slowly reaching for his weapon just in case.

"I thought so," the driver said with a grin, reaching for something on the passenger seat. Andrew was half a second away from drawing his gun when the cabby held up the newspaper that showed the photo of him on the getaway van. "Saw what you did, I can't exactly believe it, seeing you now."

"How do you mean?"

"Well, no offense, but you don't look to be the hero type. A bit scrawny for what you did."

"I'm no hero," Andrew said bitterly, relaxing slightly, "I didn't achieve anything but getting myself shot."

"All the same," the driver said, "I wouldn't mind having you on my side if I were ever taken. Quite the thing you did."

"Uh huh," Andrew said vaguely as the man prattled on for a while.

"I was there, you know," he said as they approached the address Andrew had given.

"Where?" Andrew asked, paying attention again.

"Right around the corner, a few blocks from here. Saw the van tearing away, nearly crashed into me as it ran a red. Same with that SUV that was following it. I figure it was an undercover police car or something, the way it was weaving around to keep up."

"SUV?" Andrew asked, his interest piqued, "What kind?"

"The kind you see on TV and stuff," the driver said, shrugging, "like the FBI would use. Black, tinted windows, that sort of thing." Andrew didn't reply to this. Could it have been the vehicle they switched into? Or had someone really been trying to chase the van?

His head throbbed with the unanswered questions swirling around it as they came to a stop. Andrew handed the driver a couple of bills and slid out of the taxi before heading north towards the restaurant. The scene outside had been cleared away and it was easy to spot the patrol car from two blocks down. It was sitting at the mouth of the alley where Andrew had been shot, the nose of the car spilling out over the sidewalk. It was a terrible spot to keep an eye on the building. All Andrew had to do was walk past the car, face angled away so they wouldn't see it, and was out of their line of sight by the time he was standing in front of the door to the Traveller House.

He ducked under the police tape and slipped his picks out of his pocket with a quick glance over his shoulder. The area was dead quiet after what had happened but there was almost always someone watching in New York. Andrew had the door open in less than a minute and pushed his way inside before freezing on the spot at the scene that met his eyes.

Chairs and tables were scattered around the once cozy atmosphere, thrown aside as people fled in panic. The restaurant was done up like a Victorian dining room but with a huge, gleaming open concept kitchen at the back. Evidence markers left by the police littered the floor among the pools of bullet casings. Andrew steeled himself and entered the restaurant, closing the door carefully behind himself before moving towards the largest collection of evidence markers. Cara's and Eliza's purses were lying on the ground, their contents spilling out onto the floor. Three phones lay shattered nearby as well. All in all, there was very little to suggest what had happened. Andrew scanned the room and his eyes fell on the places where the two people had been shot. The bodies had obviously been carted away but the carpet was still stained with dried blood. Both victims were closer to the kitchen than Cara and the others had been.

The kidnappers had been posing as a food delivery, which meant they had come in from the back. Andrew crossed to the back door, moving through the kitchen to follow the same path as them. He turned his back on the door and leaned forward slightly, this gave him a relatively unobstructed view of the dining room beyond. It would have been easy for them to see their targets entering from here. But then why not wait for him? Then he remembered what Duncan had said, that the kidnappers had gotten a call just before Hunter called Andrew. Someone was watching him and Cara approaching and made the call. Someone sitting outside with a view of the restaurant but who did not come inside themselves. Someone like, apparently, Diego.

Andrew steadied the rage that thundered through him and focused on the restaurant again. He walked slowly through the kitchen, relying on the light of the streetlamps outside to illuminate the scene. The first burst of gunfire had been right at the threshold between kitchen and dining room, where apparently the two had been killed. Bullet holes covered the floor, ceiling, and walls, but only on the side of the restaurant away from Cara and the others. They'd been very careful while still making it look wild and unpredictable. From there, a handful of footprints tracking through something that had been spilled showed three of the assailants crossing to their victims. Andrew studied the scene over and over, frustration building as he saw nothing useful. These people were professionals and had left very little behind.

Growing more desperate by the second, he headed for the back door where the kidnappers had entered again. He unbolted it and pushed it open a few inches. The cruiser was still sitting at the end of the alley, and he could see the two officers sitting in it. They didn't seem to notice the door opening so Andrew scanned what he could see of the alley through the gap. This proved no more useful than his search inside, especially as the snow had completely hidden the ground. He was just about to let the door swing closed again when something caught his eye. The alley walls, like seemingly most in New York, were peppered with graffiti. Some were simple scrawlings of names while others certainly had a lot more skill behind them. One image in particular caught Andrew's eye because he had seen it before.

It was an expertly painted emerald surrounded by a circle of yellow, blue, and red. He remembered Diego explaining that it was simply representative of Colombia when he'd asked about this very pattern on a ring Diego had. The emerald was apparently the national gem of Colombia, and the colors were of course the flag. If Andrew had not been feeling so helpless, or frankly pissed at the thought Diego had something to do with any of this, he may not have thought about it any further. But he had noticed it, and feeble though it may be, it was about the only lead he had at the moment. Fishing his phone from his pocket, Andrew held it up to the crack in the door and snapped a couple pictures of the graffiti before closing the door and creeping back towards the front of the restaurant.

CHAPTER 25

GETTING BACK OUT OF the Traveller House was about as simple as it had been to get in. The officers stationed in the alley were still slacking off in their patrol car. Andrew was a couple blocks away already when his phone rang in his pocket.

"What?" Andrew said shortly, not even looking at the screen as he answered.

"Good evening to you too," Duncan said on the other end, "out for a little stroll are we?"

"Something like that, just heading home."

"You might want to take a little detour up to 7th and 47th before you do," Duncan said, a slight smug tone in his voice.

"Why the hell do I want to trek up to Times Square right now?" Andrew asked, hailing a cab.

"Because our friend Diego is not only there, he seems to have snuck out past his security detail. At some club called Vortex."

"What? Why would he do that?"

"Search me, kid, just thought you might like to know. You seem like you might be in the mood for some loud music and drinking."

"You know," Andrew said, a slight, vengeful smile curling his lip, "you might be right. Thanks Duncan."

"Uh huh, just try not to kill him, that's a whole lot of paperwork nobody wants to do."

"Oh, one other thing," Andrew said quickly, "on my way here the cab driver mentioned there was an SUV that followed the van away from the restaurant. Thought maybe you'd want to check that out."

"Already done," Duncan said, "it was one of the first things the cops noticed when they looked at the security footage and whatnot."

"So, who was it?" Andrew asked, a little annoyed that no one had mentioned this.

"Relax, kid," Duncan replied, clearly knowing exactly what Andrew was feeling, "it was Diego. That's how the cops knew to talk to him, and the only reason Hunter had a shot at questioning him, even if it failed. She couldn't exactly walk into the precinct and tell her captain that one of the people an undercover operative has been spying on was supposed to be at the scene of a shootout and kidnapping that they had only just heard about."

"Oh, yeah ok, I see your point. Thanks again."

"Sure," Duncan said simply.

Andrew hung up the phone just as the cab pulled to a stop in front of him and he got in. It didn't take too long to get up to the club Duncan had said Diego was in thanks to the light traffic of the hour. Despite this lateness, however, there were still ample tourists in the square itself, staring up at the bright billboards like they were the writings of the gods. Andrew weaved between the crowd, slipped a fifty to the wall of meat standing at the entrance to the club, and climbed the stairs beyond him.

The pounding music grew louder with each step until he could barely hear his own feet stomping up the stairs. He was met with flashing lights, a couple hundred sweating bodies, and a wall of sound that could have deafened him. Andrew crossed to the bar as he scanned the crowd for Diego. A waitress bumped into him and out of instinct, Andrew caught the bottle of top shelf tequila that had tumbled off her tray. He straightened up with it and placed it on the tray again while the waitress stared at him like he was Superman. Andrew gave her a quick smile before she set off again, climbing a couple of steps at the back of the dance floor to where a group of people sat on a few couches. Diego was there, sitting with a girl in his lap who was feeding him shots.

Andrew's blood boiled at the sight. Their three best friends were gone, he had been there, and yet here he was partying like any other night. Andrew marched after the waitress, slipping through the path she had carved and nearly bowled her over as he vaulted up the stairs. It took Diego a moment for his eyes to focus on Andrew looming over him, but then his eyes widened and he stared up. He stammered something that was lost in the thrum of the music as he slid the girl off of him and tried to climb backwards over the couch, apparently to put something between him and Andrew. In his drunken state, however, Diego's foot slipped and he toppled sideways off the couch. Andrew bent down and hauled him to his feet with one hand before dragging him across the dance floor towards a door that read 'Staff Only' in bright red letters. Andrew threw the helpless Diego through it and he landed in a heap at the feet of another waitress checking her makeup in a small mirror who screamed in surprise.

"Get out," Andrew growled to the waitress who blanched under his gaze.

"B-but you aren't..." she said weakly but fell silent when Andrew held out a small roll of bills.

"I just need five minutes." The waitress took the money and fled the scene, obviously not wanting to get involved any further. The door swung shut behind her and the music was dampened slightly.

"What the fuck," Diego said weakly as he tried to get up, but Andrew pushed him back down.

"You were there," Andrew hissed, barely containing the rage, "you were at the restaurant while the others were being taken. Wanna explain that?"

"I-I don't know what you're talking about," Diego lied pathetically, "I was never there."

Andrew grabbed Diego's shirt with both hands, his shoulder screaming in protest as he lifted the man and slammed him against the wall.

"Try again," Andrew said in a deadly whisper.

"Ok fine, I got there and saw what was happening and I panicked. I told my driver to get me the hell out of there because I wasn't about to get involved. I had no idea it was Eliza and the others being taken; I swear."

"Bullshit," Andrew roared, "you invited us there, you mysteriously didn't show, and then they were taken. I was supposed to be taken too. Tell me everything."

The fear in Diego's eyes reached a new peak as Andrew leaned in closer. Between the alcohol and his own nerves, it looked like he was a few seconds away from a heart attack. "I swear I had nothing to do with it! I would never do that to any of you. My driver was running late and we hit traffic, so we didn't get there until that van was already pulling away and people were screaming like crazy."

Andrew wound back and punched Diego hard in the gut, letting him fall to the ground. The punch may have been unnecessary, but it made him feel better, at least for a second. "It wasn't a random kidnapping," Andrew said, leaning down over the coughing Diego, "we were targeted. The only other person who knew we'd be there was you and you were conveniently out of the way when it went down. Tell me one good reason I shouldn't beat the shit out of you right here."

"My uncle knew," Diego choked out and Andrew frowned at him. "He was the one who got the reservation, he said he had a meeting and wouldn't be able to use it himself, so he asked if I wanted to use it instead, to invite you guys." He said all of this very quickly, apparently in the hopes he would be spared further assault.

"Where is he?"

"What?" Diego asked stupidly.

"Where is your uncle? He's not at home and they can't find him anywhere."

"You don't think he had something to do with this, do you? I swear he would never hurt us. He's loved me like a son since the day I moved here." There was a note of genuine innocence in his face now. "How do you even know he's gone? Who's looking for him?"

"The cops," Andrew said shortly, "they want to question him about a murder, they think he's killed someone." It was mostly a lie, but Diego's reaction to these words finally convinced Andrew that he really wasn't involved. The shock and disbelief was unmistakable.

Diego swore a few times in Spanish under his breath before looking up at Andrew again. "I can't believe he would do that, or any of this."

"Where is he, Diego?" Andrew asked again, his patience running thin.

"I don't know, I swear. He sometimes goes to those resorts and stuff upstate when he needs to get away, but I don't know where. I swear, Hawk, I really don't know."

"Fine," Andrew said reluctantly, reaching out a hand for Diego who took it gratefully. He brushed himself off and gave Andrew a sort of grin right before Andrew punched him squarely in the face, sending him back to the ground of the little break room. "That," Andrew spat, "was for being such a cowardly little bitch. Now as you're trying to drink yourself into a stupor, just remember that our friends are out there, God knows where, wishing that you had been there to help."

Tears filled Diego's eyes as he clutched his bleeding nose, unable to respond to that. Andrew shook his head and left him there, pushing his way out of the club again. His shoulder was still aching in protest, not to mention his other injuries, but he finally felt like he'd actually done something to help. Hunter could safely ignore Diego in the investigation, and they could focus on finding Luca.

"Duncan," Andrew said as he strode down the street away from the club, "I've got a lead on Luca Pedroso."

"That didn't take long," Duncan said, sounding amused. "I take it the kid wasn't the mastermind?"

"Looks like he was just the fall guy. I still think his alibi is a little shaky, but he genuinely seems innocent. Not exactly an iron will on that one."

Duncan chuckled to himself for a moment before asking, "Alright, what am I looking for?"

"Diego says his uncle likes to frequent the getaway resorts upstate. I don't imagine he's using his own name or credit card, but it's something. Start with the most exclusive and work your way down."

"Can do," Duncan said, "but it'll take some time. You go home, get some rest. Got it?"

"Alright," Andrew said, admitting to himself that he was feeling exhausted already. He hung up the phone again and found a cab to take him home. This plan was somewhat foiled when he saw the mob of reporters and paparazzi crowded around the entrance to his building and the gate to the parking lot. They were being held at bay by the building's security, but it still wasn't something he was looking forward to dealing with, especially while his knuckles were still sporting some of Diego's blood.

"Change of plans," Andrew said to the cab driver before giving him Hunter's address instead.

"You famous or something?" The cabby asked, looking at Andrew in the rear-view mirror.

"Something," Andrew grunted, but did not expand on the topic. He got out in front of Hunter's building and crossed to the door, hitting the buzzer for her apartment a few times. When no response came he wondered if she was still at the precinct. Then the intercom crackled to life.

"I have a gun and I enjoy using it," said Hunter's very tired and very annoyed voice.

"Yeah, well I have two dozen reporters who are hunting me down," Andrew said, "so either go shoot them or let me in."

The door buzzed and clicked open for Andrew who pushed his way into the building. He knocked on Hunter's door a few minutes later and she answered it at once. Her red hair was messy and she was only wearing an oversized hoodie. The look in her eye could have killed him on the spot but she waved him in.

"Couldn't handle the press, tough guy?" she asked sarcastically around a huge yawn.

"Didn't really want to. I talked to Diego," Andrew began, making Hunter raise an eyebrow questioningly through the haze of sleep.

He could tell she wasn't exactly in a receptive mood, so he waved the rest of the report away. "It can wait until morning; Duncan is already on it. Nothing we can do right now."

"Great, couch," she grunted simply before ambling back to her bed and falling into it, burrowing under the blankets. Andrew settled himself on the couch where Hunter had laid out an extra blanket and pillows for him. It took a long while, but Andrew finally fell asleep, his mind racing with thoughts of Cara.

CHAPTER 26

"I HATE YOU," HUNTER mumbled from beneath the two pillows she was using to try and block him out. It was a little after dawn when Andrew had woken from a nightmare like he'd been electrocuted. He tried, for a while, to get back to sleep, watching a few snowflakes fall from the gray sky through the window. Eventually, however, he knew sleep was not about to come. Instead, he had dedicated himself to anything that could take his mind off Cara. He had cleaned the apartment, read a few chapters of the police manual on Hunter's coffee table, made breakfast, and cleaned the apartment again. Of course, none of this had worked so Andrew had waited as long as he could before braving the attempt to wake Hunter.

He stood just far enough from her that she couldn't hit him, a steaming mug in one hand and a plate of cooked bacon in the other. During their training, he had found this was the easiest way to drag her out of bed on early mornings.

"You know you have to get up anyway," Andrew said as gently as possible. As though to punctuate these words, Hunter's phone blared an alarm. She groaned loudly and Andrew reached down with his pinky outstretched from the mug to tap the phone and silence it. Hunter slowly rose into a sitting position, two blankets wrapped around her like a burial shroud. Narrowed eyes glared out at him from the blankets and Andrew held up the contents of his hands.

"Coffee first," Hunter said as a hand snaked its way out, groping for the mug. Andrew handed it over and sat on the end of her bed, waiting for her to wake up a bit. "So you spoke with Diego," Hunter prompted eventually, pulling the blankets from her head.

"Yeah, he slipped his protection detail to go get drunk in a club."

"Seems like a real standup guy," Hunter said.

"Suffice to say I scared the hell out of him by showing up there," Andrew said with a note of satisfaction.

"Do I need to be getting ahead of assault charges here?"

"Probably not, he'd have to admit he left, and I imagine the folks at the consulate wouldn't be thrilled."

"So what did he say?" Hunter asked, a piece of bacon halfway to her mouth. Andrew recounted the brief, though useful interaction with Diego. By the end of it, Hunter had cleared her plate of bacon and sent Andrew for a refill on her coffee.

"So, I've got Duncan looking for anything he can on the spas," Andrew finished as he handed over the fresh cup.

"Nice job," Hunter admitted. "It bothers me a little that you can get so much done by going around the system. It would have taken us a month and several fights with lawyers to even get in the same room as him again."

"Well, that's why I'm here," Andrew said, grinning at her. "How are things on your end?"

"Honestly it feels like we haven't gotten anywhere. There was enough blood in that van that they figured at least three people were killed inside of it. They're still trying to work on it but there is zero sign of where the bodies are."

"What if it's the guy who executed Alejandro?" Andrew asked. He went on as Hunter merely looked at him in confusion, "I've been going over all those case materials you gave me and there is only one concrete tie between all of this. Luca Pedroso. The guy whose face was smashed in and Alejandro were both killed by the same guy."

"We think," Hunter cut in.

"Ok well say they are," Andrew said, "that killer was there when they threatened Luca and killed Alejandro. If he's also now killed the crew that kidnapped everyone, then the bodies may be on ice the same way Alejandro's was. He may just be waiting for the heat to die down before dumping the bodies somewhere they won't be noticed."

"Ok sure," Hunter said, and Andrew could see her brain finally waking up as it churned through this theory, "but then why kill your own people? This job took a lot of planning and a lot of time. They went through the effort of planting people in the consulate. Why spend all that money and effort if you were just going to kill them all?"

"What if the crew and the consulate moles aren't the same people? If I was going to plan something like this then I would be going about it very carefully. All kinds of things could have gone wrong during the kidnapping, someone's mask could have come off, someone could have been injured and left behind. Why take that risk with the people you just spent so much to place here? I would have hired local talent to pull it off, told them the bare minimum, and taken care of them after the fact."

"I suppose it makes sense," Hunter said, "so then why bother getting people into the consulate if not to use them for the actual job?"

"There's more to it that we aren't seeing. With enough time and research they could have just grabbed us, but they used Luca. I think he's entered some sort of deal with a partner. If all that partner wanted was money, there are other ways to go about it. I think they wanted consulate access for a longer-term plan. The kidnapping may have just been Luca's part in all this. He gets the ransom money, keeps Diego out of the way but still enough of a suspect to deter the investigation, and stays quiet while the partner gets whatever they originally wanted. I wouldn't be surprised to hear that Luca is retiring when this is all over. Turning a blind eye with his millions on some beach with no extradition."

"You've clearly put a lot of thought into this," Hunter said quietly, and Andrew realized how much he must have sounded like a crazy person with a wall covered in red string and photos.

"It's not like I had much else to do."

"What you're saying makes sense, Hawk, but none of it is enough to act on officially. We can't even begin to speculate who this partner would be."

"It has to be someone that knows how to get to Luca, someone who has muscle to send here, and someone who might benefit from inside government knowledge."

"Someone like?" Hunter prompted.

"Someone like the Colombian cartels," Andrew said, finally getting to the centre of his conspiracy wall. "Hear me out," he added quickly when Hunter shot him a look. "The US has been putting a lot of pressure on Colombia to get its cartels under control. The influx of drugs being shipped here is astronomical. If the kingpins are worried they're about to be squeezed out of the game by their own government, wouldn't they want someone on the inside to feed them that intel?"

"Sure," Hunter admitted, "but then why not go after a more local source?"

"The consulate has the same access to the government systems and I'd be willing to bet it's a lot harder to get that access from the direct source. Remember, Duncan identified one of the fake consulate guards as a member of the Vargas cartel."

"Again though, you need actual evidence if I'm going to be able to present any of this to the higher ups. I have no problem running with it as a personal theory, but a theory isn't enough to make them deviate from standard protocol."

"I know," Andrew admitted, "which is why we need to find Luca. Hopefully Duncan finds something soon, but in the meantime I have something else I want to run with." He pulled his phone from his pocket and opened the photos of the graffiti he had taken the night before.

"What's this?" Hunter asked as he passed her his phone.

"That was spray painted in the alley next to the restaurant. I've seen Diego wear something similar. It's a symbol that only really means something to a Colombian, or someone working for a Colombian. I think it was used to mark the spot where the kidnapping was meant to take place. If I can figure out who might have put it up, then it might lead us to who else is behind all this."

"And you think you can achieve that with a picture? I know the NYPD has a graffiti database, and especially graffiti related to gang activity, but you'd have to comb through all of it to find a match. That's even assuming there is a match to be found."

"Just leave it to me," Andrew said confidently, "I have a plan."

Hunter's phone rang before she could respond to this and she answered it immediately after seeing who it was. "Yes sir," she said by way of greeting before listening silently for several beats. "Understood, thank you for the update. I'm on my way now." She hung up and got up from her bed to start getting dressed.

"What's up?" Andrew asked.

"FBI lab put a rush in on the DNA tests for the blood. There are four distinct samples and one of them came back with a match right away. Martin Hopewell, former military, dishonorably discharged four years ago after he nearly killed his commanding officer. A couple members of his former platoon are being brought into the precinct. I'm going to go question them about what Hopewell may have been up to since then."

"I'm guessing gun for hire," Andrew said, and Hunter nodded.

"You can stick around as long as you want but you're going to have to go home eventually," she said, searching her closet for a fresh shirt.

"I know, I'll figure it out. I can always play it strong and silent. The security in that building will try to shield me as much as possible. Let me know how it goes."

Hunter nodded again, "Will do. Don't do anything stupid, don't get yourself killed, and good luck with your graffiti. Hopefully it'll give us something to go on. I don't get why we haven't heard ransom demands yet and it's driving me nuts."

"Thanks," Andrew said quietly. He had been trying not to let the radio silence from the kidnappers bother him. Surely they would reach out soon to make their demands. You didn't go through a very public kidnapping of several ultra-wealthy people without asking for something.

"Hey," Hunter said more gently, putting her hand on his shoulder, "we're going to find them. I promise." Andrew nodded and Hunter gave his shoulder a little squeeze before setting off for the precinct.

CHAPTER 27

ANDREW ROUNDED THE CORNER towards his building, turning up his collar against a chill wind. He had hoped that using the parking lot's entrance would afford him a bit less scrutiny from the reporters and photographers loitering around the place. Each of them hoped to be the one to provide an exclusive about the story that was gripping the city above all others. There hadn't been a broadcast or newspaper since the kidnapping that hadn't at least mentioned it, even if there was nothing to tell. It was a little disconcerting for Andrew to discover he was one of the most talked about people in the city in hardly any time at all. Thankfully, not too many people recognised him as he walked since they only had a somewhat grainy photo of him on the van to go from. All that, he suspected, would change the moment these vultures got a hold of him.

His plan was working reasonably well at first. He slipped up the street and was nearly to the back entrance when a photographer, who had been dozing on a bench, jerked awake and saw him there.

"Mister Hawkins!" he cried at once, springing to his feet and crossing the street. "Andrew, over here, please." The distinctive clicking of a camera going at full speed grew louder as the man tried to block Andrew's path. The shout had attracted the attention of a few others who stood on the corner, apparently to keep an eye on both entrances. Soon, Andrew was surrounded by a horde of cameras, microphones, and fresh-faced journalists who took notes on their phones. Andrew suspected this last group were merely the ones that the various media outlets deemed unimportant enough to camp out in the cold for a glimpse of him. He felt a little bad for them all as he shouldered past a few, trying to silently make his way to his building.

"Where are you coming from?" one of the reporters asked before shoving her microphone in his face.

"How is your recovery going?" asked another.

"How do you feel about the lack of progress seen from the NYPD so far?"

"Who do you think is behind all this?"

"People are saying you had something to do with it and that your supposed heroic act was just a show, care to comment?" This last question made Andrew's skin crawl and it took all his willpower to not hit the man who had asked it. Andrew slowed to a stop, his fists clenched, and the reporter smiled smugly at him through the sea of faces. His cheap suit was wrinkled and he was less than cleanly shaven. He held out his phone as a microphone, waiting for a response. Then Andrew realized that this question had not only shocked him, the other reporters and photographers had gone silent beyond the occasional click of a camera.

"Look," Andrew said finally, and the mob seemed to tense, "I understand that you're all out here because there is no other news to go on. I get it. But I have nothing to tell you that you don't already know. I was there and saw what happened and I reacted on pure instinct. My friends were taken and there was nothing I could do about it."

"Why weren't you with them?" a reporter asked quietly from the back of the group. Andrew looked around at her. She couldn't have been more than seventeen years old and looked almost frightened of Andrew.

"Honestly," Andrew said defeatedly, "total dumb luck. I was walking to the restaurant when I got a call. I took it outside. I should have been right there with them and I should have been taken. I really have nothing else to say on the matter so please, don't waste your time with me."

Andrew tried to make it the rest of the way to the door after that and it seemed to break the spell he'd had over them. They all started shouting questions again and were jostling him worse than ever. Someone got pushed and they crashed into Andrew hard enough to wrench his injured arm and he cried out in pain.

"That's enough!" someone roared from beyond the throng of reporters. Andrew looked around to see both Donnie and Jack, security guards from the building, physically moving reporters out of the way. Donnie reached for Andrew, who was clutching his shoulder, and seemed to pluck him out of the centre of the group. The pair escorted him briskly to the building and got him safely inside.

"Thanks," Andrew said through gritted teeth. When was the last time he'd taken something for the pain?

"You should have given us a heads up that you were coming back, sir," Donnie said, "we'd have been out there waiting for you. We only got out there when we did because Jones noticed the reporters going mad."

"We thought you'd be gone for days," Jack said in his slower voice, as though he had to think carefully about every word before he said it, "thought you were hiding out somewhere."

"I'm not about to let them drive me from my home," Andrew said shortly. Any sense of a good mood he'd had that morning had evaporated.

"Well, let us know if you need anything. If you're going out again, we can get your driver to come right into the lot out back to make things easier."

"Appreciate it," Andrew said before crossing to the elevator and heading up to his condo. He entered the blissful dark and silence of the place, popped a couple of the pills the doctor had given him, and collapsed onto the sofa. He wasn't entirely sure if he fell asleep or not, but eventually he sat up and pulled out his phone, he needed to be doing something. The phone rang only twice before the line connected and Andrew was assaulted with a cacophony of voices.

"Andrew? Oh my God, are you alright? I saw what happened! I'm so sorry for not reaching out but I wasn't sure if you were up and about yet." Diane's voice was shrill and almost panicked, she had to practically shout to be heard over the four or five others who were yelling in the background.

"Is it really him?"

"Is he ok?"

"I want to talk to him!"

"I'm alright," Andrew said, and the voices fell silent, "really, I'm fine. How are you all holding up?"

"Not bad, all considered," Diane said, "it still hasn't really sunk in yet. None of us can focus on much right now."

"I know what you mean," Andrew said, "anyway I was hoping to see you guys actually, I have a favor to ask." Diane did not respond, though there was a sort of clattering sound on her end.

"Why didn't you save her?" a different, much younger voice demanded.

"Em?" Andrew asked.

"You saw it happen, you were on that van, why did you let her go?" The girl's voice was shaky and Andrew could practically hear the tears welling up in her eyes.

"I tried," Andrew said softly as something inside of him seemed to break all over again, "Em, I really tried, but I couldn't save her. I'm sorry."

"You should have tried harder," was all Em said, sending a shard of ice directly through his heart.

"Andrew? I'm sorry, she snatched the phone from me," Diane said, regaining control of her phone. "Look, a few of the kids and I are down in Tompkins Square. I know they'd be happy to see you."

"I'll be there soon," Andrew said as steadily as possible, then he hung up, unable to say anything further.

Ram arrived in the parking lot only ten minutes later and Andrew set out, shielded this time from the reporters who still swarmed the gates, yelling questions through the car windows. Andrew had only spoken to tell Ram where they were going and the latter seemed to understand he was in no mood to talk. His shoulder was still sore from the first run in with the reporters so he had replaced the sling, though he was very pleased he didn't need to pass through them again. Ram pulled smoothly up to the park in the East Village and Andrew got out with a word of thanks.

Diane and the kids from her group were scattered across a few benches at the edge of the large, paved area in the corner of the park. Normally, the area would have been full of ramps and rails for skateboarders, but the weather had rendered it into barely more than a large white square of snow. A few of the kids were playing some version of tag, chasing each other and sliding around on the snow. Most, though, were sitting on the benches with Diane, listlessly watching the others play.

Andrew opened a gate in the fence and a few of them turned to see who was coming, many with wide eyes. Andrew had gotten to know these kids over the time he'd been spending with Cara. Andrew spotted Em sitting on the bench right next to Diane, her hair masking her face as she looked pointedly away from him, arms and legs crossed.

"Uh, hi," Andrew said a little awkwardly to them all.

"Holy shit he really is alive," one of the older kids, a wiry boy name Oliver, said over the silence. This broke the aura of surprise as many of the kids giggled. A few ran over to him, hugging him or giving him fist bumps. Diane was still sitting with Em, unrestrained relief showing on her face. Em finally deigned to look over at him with her most severe look of wintery disapproval. He watched her eyes flick to his sling, then the healing gash on his forehead. Fresh tears filled her eyes and suddenly she was running at him at full speed. She slammed into him and Andrew caught her with his good arm.

"I'm sorry," she wailed.

"It's alright," Andrew said gently, "I understand how you're feeling. I would have done the same thing, actually I have been doing the same thing."

"What happened, Andrew?" Diane asked, getting up from the bench, "I mean what really happened, the papers don't do a great job of explaining." The kids all nodded, clearly eager to hear the story as well. So Andrew told them everything, or at least all he could reasonably tell them. Em didn't let go of him until he got to the part about being shot and falling off the van. She seemed to think she might be hurting him. He reached out a hand for her and she took it gratefully, moving to stand right at his side.

"I don't know what to say," Diane said, she was shaking slightly, "other than I'm glad you're alright. Have you heard anything about Cara and the others yet?"

"No," Andrew admitted, "but we'll get them back, trust me. I was hoping you could help me with something. It's top secret though so none of you can tell anyone else, ok?" Everyone nodded at once and Andrew briefly freed his hand from Em to pull out his phone, pulling up the pictures he had taken before handing it to her.

"What's this?" she asked.

"It was painted in the alley next to the restaurant," Andrew explained, "the police think it may have been used as a sort of signal to the people who took Cara. They haven't found anything on it yet, but I thought I would ask the people who know more about street art than anyone in the city."

Em dutifully studied the picture before moving around to show the others. They all immediately broke out into whispered conversation, huddling together to discuss. Diane took the opportunity to sidle over to Andrew and give him a hug.

"I really am glad you're alright," she whispered, "but do you know why they were taken?"

"I think it's all just about money," Andrew said, "those three make up the heirs to some of the wealthiest families in the city. There may be other, richer targets, but how often can you get several of them in the same room in public?"

"I guess it's lucky you got that call then," Diane said, chuckling weakly. Andrew was spared the need to respond thanks to the kids all turning to face him. Em strode forward, clutching the arm of a boy who didn't look thrilled about being thrust into the spotlight.

"This is Luis," Em said, "both of his brothers are in the Red Cobras."

"Red Cobras?" Andrew prompted and the boy nodded a little nervously.

"A Colombian gang," the boy said with a thick accent, "they wanted me to be a runner for them, but Miss Diane helped me get out." He fell silent again and Andrew got the impression that he didn't want anyone to get in trouble. Em thumped him on the shoulder and he stuttered into speech again. "I-I used to stand watch while my brothers tagged buildings with that symbol."

"So you've seen it before?" Andrew asked, wanting to be sure.

"A few of us have seen them around," Em said, "but something is off about this one."

"What do you mean?"

"It's a bit hard to explain and we aren't really sure, can you leave it with us for a bit? We'll get Diane to call you if we figure anything out."

"Of course," Andrew said, "I appreciate your help." Em turned back to the other kids and nodded once. Without a word, several of the older ones raced off out of the park and quickly disappeared into the city.

"Will this really help?" Em asked when it was just her, Andrew, and Diane left standing there and she handed back his phone.

"I think it will," Andrew said, and Em threw her arms around him again.

CHAPTER 28

Two DAYS PASSED WITH very little progress after Andrew had been to see the art group. The police had made no further progress after they ran the blood they had found in the van. The only piece of news on that front was that Hunter had confirmed that Martin Hopewell had fallen in with some less than reputable people after his dishonorable discharge. The man's former squad mates had not been able to say exactly what he'd been doing, only that Hopewell's wife, whom he had left shortly after his discharge, reported through the network of army spouses that Martin had fled the States for South America. Any attempt to track his movements had been difficult to say the least.

Andrew, meanwhile, had asked Duncan to look into the Red Cobras. If they really were the ones who had tagged that alley, they might be able to reveal who hired them to do it if they weren't directly responsible. He had told Hunter about the Red Cobras as well, of course, and she had even convinced her captain to reach out to Gang Squad detectives in other precincts to gather intel. The presence of a random piece of graffiti was apparently worth looking into when there was nothing else to go on.

The thing that bothered Andrew the most, though, was that there had still been no word from the kidnappers. No demands, no proof of life, not even some sort of propaganda celebrating the deaths of three wealthy captives. Andrew wasn't sure how long he could keep going like this, pacing around his condo with absolutely nothing to do. He had already converted his office into an actual conspiracy theory board, though there weren't many known connections to make just yet. He had all the evidence photos Hunter had provided, the police reports of the John Doe and Alejandro Lopez, as well as anything else he thought relevant stuck up on the walls, connecting things with string so that he could visualize it all.

Finally, on the fifth day of the hunt, Andrew was roused from his thoughts when an urgent knock came at the door. Normally the security desk called up to let him know someone was coming, especially in the evening. Andrew hurried over to the door, grabbing the gun Hunter had given him in the hospital from where it had been stuck in his sling.

"Yes?" Andrew called, the barrel of the gun level with where someone's head would be.

"It's me," Hunter called, "let me in. They're alive."

Andrew's heart leapt practically out of his chest as he processed her words. He set the gun down and fumbled with the lock before wrenching the door open. Hunter stood there, her phone in one hand and a tablet in the other. She had a sort of wild excitement in her eyes at the prospect of a lead. Hunter walked through the door without any invitation and passed right through to the kitchen. Andrew followed on her heels and waited impatiently for her to prop the tablet up on the counter and set her phone down.

"Hey kid," Duncan's voice said from Hunter's phone, "I've been trying to track it, but they knew what they were doing when they sent it to the families."

"What are you talking about?" Andrew asked. His blood was thundering loudly in his ears at this point.

"This," Hunter said simply as she pulled up a direct link to an IP address on the tablet. The screen filled itself with a video feed from a pretty decent camera looking down from the upper corner of a plain stone room with a single, heavy looking wooden door. Chained by the ankles to the wall opposite the door were three people in fine clothing who were all looking a little disheveled. Andrew's eyes widened as they fell upon Cara, sitting on the dirty concrete floor with her back against the wall in plain view of the camera. It looked like her dress had a few small tears in it but otherwise she looked alright. A couple of thin blankets were bundled up underneath her. The other two, though not facing the camera, were clearly Dirk and Eliza. One of Dirk's shoes was missing, and Eliza was huddled on her own blankets, but there was no obvious sign of damage to either of them either.

"How..." Andrew said, his throat suddenly dry, "how do we know this isn't prerecorded."

"Just keep watching," Hunter said gently as she flicked on the TV in the kitchen and flipped to CNN News. About a minute later, a small screen in the far corner of the room, out of reach of the captives, flickered to life and displayed a CNN broadcast. Andrew looked quickly between his TV and the little one in the security feed. They matched. There was a delay of several seconds, but it was definitely the same broadcast. Andrew couldn't speak again, so simply looked at Hunter questioningly.

"They turn it on for two minutes at the top of every hour," she explained, "it's how they prove it's a live feed. They're alright, Hawk, they're all alive."

"And we really can't track it?" Andrew asked.

"I've been trying," Duncan replied from the phone, "but like I said, they know what they're doing. Each of the families were sent an email with an IP address and the demands. The emails also came with a nifty little virus that scrubbed its own footsteps as it traveled. The feed itself is being routed through so many different places it's got me running in circles."

"Surely there is something at the end of those circles," Andrew prompted.

"Oh definitely," Duncan said, "but every time I get close to the actual origin, the entire routing pattern changes. Someone has set up a *very* sophisticated little algorithm to keep people like me out of there. I'll keep trying, but I wouldn't hold my breath."

Andrew's eyes traveled greedily over Cara again, taking her in and trying to determine how she was based on the small image of her. If the three of them knew there was a camera, they were either ignoring it or didn't know that they were being watched by anyone other than their captors. The small screen displaying the news went out. None of them had even glanced up at it.

"What do they want?" was the next thing Andrew was aware of actually saying out loud. It was the only question of those that he was thinking that seemed important enough to actually voice.

"A hundred million from each family," Hunter said, "and they have made it very clear that failure to meet those demands will end very, very badly for the ones they took."

"I know the Warpoles and the Samson-Wallers have that sort of money, but what about the Randals?" Andrew asked uncertainly. "I know George is former director but that can't mean that much money."

"His wife is the real rich one," Hunter said, "her family is worth more than the others put together. They all have the money and they are all already working on getting it together. The deadline is five days from today and exchange instructions will be sent the day before."

Andrew took a deep breath, his eyes never leaving the feed. "Ok, so worst case they pay the money and we get them back, right? But surely we're still working to find them."

"Of course we are," Hunter said reassuringly, "the exchange is an absolute last resort, we just want to be ready for it. George Randal has already stepped forward and offered to be the one to make the exchange. Given his career history, the NYPD and the FBI are both in agreement. In the meantime, we keep running the leads we do have, small as they may be."

"What do you need me to do?" Andrew asked at once.

"Nothing," Hunter said, "I only wanted to let you know what was happening. Keep doing what you're doing. Lay low, keep digging for what I may have missed in the murders, and I'll let you know when something else happens."

"We're all still working around the clock on this, kid," Duncan put in, apparently to try to reassure Andrew, "I'm scouring the state for Luca, but there are a shocking number of spas and resorts out there."

"Alright," Andrew said, "thank you. Both of you." Hunter nodded and gave him a brief one-armed hug before scooping up her phone and heading for the door. Andrew remained standing in his kitchen, staring at the tablet that Hunter had left behind. As he watched, Cara adjusted the cuff around her ankle and laid down on the floor. She shot bolt upright again as the door opened. A man wearing a ski mask appeared there, tossed a plain white plastic bag into the room, and slammed the door again. Cara got to her feet at once, the heavy chain secured to her dragging as she retrieved the bag and approached the others. She handed out bottles of water and what looked like sandwiches wrapped in cellophane. None of the food had any kind of label that Andrew could see and he supposed the kidnappers didn't want to make it too easy to track them down.

Eliza and Dirk took the offered food and water, both consuming it greedily as Cara sat back down and unwrapped her own sandwich. She seemed remarkably composed given the situation and Andrew's heart swelled with pride and affection. He watched Cara finish her less than substantial meal and lay back down. She turned to face the wall and seemed to be doing something with her hands, but he couldn't see what. Andrew watched until she fell still and the lights in the room were turned out, plunging the scene into total darkness.

After several long minutes of watching the dark screen, hoping something else would happen, Andrew's phone rang, making him jump slightly. He reached for it and saw that it was Duncan.

"Duncan?" Andrew said, a little unsure why, if he had anything to say, he hadn't done so while Hunter had been there.

"I'm assuming you're going to do something stupid now that you've been left alone again?" Duncan stated as a question.

"I wasn't really planning on it," Andrew said defensively, "besides, what would I even do?"

"Oh, I dunno," Duncan said casually, "break into Luca Pedroso's house?"

"Why would I want to do that?"

"Come on, kid, you aren't that slow. I've been searching for days for the man, with nothing to show for it. We know he's involved but Hunter can't get a warrant. I suspect that if there is any clue to follow, it's at his house. I'd do it myself but I'm not exactly as spritely as I used to be."

"Aren't you supposed to talk me out of things like this?" Andrew asked. "I can't imagine the company would be thrilled about me breaking into a Colombian state official's house...again."

"The company likes to turn a blind eye to most spur of the moment decisions from their operators. They can always disavow you if you go too far."

"Comforting," Andrew said bitterly.

"Come on, kid, this is all I've got. If I could hack into the contents of his house then I would. As far as we know there has been no one in or out since Luca left so he may have left something behind."

"Alright fine," Andrew said, shutting off the tablet, "I can't say I hadn't thought of it myself. Just don't tell Hunter if we don't find anything. I really don't need her yelling at me."

"No worries there, she scares the hell out of me. Call me when you get there and I'll get you inside, just like last time." Andrew hung up the phone and undid the clasps of his sling. Truthfully, it had been driving him nuts and even if it did help with the pain, he wanted it off. And burned. And the ashes scattered to the wind. He was done being the victim.

CHAPTER 29

As ANDREW WALKED TOWARDS Luca's house for the second time, he felt the training that had been drilled into him take effect. He had total awareness of his surroundings even while maintaining a decidedly calm demeanor. He was on high alert. Even if he wasn't expecting trouble, the reporters waiting outside his building had a nasty habit of popping up wherever he happened to be. It had taken him an hour of doubling back and random driving before he was confident none of them had followed him.

Admittedly, the mob of them had shrunk as the days had passed and nothing new came to light. The moment the press found out there was a live stream of the kidnapped socialites, however, they had returned in force that very evening. Given the speed of the response, Andrew suspected someone in the NYPD was selling their inside knowledge. Regardless, by the time Andrew had parked a reasonable distance from Luca's house, he was sure that no one was following him. Duncan was already on the line in his ear and he didn't even reach for the door before the electronic lock clicked open. Andrew slipped inside quickly and turned on a small flashlight he pulled from his pocket.

"Alright what am I looking for?" Andrew asked, scanning the beam over the lavishly decorated entryway.

"Anything you didn't look for last time you were here. We just need some indication of where he may have gone. One interesting thing, however," Duncan added, typing away in the background, "when I was digging a little deeper into Luca, I noticed that for the past several months his house was drawing more power than normal. As much as it would shock me, he may be hiding something like a server bank or similar. I would normally find this kind of reading when someone is trying to cool something big."

"Well, there definitely wasn't anything like that in his office," Andrew said, his eyes scanning as he passed into the living room.

"Up or down then?"

"I'll try down," Andrew replied, crossing to a door that hid the staircase to the basement of the house. "I'd be more likely to hide something in a basement."

"Good to know," Duncan commented idly.

Andrew opened the door and was met with the upper landing of a set of carpeted stairs. He descended them slowly, one hand constantly on the gun he had hidden in his coat. The narrow staircase opened onto a surprisingly small, though still very comfortably furnished basement. Someone had clearly, like the rest of the house, ripped the basement down to its studs and replaced everything with dark woods and gilt accents. Andrew turned slowly on the spot, taking in the man cave Luca had built for himself. Clashing terribly with the rest of the decor was a truly ugly recliner that looked like it was from the nineties pointed at a wall-mounted, 100-inch TV. A small bar was pushed against one wall, overflowing with expensive bottles mingling unashamedly with cheap beer.

"This is wrong," Andrew muttered as he paced the length, then the width of the room. "Duncan, the basement is too small for a building like this. I'm looking at a single room that's about fifteen by fifteen."

"You're not wrong, it should be at least double the size. Looks like our man was hiding something after all. Check for concealed doors or false walls."

Andrew approached the back wall of the basement, opposite the massive TV, and began tapping his knuckles against it every few feet. To his satisfaction, a section in the middle made a thunking sound like it was hollow. But there was no obvious handle or knob to open it. He contemplated for a moment and was just about to start bashing it down when his eyes fell on one of the ostentatious candle brackets hanging nearby.

"Oh no way," Andrew said, barely suppressing giddiness from his voice as he reached up. He held his breath and pulled the bracket which swung down with a telltale click and the section of wall swung outward a few inches. Pausing only briefly to admire the spectacular cliche, Andrew pulled the door open and froze at the sight that met his eyes. LED lights flickered to life all on their own, illuminating one of the most horrifying scenes he'd ever witnessed.

"Jesus Christ," Andrew exclaimed, taking a full step away from the door.

"What is it?" Duncan asked at once. "Kid? Andrew? Talk to me."

Andrew took a deep breath, steeling himself this time before stepping into the room. One corner of the room was dominated by a large, circular, rotating bed. The walls were adorned with a truly disturbing number of sex toys, many of which Andrew couldn't even guess the function of. Then, in pride of place in the centre of the room was a large wooden cross that was clearly meant to have someone tied to it.

"It's a fucking sex dungeon," Andrew groaned.

There were several moments of dead silence before Duncan burst out laughing. It was a dry, wheezing sort of laugh, a sound that Andrew realized he'd never actually heard from Duncan before. "On a scale of weekend hobby to dominatrix, what are we talking?"

"Worse," Andrew said, trying very hard not to picture Luca anywhere near the room before him, "much worse. Hang on though." Andrew had just spotted another door in the room; it was made of thick glass and was the only thing that hadn't lit up when the room had come to life. He walked over to it, pleased to turn his back on the rest of the room, and found a switch next to it. He flicked it on.

"Whacha got?" Duncan asked.

"A sauna," Andrew replied, "a fancy one too. I guess this answers your power draw question."

"Ah well," Duncan said, still laughing a little, "hopefully there is more to Luca than a greedy pervert. Keep looking."

Andrew frowned, more than a little let down by the discovery, and was about to leave the room when he saw a pair of slippers by the sauna door. It wasn't that they were out of place or anything, rather that they looked cheaper than he would have expected. Knowing Luca's other tastes, Andrew would have assumed he would have some sort of designer slippers that cost more than a car. These, however, were the plain white kind you got for free in fancier hotels. Then again, Andrew supposed, as someone trying to look rich while truly being a cheap bastard, why shouldn't Luca take the slippers from a hotel.

"Hey Duncan," Andrew said, picking up one of the slippers to examine the embroidered logo on the toe, "I don't suppose one of those resorts you've been looking into has a logo of what looks like a lotus with a crown over it."

"Hang on..." There was more furious typing over the call and Andrew waited as patiently as he could in the room of nightmares. "In fact there is. Fittingly it's called the Crowned Lotus resort and spa up near Lake Placid."

"Any way to tell if Luca is there?" Andrew asked, dropping the slipper and leaving the room, careful to shut the hidden door again.

"If there is, I'll find it. Looks like I might be able to punch through into their booking system, but if he was under his own name, I likely would have found him by now. Give me a couple hours to parse through this and I'll let you know. Good job."

Andrew made a cursory search of the rest of the house, looking for anything that might give a more concrete answer. For the most part, however, there was nothing to find. Half of Luca's closet was empty, complete with hangers laying on the ground from where they had fallen. Evidently their contents had been taken in a hurry. Luca's car keys were still by the front door, which tracked given that Duncan had found no sign of his car leaving the city. In the end, the slippers were really the only substantial lead that Andrew could find, and substantial was pushing it a bit.

He slipped back out into the darkness of the city, Duncan locking the door behind him, and he returned to his car. The last thing he was expecting at that moment was to see Diego leaning against the car. Yet there he was, slumped against the side of it with a mostly empty bottle of tequila in his hand, knocking pathetically on the window with his free one.

"Come on," he whimpered pathetically, "let me in, Hawk. Please? I'm sorry."

"What the hell are you doing here?" Andrew demanded as he approached, anger flaring up at the sight of him. Diego whirled around, nearly falling over in the process, and tried to focus on Andrew.

"How did you get there?" he asked stupidly, apparently still under the impression that Andrew should be in his car. Then he blinked a couple times and said, "I was coming to see my uncle. I want answers, Hawk."

"Yeah, well so do I," Andrew said bitterly, "but your uncle isn't home, I was just there."

"Oh no," Diego whispered.

"Aren't you supposed to be at home with an army of security?" Andrew suspected, and it seemed he was right, that Diego was far too drunk to recognize that he had no business knowing this.

"Those guys are idiots, getting out is easy. I wanted...I wanted to help after I ran away at the restaurant."

"Then make an actual statement to the police, don't let the consulate stop you. Tell them everything you told me, and it might actually help."

Diego's eyes widened in terror. "I don't want to go to jail, Hawk," he whined pathetically.

"Did you do something illegal?"

"Uh, no," Diego said, thinking hard.

"Then you won't go to jail."

"Oh, ok then. Can you take me there?"

"I'll do you one better," Andrew said, pulling out his phone. It rang a few times before the call connected and he heard the symphony of sound that came with a police precinct.

"Hawk?" Hunter said, "What's up?"

"How would you like everything Diego told me on the official record?" Andrew asked.

Hunter snorted, "Yeah that'd be great, got a way to call off his lawyers?"

"What if I told you he wants to come in *and* he'll waive his right to counsel?" Diego nodded earnestly.

"You're joking."

"You might have to sober him up a bit for it to not look like coercion, but no, I'm not joking."

"Where are you? I'll have a patrol car pick him up."

CHAPTER 30

WITH DIEGO SAFELY OUT of the way, Andrew returned home to find Hunter waiting there for him. She stood in the lobby of his building under the watchful eye of security who had evidently not allowed her up while he was away. Andrew nodded to them and gestured for Hunter to follow him towards the elevator. The moment the doors closed, she turned to him.

"How did you get Diego to agree to that?" she asked at once.

"It was mostly his idea," Andrew replied, "I think he genuinely feels guilty about running away that night. Shouldn't you be there when he gets to the precinct?"

"I asked a couple of the officers to pump him full of coffee and keep an eye on him while I'm away. I'll head back later to talk to him. Where did you find him anyway?" The elevator chimed and the doors slid open. Andrew gestured for Hunter to precede him before answering.

"Total random chance. I was leaving Luca's house and he was at my car, drunk off his ass."

Hunter closed her eyes as though praying for patience while Andrew searched his pockets for his keys. "Breezing past the flagrant breaking and entering," she began.

"Technically Duncan did the breaking, I only entered."

"Whatever, what were you even looking for?"

"Some indication of where he might have gone," Andrew said, shrugging, "and it worked out too. We might have a lead; Duncan is running it down now. I knew you couldn't get a warrant without more to go on so I figured I would help."

"But with Diego's statement we actually could get a warrant."

"A statement you would never have the chance to get if I hadn't gone to Luca's." Hunter bit her lip in the way that meant she knew he was right, even if she didn't like it. He opened the door and they stepped into his condo while he explained the lead he had found.

"Not exactly a smoking gun," Hunter commented when he was finished.

"I know," Andrew said, "but it's better than the nothing we've been working with up until now. I know we've got contact from the kidnappers and that's great, but should we not be exploring every possible avenue besides that? Even if it means breaking into the house of a corrupt diplomat."

"Yeah alright," Hunter said, curling her legs beneath herself on the sofa, "just maybe keep me updated from now on. It's sort of my job to know what you're up to."

"I'll do my best," Andrew said with a grin.

They chatted for a while about the progress, or rather lack thereof, that the FBI had made with the proof of life feed. Obviously they were running into the same issues as Duncan whenever they tried to trace the source. The emails that had been sent to the families were equally as encrypted but apparently they had at least been traced back to the North-Eastern states, though nothing more specific than that. When Andrew's phone rang again, he answered it on speaker.

"Duncan," he said by way of greeting, "I'm here with Hunter too."

"Hey kid, ma'am," Duncan said, "I found him. Or at least I think so."

"Seriously?" Hunter asked, meeting Andrew's eyes.

"Uh, yeah, I got lucky actually while I was poking through some of the resorts upstate and-"

"It's alright," Andrew interrupted, "she knows I broke in again."

"Oh great," Duncan said at once, "so I was looking into the slipper logo you found in the sex dungeon, and I think I found him."

"There was a sex dungeon?" Hunter asked, humor and surprise playing in her eyes.

"Moving on," Andrew said sharply.

"Right," Duncan said, sounding ready to laugh about it all over again, "well the Crowned Lotus is exclusive. As in show up with a referral or a Black Card, no exceptions. Their reservation services are stored electronically so it wasn't difficult to poke around a bit. But there is no sign of a reservation for Luca Pedroso."

"But?" Hunter prompted, sensing that Duncan was just trying to build the suspense.

"But" Duncan said smugly, "there was a reservation made, last minute, for two suites in the even more exclusive VIP wing by a Mister Fabian Martinez."

"And who is Fabian Martinez?" Andrew asked.

"A member of the Bogota FC from '88 to '90," Duncan replied, as though this explained everything.

"Ok so some retired soccer player bought himself a pricey vacation, how is that tied to Luca?" Hunter asked.

"The Crowned Lotus doesn't simply let you walk in off the street and gain access to the VIP amenities, no matter how wealthy or connected you are. You have to build a reputation with them, namely, you need at least ten previous stays with them of a certain value. Not only has Fabian Martinez never been a VIP, but he's also never even been to the resort before so he can't have been allowed to make the reservation."

"But Luca could have paid someone to put it in under a fake name," Andrew said, his eyes widening. "Feed them some story about a nosy wife and line a few pockets and you've got a five-star hiding spot that offers daily massages."

"Exactly my thinking," Duncan said, pleased that Andrew had caught on.

"Alright so I'll head up there," Andrew said, getting to his feet, "I should be able to get in alright and I'll find Luca."

"Hawk," Hunter said, trying to cut him off, but Andrew plowed ahead.

"Hunter, this is the best shot we have at being able to talk to him. He won't be expecting someone to find him there and he may very well know exactly where Cara is being held."

"Who is the other room for?" Hunter asked.

"What?"

"The reservation was for two suites, not one. Who is the other one for?"

"What's it matter?" Andrew could feel his temper rising again. He wasn't sure he was ready to hear Hunter tell him that they should leave Luca alone.

"You watched someone get murdered in front of Luca just to prove a point. If he's gone there with some sort of protection, or for that matter, someone to keep him in line, then you could get yourself killed. Use your head, Hawk, I know you're smart enough to have thought of this too."

"I won't just let him get away with this because there may be someone there with him. I'm not letting Cara and the others sit chained to a wall for a second longer than I have to! I'm going up there."

"I'm not saying that you shouldn't," Hunter said more softly, "I'm just saying you should go with backup. I'm coming with you." Andrew didn't respond, he merely looked Hunter in the eye and a lot of information seemed to pass between them. It was a trick they had picked up during training. The ability to have most of a conversation without uttering a word was more than a little useful in covert tactical situations. Andrew searched her face for any sign that she wasn't being serious and when he found none, he nodded.

"Duncan," Andrew said after a full minute of silence, "think you can get me a reservation?"

"Already done," Duncan replied, "and bringing a plus one shouldn't be a problem. She'll have to look the part though."

"Meaning?" Hunter asked.

"Meaning you can't show up there in jeans and a scuffed-up leather jacket," Andrew supplied, and Hunter stuck her tongue out at him.

"Fine," she said, "tomorrow we'll go shopping then head upstate. I'll get another detective to take over Diego and I can tell the captain that I'm following up on another lead. The NYPD is desperate to play in the same sandbox as the FBI so they'll take anything they can get without too many questions."

"Great," Andrew said, truly excited, "I'll pick you up at nine."

The following morning Andrew was up at seven. He'd packed and repacked a few days worth of clothes in one of the soft leather bags from his closet. He also packed both pistols, extra ammunition, and the silencer for his Glock. Unable to settle to anything after that, he swung on his coat and headed down to the lobby. The guards were just changing shifts as the elevator doors slid open and all four of them looked up to see him. Donnie nodded politely as he passed.

"I'll get the parking gate for you on my way out," he said, pulling on a jacket, "when should the boys expect you back today?" This had become the standard question whenever Andrew left the building. It allowed one or more of the guards to be ready to chase away the swarming reporters, avoiding another scene.

"I'm actually going to be away for a couple of days," Andrew replied, slowing a bit to let Donnie catch up, "need a bit of time away from all this."

"Probably for the best," Donnie said darkly as he reached to open the door for Andrew. The moment they stepped out into the parking lot, a wave of shouts and the clattering of many cameras fell over them. Andrew looked around in surprise to see at least twice the usual number of reporters. "They caught wind of the proof of life stream last night," Donnie went on morosely, "and they've been absolutely feral ever since. We chased half a dozen of them out of the building already and a couple ended up throwing punches, trying to get past us. We're dealing with them as best as we can, but you shouldn't have to go through this on top of everything else. Some time away might just be the best thing for you."

Andrew nodded seriously, "I sure hope so."

Donnie and the guard stationed by the locked gate to the parking lot managed to punch a hole in the swarming reporters so that Andrew could slip through them. He felt a little guilty that the other tenants of his building, none of whom he had interacted with beyond the occasional elevator ride, were being forced to deal with this too. Then again, Andrew figured, if they were wealthy enough to live there, they must have seen this sort of thing many times.

It took Andrew the better part of thirty minutes to lose the last of the people following him. Finally, with a dangerous swerve through an intersection that left a news van stranded in the bumper-to-bumper traffic crawling through the Holland Tunnel, he was free to go about his business as usual. Stopping only to grab pastries and coffee for Hunter, he pulled up to her building and waited. Right at nine the passenger door opened and she slipped in, still rubbing sleep out of her eyes. Hunter tossed her bag into the back seat of the car and Andrew promptly handed over the coffee before she could say anything. They drove in silence towards the higher end stores of 5th Avenue, Hunter sipping her coffee and Andrew keeping an eye out for more reporters.

"Why are you watching so carefully?" Hunter eventually asked.

"Can't you just imagine the scandal they would invent if I suddenly seemed to have moved on from Cara while she's still missing? I don't really need more reporters camped outside, thanks." Hunter grimaced at this, imagining herself as the target of the media's attention. Andrew pulled to a stop and held out the little titanium rectangle that was a Black Card. She grinned and snatched it before hopping out of the car with a surprising spring in her step.

CHAPTER 31

ANDREW HAD NEVER EXACTLY considered Hunter to be a girly girl, but apparently even she was not immune to the prospect of a nearly limitless budget at some of the most expensive stores in the country. It took the better part of three hours, dragging Andrew along the entire way as she tried on clothes and racked up a bill that would surely raise a couple eyebrows from the higher ups. About halfway through the shopping, she realized that the small bag she had brought wasn't going to cut it so topped off the whole experience with a designer luggage set into which she stuffed with a dizzying array of extravagant clothes.

"We're only going for a few days," Andrew mumbled after the fourth store.

"You never know what might be waiting for us," Hunter said. "Boys have it so much easier, you can practically wear the same thing every day and no one cares."

"You sound like Cara," Andrew said, a little glumly. This comment had the fortunate effect of hurrying Hunter along enough that they were on the road and leaving the city around noon. She had changed into a pair of dark green pants and a cream sweater along with several thousand dollars worth of diamonds in an effort to look the part. The urban sprawl of Manhattan and the surrounding areas were soon lost in a tangle of dense trees that seemed to take over the farther north they went. The slushy, wet accumulation of snow was replaced by gentle hills capped in fluffy white. They had stopped for lunch in one of the many one-horse towns along the way, eating greasy burgers and fries in Andrew's car, when Hunter got a phone call.

"Hang on," she said around a huge mouthful, turning down the radio which she had firmly dictated was to be set to an eighties station and nothing else, "it's my captain." She swallowed hugely and answered the phone on speaker in a voice of clipped efficiency, "Sir, is everything alright?"

"Well," the captain said, sounding utterly defeated, "we've gotten news from those tech whiz kids from the FBI, are you alone?"

"Yes, sir," Hunter said at once, making sure Andrew stayed quiet with a look.

"When the captors dropped in the bag for the morning food delivery, Cara Randal unpacked it as usual and something fell out. It was a receipt," the man's tone was so heavy it was practically weighing Andrew down. "As soon as the captors saw it, they rushed in to take it away, but the damage was done. The techs grabbed a screenshot and have been working on enhancing it. They got the name of the store they've been buying the food from."

"Where?" Hunter asked a little uncertainly.

"It's a little grocery store in the heart of Bogota. It looks like they're all being held in Colombia." Andrew felt a part of himself die at these words, unable to process properly, he gestured at Hunter to follow up.

"Sir, how sure are we? They're planning a ransom exchange."

"It looks like that might have been a bluff to get the money. They're working on confirming now but the FBI is fairly certain. It also explains why there was such a delay between the kidnapping and the proof of life. They would have had to smuggle the captives out of the country through less than conventional means. It also explains why it looks like they hired an outside crew, didn't want to risk too many boots on the ground themselves. Honestly, them being in Colombia explains a hell of a lot. You yourself brought Diego Pedroso's potential involvement to our attention, you must admit it makes some sense."

Andrew's fingers had gone numb and he dropped his burger back into the paper bag awkwardly. Blank disbelief washed over him. It did make sense, though, everything that the captain had said. Luca's involvement made even more sense considering the final destination. He may have even helped with the transport, labeling whatever they had used to transport Cara and the others as a diplomatic pouch. He'd come to terms with the fact that Luca was a greedy son of a bitch, but this was well beyond that. Vaguely, Andrew could hear Hunter still talking to her captain and he tuned back into the conversation.

"...already handed off the investigation completely to the FBI and they will be working through political channels to get them back," the captain was saying. "But, as you know, Colombia isn't exactly playing nice at the moment, and they may not be prepared to invite a whole host of agents to poke around. It doesn't help that this just emphasizes how much the Colombian government has been slacking in regards to organized crime. Look, feel free to follow your lead, but the NYPD is officially ordered to stand down."

"Understood, sir, thank you for letting me know," Hunter said and hung up. She looked over at Andrew who was now gripping the steering wheel tight enough to break it. If she had anything to say, she couldn't seem to find the words. Anger was starting to surge through Andrew now. Anger at Luca for orchestrating something so evil. Anger at the bastards who had shot up the Traveller House. And anger at himself for not having done more at the time.

His lip curling, Andrew punched the ignition button and the high-powered engine purred to life. He slammed it into gear and screeched out of the little truck stop parking lot. A car had to swerve out of the way as he rejoined the slow traffic headed north and Hunter looked at him with slight panic in her eyes.

"Hawk, what are you doing?"

"I'm going to kill him," Andrew growled softly.

"Slow down," Hunter said gently, not talking about his driving, "you can't just barge in there and shoot the place up."

"Watch me."

"Hawk...Andrew, listen to me," Hunter pleaded. The use of his first name earned her a glance and she pressed her advantage. "If it's true, if they are in Colombia, then Luca might be one of the only people who knows where they are. I know things are rough between us and Colombia so I'll go with you myself to get them if that's what it takes, but we can't do that if we don't know where they are. Please, Hawk, let's just stick to the plan and talk to him. We'll get him to talk."

He was grinding his teeth, trying to displace some of the anger, and didn't respond right away. Not because he was going to disagree, but because he was sure Hunter was right and that was causing a whole dizzying argument to take place in his brain.

"Fine," he said eventually through his clenched teeth, "we'll talk to him. We'll get him to talk." Hunter nodded and patted his arm consolingly as he continued to break several traffic laws. The BMW slid around other cars, barely a few inches between them. At one point, on a lonely stretch of road that cut like a knife through the forest, a single police car was lying in wait to look for speeders. By the time the red and blue lights lit up the trees around it, Andrew was already rounding a huge bend with no hope of being caught. An hour of painful, tense silence passed between him and Hunter before the car nosed its way onto a frozen gravel driveway that led directly into the darkening trees with a soft crunch.

"Hawk," Hunter said, speaking for the first time since he'd agreed not to simply execute Luca, "I know it's going to be tough, but you have to try and act natural until we can get a lay of the land. It'll take a bit of time before we know how to handle this." Andrew was about to argue that they didn't have much time left but Hunter headed him off at the pass. "The supposed exchange isn't for another four days, which means they have to keep up the act until then. We can afford a couple days here to make sure we do this right and then we'll be able to sort it out, but only if we know where to go. Ok?"

Andrew nodded and did his best to start packing away the raging emotions he was experiencing. Thankfully, he had a full ten minutes of driving along the gravel road before the resort swam into view. The owners had carved out a piece of prime real estate along the shores of East Lake, clearing just enough of the trees to plant the building without disrupting the natural feel. The resort itself was a masterpiece of wood and glass that managed to not look out of place amongst the snow-laden trees. Soft orange light was spilling out of large windows along the front of the building, staining the ground with color. Andrew pulled up to the doors where a pair of valets were standing ready, apparently impervious to the cold. One of them opened Andrew's door while his counterpart hurried around to Hunter's.

"Good evening, Mister Hawkins," he said crisply as Andrew got out, "I trust your drive up was a pleasant one?"

"It certainly had its moments," Andrew said jovially, plastering a smile on his face as he handed over the keys to his car.

"Well, I'm sure you'll find our accommodations more than enjoyable, we shall see to your bags and you may head inside."

Hunter took Andrew's arm, looking around at the building with a sort of awe while he slipped the valet a hundred from his pocket. "Thank you very much, I'm sure it'll be exactly what we need."

CHAPTER 32

"I SUDDENLY REALIZE I don't know how to act rich," Hunter whispered as they walked into the hushed lobby of the Crowned Lotus. Their footsteps echoed off the polished marble floors, making a young woman look up from a computer screen behind a long reception desk of sandy colored wood. The whole place was open and airy with minimal furniture and adorned with a tasteful number of potted plants.

"It's easy," Andrew whispered back, "just wear what everyone else does and act like a bitch. Top two rules of being entitled." Hunter snorted softly before turning a dazzling smile upon the receptionist behind the desk.

"Good evening," the woman said in a low and breathy voice, "and welcome to the Crowned Lotus Resort and Spa. You must be Mister Hawkins," she finished, turning to look at Andrew.

"Yes, that's right," Andrew said, smiling politely, "we've heard such great things about this place, so we just had to try it out." Hunter squeezed his arm and rested her head on his shoulder, selling the bit.

"Wonderful," the receptionist replied with a slightly robotic smile, "well you are most welcome. Our kitchens are open twenty-four hours a day for your dining pleasure either in one of our two restaurants or delivered to your suite where you will also find a list of our spa services. Almost all of our services are available in your suite or else in our world class facilities, either of which offer maximum privacy. Your luggage shall be taken to your suite at once and you are free to follow them or else explore our common areas before retiring, please do let me know if there is anything you need." All of this was stated with a clinical efficiency that left Andrew feeling slightly creeped out. The receptionist slid a pair of gold keycards across the desk for them.

"Right," Andrew said, "actually I was wondering about some of your other services. See I have a friend, Luca Pedroso, who takes advantage of your VIP services, how do they differ from a standard stay here?" Andrew kept his tone casual, even as the name made his heart pound with fury all over again. He was watching the receptionist very carefully for any reaction to the mention of Luca. He was rewarded for this by a slight twitch in the woman's otherwise tranquil expression.

"Of course," she said, betraying nothing in her voice now, "well as I'm sure you are aware, the VIP services are available only to our most elite clientele. They are offered a separate, private entrance in the west wing of the resort. Naturally between this and the total privacy offered by their more expansive suites, it draws our most discerning guests who appreciate the opportunity to relax in peace."

"Sounds lovely," Hunter said with a smile as she took her key before adding to Andrew, "shall we?"

"Absolutely," Andrew replied, taking his own key and nodding his thanks to the receptionist. They walked together through the lobby and into a large open space with an array of sofas and chairs arranged around freestanding fireplaces or else around the massive windows that looked out over the lake. A bar was nestled against one wall and the entrance to a large dining room on the opposite side. A waitress in a simple black dress delivered a couple of drinks to a pair of women lounging on a sofa together before one of the fireplaces.

"She was a little creepy," Hunter said once they had sat down in a pair of comfortable chairs and ordered drinks.

"No kidding," Andrew said, "did you catch it when I mentioned Luca? That little twitch?"

"Yeah, she certainly recognised the name, you could see it in her eyes for a second there. Think that means he's here?"

"I'm thinking so, yeah, if he's come here enough to be known by the staff, he probably thought to hide out here. We'll need to get a look at the VIP area though, if we're going to find him." The waitress returned with a scotch for Andrew and a martini for Hunter, setting them down on a low table. Andrew sipped the scotch slowly, scanning the room. There were about half a dozen others there with them and a few more that he could see in the dining room.

"Hawk," Hunter said softly when the waitress had left again, "I meant it before, we can't be stupid about this. If Luca knows where they are then we have to find out. He'll pay for what he's done, but you can't take that into your own hands."

"I know," Andrew said, and he really meant it. Luca was now the only person who even had a chance of knowing where Cara was and he was going to get it out of him, one way or another. "Creepy robot lady said the VIP entrance was in the west wing, yeah?"

Hunter nodded and he looked for any obvious way to the west side of the resort, but it seemed to end at the dining room in that direction. There were hallways from the lobby and past the bar which headed east through the resort, but that was it. They finished their drinks, trying their best to look like they were actually on vacation, before Andrew stood and offered his hand to Hunter. She took it and the pair of them left the lounge arm in arm towards the east wing. The halls led past a variety of spa services, all of which featured elegant glass signs declaring what they were and had strategic walls or panels to block the view from the halls. Hunter steered them up a short hallway to a set of stairs that led up.

Where the ground floor was dedicated to the spa services, the upper two were the suites. Checking the number etched into the gold keycards, they proceeded up to the third floor where they found their room. The suite consisted of a lavish bedroom and sitting room, both of which featured views of the lake and surrounding trees. Andrew crossed immediately to the bedroom where his bags had been left, checking his watch. He figured he had a few minutes before it was too late. He fired up the tablet Hunter had left in his condo and it opened at once to the live stream.

There came a twist in his gut as he thought about just how far away Cara really was from him. The worst part was that he could see it now. The amount of water they were being given, Cara fanning herself with what looked like a flattened aluminum tray, and none of them were actually using the blankets they had been provided. Between all that and the slight sheen of sweat on their skin, it pointed to a room that was constantly warm. How could they all have missed it? Hunter appeared over his shoulder and peered down at the stream as well before putting a hand on his arm.

"It'll be alright, Hawk, I swear it will."

"I know," Andrew said automatically. People kept saying things like that to him and he couldn't let himself express the deep fear that it would not be alright. That would make it real. He tore his eyes away from the tablet and shut it off again before tossing it on the bed and opening his bag.

"I'm going to try and get a look at the VIP area," he said, pulling on gloves and shoving the Glock into his waistband.

"You're going to walk through this place armed?" Hunter asked skeptically.

"Of course not," Andrew said with the kind of grin Hunter knew meant she wasn't going to like his plan.

It took five minutes of slipping and swearing, but eventually Hunter agreed to help and boosted Andrew up on the balcony of their suite. He had sworn up and down that this was purely a reconnaissance mission to try and get eyes on Luca. Andrew clambered up onto the gently sloping roof of the resort, punching a hole in the foot of snow there. Hunter pointed out that it would leave an obvious trail straight back to them but eventually agreed that no one was likely to see it from the ground or even a neighboring balcony. Once he was up, Andrew leaned over the edge to catch the small backpack he'd stuffed with spare ammo, binoculars, and rope. Both the rope and the ammo were only to be used in an absolute emergency, a criterion of Hunter's help.

It was slow moving as Andrew carved his way through the snow, careful not to slip and tumble off the side. Finally he managed to scramble down the slant that connected the roof of the suites to that of the lobby and lounge areas. Here he had to be very careful not to tread on the many skylights, only visible by a warm glow through the snow. He could see the far side of the roof now and the drop off where the VIP section of the resort must be. He quickened his pace, keen to see the layout below. As Andrew took another step towards it, however, his foot hit something hard. Some sort of vent, buried in the snow, had been seemingly lying in wait for him and it sent Andrew tumbling towards the edge of the roof.

CHAPTER 33

ANDREW SWORE SILENTLY AS he fell, desperately trying to grab onto something as he slipped and slid inexorably towards a fall that would either kill him or else get him caught and probably arrested. He felt his face go from plowing through snow to falling through cold air. Opening his eyes revealed the forty foot drop into a private courtyard below. At the last second, as his arms slid over the void as well, his fingers found a grip on the very edge of the roof and clung on for dear life. He swung awkwardly, twisting painfully around his arm before slamming into the wall, knocking the wind out of him. It took all his strength to keep holding on, but he managed. Just as he was about to pull himself back up, the sound of an annoyed voice reached him from below.

The VIP wing was laid out as a single story of much larger private rooms, each featuring a sort of courtyard that was equipped with high walls on two sides to maintain privacy without ruining the view. The voice was coming from the suite right below Andrew, whose large glass door had just opened. A short, slightly pudgy man in a bathrobe and slippers was exiting the suite, clearly heading for the large hot tub set into the ground which steamed gently in the January air.

"I'm sick of it," the man said, and Andrew immediately recognised Luca's voice as it shot a fresh arrow of fury through his heart. He fell completely still, praying that no one would see him hanging from the roof as a second man dressed in all black followed Luca out. The second man didn't look like much, but the rather large pistol in hands told a different story.

"I don't really care," the second man said, his voice thick with a Mexican accent, "we're under orders to keep an eye on you. You know that."

"I do know that," Luca replied, still annoyed, "and I most graciously agreed to keep a low profile here at the resort. I even got you your own suite. What I did not agree to was you breathing down my neck 24 hours a day. How am I supposed to relax with you always watching me from the corner? You nearly shot my masseuse when she knocked on the door and you already stick out like a sore thumb. Go back to your suite, order room service, get a massage, I don't care, just leave me alone for a night. Would that be so terrible?"

"Do not forget who is in charge here," the second man said with a sneer. "It was hardly my first choice to babysit your pampered ass *pendejo*, but here we are. If you don't start showing some respect, then a frightened masseuse will be the least of your problems. I voted to put you down when we were done with you, but the boss seems to think you still have some use. So don't push your luck."

"Fine," Luca said, practically shouting now, "then enjoy the view, you people paid an awful lot of good money for it." Luca dropped his robe, revealing a stunning lack of anything beneath and waded into the hot tub, hitting a button that turned on two dozen jets throughout the whole thing. The second man made some sort of exasperated noise and turned on his heel, heading back into the suite and slamming the glass door. Andrew, whose muscles were throbbing now, even if it wasn't his injured arm, watched as a woman appeared in the suite as well, playing with a butterfly knife idly as she ate an apple. The man started gesticulating wildly towards Luca, waving his gun wildly while the woman frowned at him and paused in her chewing. She pointed at the man with her knife, then at Luca through the windows, and the man seemed to deflate slightly before arguing back, though with less vigor.

Andrew turned his attention back to his current predicament while their attention was diverted. He swung himself around, reaching up with his other hand to get a better grip on the roof before hauling himself, panting and cursing, back into the deep snow. Once there he crouched and turned to see what else he could see. The two people inside were still arguing, apparently over their less than stimulating assignment, in Luca's suite. Andrew pulled the binoculars from the little bag he had and directed them to the suite next to Luca's. He couldn't see as much of this one, both because of the privacy walls and the fact that there were no lights on. He could, however, still see a pair of bags thrown on the bed, still packed, save for two AK-47s which had been laid out for ease of access. They gleamed slightly in the moonlight which poured in from the windows.

So then, Andrew thought, this must be the suite Luca had reserved for his guards. Andrew didn't exactly feel like getting into a shootout with two far better equipped guards, but the fact that the guns were left in the suite suggested they were for emergencies they knew were coming. Likely they were there to defend Luca if they caught wind someone was coming for him. Andrew turned his binoculars now on the man he was here for. Luca was lounging without a care in the world barely eighty feet from him. It wouldn't be hard to simply pick him off from here. Yes, his own pistol wasn't meant for sharpshooting, but Luca was just lying there in the water and Andrew had aced his firearms training. It would be simple.

He found himself reaching for the gun, drawing it from the bag and leveling it with Luca's head. Just one little squeeze and his revenge on the man would be final. No one knew he was there; the guards would barely have time to hear the shot before Andrew was crossing the roof again. But Hunter's voice sounded in the back of his head, trying to drown out the angry buzzing that was filling his ears.

Luca was the only person they knew might know where Cara was. Was getting revenge worth losing their only major lead? Perhaps, but there were other ways Andrew could get his revenge too. He lowered the gun, comforting himself with the thought of Luca behind bars and silently swearing to make that visit. Andrew continued to watch as the pair of guards finally finished their argument and the man, defeated, flopped into a leather armchair to watch Luca closely. The woman, who did not seem to care nearly as much about being stuck in a five-star safehouse, lounged on the massive bed and flipped through channels on the TV as she ate another apple.

It wasn't until about an hour of growing steadily more freezing on the roof that something happened. Luca stood in the hot tub and Andrew did his best not to watch as he strode, still fully naked, back into the suite and right past his guards. Andrew had to reposition himself slightly but caught sight of Luca opening a different door in the suite. Based on the cloud of steam that emanated from it, he guessed it was a personal sauna, just like the one in his house.

Figuring that this was enough to be getting on with for the time being, Andrew stood, his knees popping slightly, and made his way more carefully back across the roof. When he was back to the balcony of his and Hunter's room, he poked his head down to make sure she was alone. When it was clear that she was, he swung down and landed heavily on the balcony, making her jump slightly. In his absence she had gone native. She was wearing one of the plush bathrobes provided by the resort and there were no fewer than twelve different plates of food scattered across the low table in front of the sofa.

"Glad you're enjoying yourself," Andrew said as he closed the balcony door behind him.

"Just keeping up appearances," Hunter said with a grin, popping a toast point into her mouth, "find anything?"

"Found Luca," Andrew said darkly, "and the ones keeping him safe."

CHAPTER 34

"OK, RUN ME THROUGH it again," Hunter was saying as she flopped down on the king size bed in the suite, her head hanging off the end to view Andrew upside down. It had been two full days of watching Luca now and Andrew was getting restless with it. He let out a small huff of annoyance and gestured to the crude map of Luca's VIP suite that he'd been able to piece together from his rooftop spying trips.

"From what I can see of his rooms, it's mostly a large bedroom leading out onto the patio. Based on the times he's left the room and how big the building itself is, we can assume that there is something like a sitting room and possibly a dining room in the back. There is always at least one of the guards with him at any given time and they are always careful not to be seen by the resort staff."

"But the guards still use their rooms, right?" Hunter asked, pointing to the neighboring section of map.

"Only to sleep, which they do in shifts. Everything else, including eating, is done where they can keep an eye on Luca. Based on what I've overheard they are acting both as protectors and also jailors in a way. They definitely want Luca out of the way during this part of the plan but not to the point of actually killing a government official."

"So you want to sneak down there, from the roof, while an armed guard is waiting in the room, to have a conversation with the man they are trying to keep hidden." Hunter said it as a statement rather than a question. "Do you see the problem there?"

"So, we deal with the guard first," Andrew said, stabbing a finger at the drawn out courtyard area. "Every night after he eats, Luca has gone out to the hot tub before going back inside to the sauna. His activities during the day aren't exactly predictable as he seems to be trying to receive every treatment this place has but the night routine never changes. When he goes inside the sauna, one of the guards leaves after a few minutes to get some sleep."

"Ok so obviously the best time to strike," Hunter put in and Andrew nodded in agreement, "but the two of us rappelling down the building won't exactly go unnoticed. We'd be better off getting the guard to come outside with some sort of distraction and dealing with them out there. Luca won't hear anything, and we'll have more room to maneuver."

"Ok sure," Andrew said, "what did you have in mind? It can't be something so crazy that he goes for backup or a bigger gun before going to look."

"You said that there was a door on the wall closest to us, right?" Hunter asked.

"Yeah, I went looking for it on this side and it looks like it's just some emergency exit or something, only opens from the inside."

"Perfect," Hunter said with a grin, "I'll take care of it then. I'll need you on the roof right above the courtyard for the takedown. The lower one, I don't need you breaking your legs."

"It's still a twenty-foot drop," Andrew said, frowning slightly, "I'll need a minute to get down before I even think about dropping. Think you can get him out far enough to not see me?"

"Oh absolutely," Hunter said, still with an inverted Cheshire grin from the bed.

They waited until after dark to put their plan into action. Andrew was to take a full bag of equipment this time, including whatever Hunter might need once the guard was dealt with along with ropes and a harness for him, across the roof to wait. He crouched in his usual spot after following the path that he'd carved out without the nearly fatal faceplant this time. Right on cue, Luca pushed open his door and strode out to the hot tub, shedding his robe in the process.

The two guards were sitting at a small glass table inside, watching him periodically as they ate what looked like caviar and sipped champagne. Complain as they might, Andrew thought, they had a pretty easy job here. At least until now. The woman had set her butterfly knife down on the table to eat along with the man's large pistol. Both close enough to grab if something happened.

Andrew stood ready, waiting impatiently while he fiddled with a metal loop on the harness he'd put on. There was a metal rail along both this roof and the lower one of Luca's suite, he'd be able to tie himself off to those and lower down pretty easily, but not until he'd seen Luca go into the sauna and one of the guards leave. After what felt like an eternity, Luca dragged himself up from the hot tub and hummed contentedly as he strode back into his room and to the sauna door, opening it with its usual cloud of steam.

The two guards followed Luca's progress and the moment the sauna door shut they turned to each other; fists extended. Both fists pumped three times in the air before the woman held hers out and the man extended two fingers.

"Every fucking time," Andrew muttered as the man slumped in his chair, defeated. He had picked scissors every time Andrew had watched this little exchange. The woman downed the rest of her champagne in one go and got up from the table triumphantly, winked at the man, and left. Andrew waited until he saw her enter the bedroom next door, move the automatic rifles aside, and fall into the bed before making his way over to the first rail. He had the rope tied off and was lowering himself expertly in a matter of seconds.

He landed softly in the fresh snow of the lower roof and moved towards the edge, careful not to shove snow off of it where the guard might see. Once he had cleared a spot and tied off the second rope, he pulled his phone from his pocket and sent Hunter the go signal. A moment later, the emergency exit door burst open and Hunter half fell out of it.

"Jesus Christ," Andrew muttered under his breath. The door swung shut on its own with a loud bang, leaving Hunter stranded outside in nothing but a shockingly short towel. How she had gotten past the staff, not to mention a lounge full of guests like that, Andrew would never know.

"Oh shit," Hunter cried as she stumbled into the frozen courtyard, looked around in a slight panic, and tried prying at the door where a handle should have been. "Shit, shit, shit," she said desperately, already shivering dramatically. Andrew heard Luca's door open beneath him and the man's voice calling out.

"What the hell are you doing?"

Hunter turned quickly, her bare feet slipping on the snow, and tumbled to the ground, giving the guard a generous view. "Ow, fuck," Hunter said, trying and failing to get back up, "Can you help me please? I took a wrong turn and ended up out here by accident. It's freezing!"

The guard stepped out beyond the overhanging roof and Andrew could see the gun stuffed into the back of his jeans, but he wasn't reaching for it. Evidently, the presence of a mostly naked woman had driven that thought from his mind. Thank God this guy sucked at rock paper scissors was all Andrew could think as he readied himself. The man approached Hunter and reached out his hands to help her up.

"Come on," he said, annoyance replaced with a husky sort of chivalry, "let's at least get you warmed up inside."

"Oh thank you," Hunter said, reaching up with both hands to take his as Andrew swung backwards off the roof and lowered himself down. In the effort to get up with the man's help, Hunter's towel fell off completely. Andrew couldn't see his face, but figured he was having some sort of minor heart attack.

"*Dios mio,*" the guard said softly, looking Hunter up and down. Andrew shook his head, surely there was an easier way than this. He touched down on the ground and unclipped himself from the rope before prowling towards the man.

"There's just one thing we have to take care of before you warm me up," Hunter said quietly, biting her lip slightly.

"W-what is it?" the man asked stupidly.

"Him," Hunter said, pointing behind him. The guard, apparently reluctant to look away, took only a quick glance behind him and did an almost comical double take. He whipped around properly to find Andrew there with a baton that he flicked out to full extension.

"Hi there," Andrew said brightly before clubbing the man upside the head with all his strength. His legs crumpled instantly and he fell, half buried in snow. "Seriously?" Andrew asked, casting a withering look towards Hunter.

"What," she said unashamedly, shrugging, "would you like to have been the naked damsel in distress?"

"Why did there have to be any naked damsel in distress?" Andrew asked, pulling a smaller bag that Hunter had packed from his own larger one. She pulled out jeans and a black turtleneck from it and pulled them on.

"You asked for a distraction that would keep him fully occupied, I supplied. I fail to see the problem." Andrew rolled his eyes and passed over her service weapon.

"I remember when you were reserved and professional."

"Yeah right," she snorted, "we doing this or not?"

"Definitely doing this," Andrew said, checking his own weapon before holstering it on his hip and heading back towards the suite.

CHAPTER 35

ANDREW STRODE STRAIGHT THROUGH the open door, passing the table where the caviar lay abandoned with the woman's knife, grabbing a chair on his way. The thing was surprisingly heavy and he had to drag it along with him, leaving two long scuffs on the highly polished floor. As he approached the door of the sauna, he could see the blurry outline of Luca sitting there through the foggy glass. With a slight grunt, Andrew propped the chair right up against the handle, holding the door shut. He reached out a hand towards the temperature controls when an opening door made him freeze and look around.

"Hey," a woman called out in Spanish from the next room, *"did I leave my knife in here?"* Andrew's gaze slid slowly from the closed bedroom door to the table where the gold knife was still resting.

"She's coming back," Andrew whispered, and Hunter nodded once in understanding, taking up a position that would put her behind the door when it opened. Andrew flattened himself against the wall and raised his gun, but Hunter shook her head violently. He understood, a gunshot would draw far too much attention right now, they still needed time. Instead he tossed Hunter the baton he'd used on the first guard and waited.

The door between them opened and the woman walked right past Andrew without glancing over, spotting her knife on the table. Andrew and Hunter both crept forward as she reached for it, prepared to take her down quietly. Then she realized the man wasn't there at all. Looking towards the open door revealed the truth, she glimpsed Hunter's reflection winding up behind her and she whipped around with lightning speed, the knife clicking slightly as it opened. Dropping to one knee as part of her turn sent the baton sailing over her head and the knife flashed dangerously towards Hunter's stomach.

Andrew reacted instantly, kicking out and connecting with the woman's wrist which sent the blade skittering across the floor. Hunter followed this up with an arcing blow that should have killed the woman, but she dodged, tilting her head just enough to send the baton into her shoulder. There was a loud crunch of bone and the woman screamed. Andrew's heart leapt in panic and he dove on her, wrestling her across the table and to the ground. The caviar and Champagne went flying as they fell, but he managed to clamp a hand over her mouth to muffle the scream. She thrashed and squirmed, but a kick to her stomach from Hunter knocked the wind out of her and Andrew shifted his grip. The woman choked and gurgled softly as he squeezed her neck in the crook of his elbow, pressing down on the back of her head to add force. Finally, she went limp, and Andrew let go, panting slightly and pushed the woman off him. A dull pounding reached their ears along with Luca's voice from the sauna.

"Hey," he called, "what the hell is going on? Let me out."

"I'll make sure she stays down, and I can get the other one," Hunter said, "you go deal with him." Andrew nodded and got to his feet, brushing himself off with murder in his heart.

Luca's face was pressed up against the glass, trying to see through a spot he had cleared of the fog. Andrew made sure to enter his view from the side, mostly to increase the dramatic effect. Luca's eyes went wide at the sight of him, and Andrew took up a position in front of the door, less than a foot away from the man.

"Hello Luca," Andrew said with deadly calm, "I think we should have a little chat."

"A-Andrew?" he stuttered, taking a step back from the glass. He seemed unsure how to process the sudden confrontation and landed on the doting uncle route. "Thank God you're alright, I-I heard what happened to the others."

"Did you?" Andrew asked, "I'm surprised you've heard much of anything after you locked yourself away up here. I'll admit it took a while to find you."

Clearly picking up on the mood Andrew was trying to set, Hunter chose that moment to drag the unconscious body of the woman into Luca's line of sight, dropping her on the floor. Luca swallowed, which seemed to take a great effort as his eyes darted between Andrew and the guard.

"Have you killed them?" Luca whispered, fear gripping him entirely.

"Of course not," Andrew said dismissively, "how else could they go running back to their boss and tell them you escaped their watch. I imagine they'll kill you rather than let you run around on your own." All pretense was gone now and Luca fell to his knees, mouthing soundlessly. Andrew casually reached over and flipped a switch on the sauna controls, cranking the heat to maximum. Steam billowed into the little room and Andrew crouched down as Luca crawled towards the door. "Then again, maybe I'll just let you roast in here and save them the trouble."

"Why are you doing this?" Luca asked desperately and Andrew slammed a fist against the glass, making him flinch violently.

"I know what you did," Andrew said furiously, "I know everything Luca. I know about the money, I know about the plan to have us all kidnapped, I even know you set up your own nephew to take the fall for it. I know that the ransom drop is a lie, just a con to get the money. There is just one thing left that I don't know and believe me when I say that it is the only thing keeping you alive at this point."

"Please," Luca said, sweat and tears pouring down his face in equal measure, "it wasn't supposed to be like this. They...they killed my friend; they'll kill me if I talk."

"You think I won't?" Andrew shouted, standing up straight and leveling his gun with Luca's head through the glass. Luca froze in place, staring up at Andrew with sheer terror. A heavy thud from behind him told Andrew that Hunter had dragged the other guard back in. She appeared in the corner of his eye, leaning against the wall with her arms crossed.

"Hawk," she said warningly, but he ignored her.

"Tell me where they are," Andrew said, pressing the gun against the glass.

"I-I swear I don't-" Andrew roared with fury and kicked the chair aside. Pulling the door open he marched through the cloud of steam and grabbed Luca's thinning hair in one hand, jerking his head back and pressing the muzzle of the gun into his forehead.

"Talk!"

"I need protection," Luca wailed, his eyes rolling in terror, "promise me that and I'll talk." Andrew looked over his shoulder to where Hunter had shifted and she gave a sort of shrugging nod.

"Fine," Andrew said, dragging him out of the sauna by the hair and tossing him on the ground next to the unconscious guards. Hunter grabbed a towel from the stack next to the sauna and threw it at Luca who covered himself as best he could without actually getting up. His eyes kept darting between Andrew's face and the gun still pointed at him.

"I need a guarantee," Luca said softly, "proper protection from these people."

"This is Detective Caitlin Hunter with the NYPD. If your information proves to be useful then she'll arrange for you to be placed in protective custody. Both from whoever is paying you and from me," Andrew finished in a deadly voice. Luca turned a stricken face to Hunter, color draining from him.

"You're police?" he asked indignantly, "And you're condoning this lunatics actions?" Andrew's knuckles turned white on the gun, but Hunter gave a little shake of her head and he dropped his arm to his side.

"I'd be careful who you call a lunatic," Hunter said calmly, "given that he's still the one with the gun. Normally I would never approve of something like this, it's quite literally my job to make sure it doesn't happen like this, but you're quite the special case Luca Pedroso. But, before we discuss ethics or your deal any further, you need to tell us where they are holding Cara, Dirk, and Eliza. A gesture of good faith if you will. We know they're being held in Colombia; we just need to know where."

Luca blinked stupidly several times, looking between Hunter and Andrew. "The kids aren't in Colombia," he finally said to Hunter, "they never left New York."

CHAPTER 36

"EXPLAIN," ANDREW SAID, HIS last nerve waning rapidly. A full minute of stunned silence had passed after Luca's declaration, after which Andrew had tried to lunge for Luca, planning on beating more answers out of him. Hunter managed to hold him back while Luca scrambled away. Now Luca was sitting in a chair at the table, a large glass of cognac next to him, with his face in his hands. Andrew had begrudgingly agreed to hear him out properly and was now pacing back and forth before the man while Hunter sat in front of him.

"It started about a year ago," Luca began heavily, "when I got a letter explaining that they would pay me a hundred thousand dollars to deliver a blank consulate ID. I figured it was just some joke or something, but they had some rather...indecent photos from my last trip to Colombia. It started as blackmail, please understand that, whatever it may have turned into. I did what they said and it earned me my money and another offer. I began a sort of partnership with them. I was their man on the inside and so much of it was harmless information."

Luca paused here to take a large swig of his cognac. It had been poured from a very expensive looking bottle that went so far as to label itself as one of only five hundred in the world. Neither Hunter, nor Andrew prompted him to go on. They were both desperate for the information this man had, both for their own reasons, but neither wanted to be the reason he stopped. So they waited through the long pause as Luca took a shaky breath and rambled on.

"The next time I traveled home to Colombia, they were waiting for me. I'd been asking for a face-to-face meeting for a while, but they kept on saying that the time wasn't right. Then there they were. I met with two people. One was a hired gun, the man who murdered Alejandro, the other was Elena Ramos. Yes," Luca added, nodding at the shocked look on Hunter's face, "as in Elena Ramos, the leader of the Ramos cartel."

"The third most powerful in Mexico," Hunter whispered to Andrew who nodded once to say he understood.

Luca wiped a hand over his face and went on, "Elena had me brought to a town car where she and her little *asesino* were waiting for me. While we drove, she explained that she had been the one sending me money and it was her men who I had been sneaking onto the staff at the consulate."

"Hang on," Andrew blurted out, unable to contain himself any longer, "when they ran the prints of one of those men it came back as someone belonging to the Vargas cartel in Colombia."

Luca nodded sadly as he poured himself more of the cognac. "One of the many things I did for Elena was covering up who her men were and instead linking them to a rival organization. It wasn't difficult, to tell you the truth, my country has a large database of those connected to the organized drug trade, I just slipped them in. Anyway, once Elena explained who she was and a bit of why she wanted me, the car stopped. I was surprised to find that we were at the house of my first wife, Isabel. Her man hauled me inside and she followed to show me exactly what would happen if I ever turned on them. Isabel was on the floor, blood everywhere and I was made to watch as that man...that monster cut her into pieces. Nobody ever found out what happened to her, it was as though she simply vanished from the world. But I knew, and I knew they would do it to me, so I played along.

"The money made it easier to ignore what I was doing, I pretended not to be putting the pieces together and instead I drowned myself in distraction. Finally, the last orders came through. I was to provide one last set of false consulate security badges, send a list of Diego's most influential friends, and get ready to disappear. I knew what was going to happen, of course I did, but I also had seen what would happen if I refused. Elena swore that no harm would come to the ones she took."

"So, this was all just about money for her?" Hunter asked and Luca looked up from the floor as though waking from a dream.

"No, of course not," he said, "Elena Ramos has clawed her way to become one of the most powerful and wealthy people in Mexico. She has more money than she could ever need. No, her plan was far more than that. If the police have figured out that the children are in Colombia, or think they are anyway, then it should be any time now that they trace the stream to a property in Bogota owned by the Vargas cartel. United States law enforcement will attempt to rescue them, but my government is unlikely to allow such a thing. The resulting feud will end up diverting a significant amount of resources towards fighting what Colombian crime they can.

"The DEA will focus on Colombian shipments, the United Nations will undoubtedly pressure my country for the return of the hostages, and my brother will do what he has always done when confronted with aggression, fight back, even if he knows he is wrong. Even if Colombian police raid the property, they will not find any hostages. All attempts to explain this will simply look like they are trying to cover something up. Then, while all of this is going on, while all attention is focused on Colombia and its failings, the Ramos cartel is poised to fill the vacuum left behind when Colombian distribution is halted. Elena has crafted herself a perfect little scheme to become one of the only names in the drug trade."

Luca finally fell silent. Hunter was sitting with her hands clasped tightly, putting it all together in her head. Andrew meanwhile, stopped his pacing and turned to face Luca properly.

"Where. Is. Cara?"

"I don't know," Luca said at once, "I only know that she and the others never left the city. It would have been too risky to try and move them with the police on high alert. They hired a crew to kidnap them, and Elena's mercenary killed them when the job was done. Only Elena, that man, and a tiny handful of others know where they are. I swear, Andrew, I don't want them harmed any more than you do." This was rich, Andrew thought, coming from the man who had sold them out. It was taking a great deal of effort to not throw Luca back to the ground.

"Do you know who this might have been?" Hunter asked, showing Luca something on her phone. Andrew glanced over and saw a picture of the man from her cold case, the one whose face had been smashed in beyond recognition.

"*Dios mio,*" Luca muttered, "I cannot say for certain, but this tattoo," he zoomed in on a portion of a tattoo that was visible under the man's sleeve. The artwork had not returned any hits when Hunter had had it scanned, but Luca certainly seemed to recognize it. "I do not know his name, but I believe this is the man Elena used to purchase false identities for her men. He provided passports, driver's licenses, that sort of thing."

"That fits," Hunter said, looking up at Andrew, "this guy would have been the only other person who could point out every Ramos cartel member in the States. Makes sense that she'd have him taken care of too."

"This is great and all," Andrew said, "but we still don't know where Cara is."

"True," Hunter said gently, "but we know she is in the city, and we know who's really behind this. That's something we can work with. We need to get back to the city."

"Right," Andrew said, "let's go." Hunter got up as Andrew made to leave and Luca scrambled to his feet as well.

"Wait," he cried, "what about our deal? You said you'd protect me!" Hunter and Andrew shared a look. She knew exactly what his opinion was on this matter.

"I'm sorry," she said bitterly, letting some of her own emotions bubble through, "but I'm afraid I don't hold the authority to actually offer protection. I'd wish you luck, but I truly don't like your odds." She walked away without another word, leaving Luca stricken. He recovered himself in time to lunge furiously at Hunter, but Andrew saw the move coming a mile away. One well placed punch was all he needed to send Luca sprawling to the floor, wheezing and gasping for breath.

"Well," Andrew said, crouching down in front of Luca, "looks like you have some decisions to make. I'd recommend doing so before they wake up," he nodded towards the guards. "I can't say how long it'll take for them to hear that you squealed, but I imagine it won't be a fun conversation. Good luck."

Andrew left him there, blubbering incoherently as he tried to crawl after them. Hunter opened the door of the suite and held it for Andrew who quickened his pace. The security standing at the entrance to the VIP wing of the resort didn't even glance twice at them since they had apparently been allowed inside. Andrew forced a smile as the beefy man inclined his head to them and they half walked, half ran towards the main door.

"Bring my car around now," Andrew spat at one of the valets who leapt to his feet in surprise at the sight of them. The valet's response was lost as Andrew and Hunter burst through the front door and raced to their room. It took them only a minute to grab the essentials, mostly those things that would be somewhat incriminating if found by housekeeping. By the time they were jogging past the serene receptionist again, the valet was pulling up at the front door in Andrew's car. Within minutes they were racing down the highway at breakneck speeds. They were closer to finding them now than they had been all week and there was still time before the deadline.

CHAPTER 37

"I'LL EXPLAIN LATER," BOTH Andrew and Hunter said into their phones at the exact same moment. They shared a look of exasperation that those they were talking to were not acting as quickly as them.

"It doesn't matter who that was," Hunter said, talking to her captain, "sir, you have to believe me. No, by the time any of you got out here or we were able to get Pedroso processed it would be too late. Besides, I already told you that it wasn't a proper confession." This was the story she was forced to go with to maintain both hers and Andrew's covers, that she had gotten a third party to tell her something Luca had said.

"Alright, kid," Duncan said in Andrew's ear, "I've pulled up a list of all the properties that are known or suspected to be owned by the Ramos cartel. What the hell am I looking for?"

"We think that Cara and the others are being held in the city. Start going through them and looking for somewhere that could be used."

"Hang on," Duncan said, "that's what this is? Didn't Caitlin tell you that they traced the stream to a building in Bogota?"

"I have reason to believe that was a false trail left by the real kidnappers," Hunter said to her captain, as though responding to Duncan's question.

"Please just do it," Andrew begged, "I need you to trust me."

"Alright, alright I'll let you know what I find, calm down." Duncan ended the call and Andrew tore the headset from his ear, tossing it behind him.

"Yes sir," Hunter was saying, "I understand, I'll be there soon."

"Well?" Andrew prompted her as she hung up.

"He can't authorize any kind of search without actual proof that isn't an admittedly coerced confession from a man who we then left behind to be dealt with by a cartel. He wants to believe me, but the case has already been handed off to the feds who sealed it up immediately. They don't like letting the NYPD tell them what to do."

"Bullshit," Andrew said, banging the steering wheel before swerving around a car that was sedately crawling down the road.

"He wants me to come in to talk to him in person, I'll get him to come around. If Duncan can at least get a suspected location then we can send units to investigate regardless. I know you're going to hate this," she went on, "but I need you to drop me off then go home. Stay put until we know more."

"What? How am I supposed to just sit things out now?"

"I can't have you marching into the precinct, and I know you know that. I'll keep you updated, but officially you're a civilian." Andrew seethed for a moment. He knew she was right, but it still felt awful.

"I know, but the exchange is supposed to happen in just over a day, we still have time but it's running very short. I have no idea what's going to happen after the ransom deadline, but I don't imagine it'll be a happy reunion based on Elena's plan."

"I know, Hawk, I'll get it done."

They drove the rest of the way in silence and Andrew only nodded to her when he pulled up in front of her precinct. His drive home was viewed through tunnel vision, barely acknowledging the sights or sounds of the city waking up. It wasn't until he had made it through the reporters calling out for his attention and was walking into his building that a voice caught his attention.

"Andrew Hawkins, stop being a little bitch and look at me!" It was a shrill, small voice that nevertheless carried over the cacophony of the reporters. There, standing right at the gate into the parking lot, pressed against the bars by the throng, was Em.

"Em?" Andrew said in a slight daze, walking back towards her.

"We need to talk," she called, holding up a phone so that he could see a picture of some graffiti. It must be Diane's phone, he thought, but then what was she doing here instead of calling him?

"Let her in," Andrew called to the security guard standing at the gate. He looked a little wary but opened the gate just enough for Em to squeeze through and run over to Andrew. The reporters, obviously seeing this, began hurling questions to both him and Em, trying to determine what relationship there was between them.

"Finally," Em said as Andrew ushered her inside, "I've been trying to call you for hours."

"Right," Andrew mumbled, "sorry, I sort of wasn't checking my phone. What did you want to show me?" Em stopped in the lobby and held out the phone. Andrew did his best to shield her from the security desk, making it clear that this was not the time for interruptions. The image displayed on the phone was of a red brick wall with a shockingly detailed mural of an eagle ripping a red snake in half with its talons.

"We found ten of these painted all over the place," Em reported dutifully, "all of them are painted by the same guy. This same tagger is the one who painted that wall you showed us."

"Ok great," Andrew said, trying to understand the grin on Em's face, "so what's the part I'm missing?"

"The walls where these were thrown up are all in the territory of a different gang, not the Red Cobras. It proves that we were right, someone painted that crest to make it seem like the Red Cobras were involved, but the Red Cobra who does their tagging definitely didn't paint this."

Andrew's heart leapt. This might be exactly what they needed. "Em," he said, "do you know exactly where these were painted?"

"Of course," she said, looking up at him with a suddenly serious expression, "will this help Cara?"

"You might have just saved her," Andrew said with a little laugh before hurrying over to the elevator, "come on." Em followed him through the golden doors which slid shut silently behind them. Andrew was already on his phone before they started moving.

"Who are you calling?" Em asked curiously.

"A friend," Andrew said before the line connected. "Duncan, does the Ramos cartel have any symbolism directly associated with them? Something like an eagle maybe?"

"Yeah," Duncan said at once, "the Ramos family crest features an eagle, why?"

"Because I think I just narrowed down our possible locations, how's that list coming?"

"I've found around seventy places where the cartel either owns it or has done business there, but there might still be more. What the hell is going on, kid?"

"I'm about to put you on with a friend of mine," Andrew said, smiling down at Em, "she's going to give you ten locations to dive into more deeply. I think they will be our best bet. Do me a favor and look into them closely."

"Alright, kid, whatever you say," Duncan said, still obviously confused. Andrew passed the phone over to Em and she held it to her ear.

"Ready?" she asked with a perfect businesslike tone. "Em," she said in response to something Duncan said, "no I don't have a last name....thirteen, but...fuck you old man, at least I'm not asking stupid questions right now, are you going to listen or not?" Andrew snorted with laughter as apparently Duncan acquiesced and Em started listing off addresses all over the city. He guided her from the elevator to his condo and let her in, leaving her in the kitchen to vault up the stairs.

He hadn't exactly been given a plethora of tactical gear when they moved him to New York, but he worked his way around the bedroom, collecting spare ammunition and a couple of knives in a bag before heading back down. He found Em raiding his fridge, the phone set on the counter.

"Your 'friend' said he'd call back when he found something. Who is that guy anyway?"

"Someone who is very good at finding things, I trust him." This seemed to be enough for Em who was busily constructing herself a sandwich. Once she had completed a triple decker masterpiece and found a bag of chips, she settled herself at the kitchen island and began attacking it.

"Hey Em," Andrew said cautiously, fighting the urge to run out to find Cara until he heard back from Duncan, "are you, you know, being looked after?" She looked up at him with an expression he recognised all too well from his own childhood. Before he had been officially taken in by Eddie's family, he had been placed in the system following his parents' deaths. So many of the kids had this same sort of look. The kind that meant they knew what it was like to be bounced around from home to home and the horror of being sent back to a group home when they tried to make it on their own.

"Sure," she said, wiping her mouth, "real nice family adopted me and everything. I got the form if you wanna see it."

"You carry it around with you?" Andrew pressed and he could see the slight panic flicker in her eyes. How long had she been on her own?

"Never know when someone nosy will come looking for it," she said as casually as she could.

"Well," Andrew said, "I'm sure your family will be wondering where you are sooner or later, I can take you home."

"That's ok," she said quickly, "they don't mind."

"Em," Andrew began, but he fell silent when her eyes filled with tears.

"Please don't," she whispered, uncharacteristically vulnerable, "don't make me go back. He beats the kids, all of them. I won't go back there, ever. Cara used to pretend she didn't know I was stealing her food...but then she went away."

"Where are you staying?"

"Wherever I can," Em replied, "but there are some people out there who make sure kids like us have somewhere warm to stay in the winter. I promise I'm alright, please just don't make me go back."

Andrew was silent for a long moment. He wished he could tell her that he knew exactly how she felt, but it wasn't exactly in line with who he was now. "How many homes?" he finally asked.

"Sixteen," she said, "not including the group homes." She was trembling now, apparently convinced that Andrew was about to haul her back to whatever hell she had escaped from. He'd never seen her like this, and it broke his heart. Em jumped slightly when he set down a large glass of milk on the counter next to her and she looked up at him confused.

"Well, it's a good thing you found a nice family in the end," Andrew said with a significant look. It took Em a moment to clue in, but then a grin spread across her face.

"Right? Not everyone gets lucky like that," she said before gulping half the milk down greedily.

"Now that I think about it though," he said, "I leave this place a lot these days and between you and me, I don't really trust the security. It might be nice to have someone check in on it now and then, should the need arise." He walked over to the door and grabbed a spare key from the little bowl there, tossing it to her.

"You mean it?" she asked, letting the charade slip a bit again.

"Whatever you need," he said. "I can't promise I'll be here when you come by, but my fridge always has more food than I need anyway. Just make sure you take care of yourself, ok?" Em nodded solemnly and returned her attention to the sandwich, seemingly unsure how to say thank you.

CHAPTER 38

HOURS LATER, AS THE sun began to set, marking the eve of the ransom deadline, Hunter had only reached out to tell him that the NYPD was still standing down. The FBI had hopes of catching whoever showed up to collect the money from the drop, but otherwise they were still trying to gain access to Colombia. They had passed on the information of the suspected location they had traced from the stream, but the Colombian government had simply said they'd look into it. Andrew had long since packed everything he could think of into a small bag and changed into clothes more suited for action, waiting for the moment that Duncan called back.

Em had curled up on one of the reclining chairs in the theater room, flicking through the seemingly endless channels to her heart's content. It felt good to help her, considering everything that had happened. Sort of a tribute to the kind of person Cara was and an homage to the boy he had once been. Right when Andrew just about had enough of waiting, Duncan called.

"Did you find it?" Andrew asked in greeting.

"I think so," Duncan said solemnly, "that list the kid gave me are all active suspected properties of the Ramos cartel. Five of them are businesses they use as fronts, a few are apartment buildings, and the rest are storage buildings of one type or another. I investigated each, found building plans, tax records, and even power usage."

"So where are they?" Andrew asked impatiently.

"In an industrial park on the Gowanus Canal, a refrigerated warehouse. It's been drawing power like crazy."

"Wouldn't that be pretty standard for a refrigerated warehouse?" Andrew asked.

"Maybe," Duncan replied, "but this power usage started the day before the kidnapping. When I took a peek at some definitely unsanctioned satellite thermal imagery, I saw that the building is radiating an awful lot of heat for something that should be frozen."

"Which is how they gave the impression that they were being held somewhere hot," Andrew said, finishing the thought.

"Exactly, I just sent you the address and routed a request through NYPD dispatch to send a patrol car to check it out, just a casual recon. I'll call Hunter next and let her know we found them, and she can try to organize a more substantial force to raid the place."

"Let me do it," Andrew said at once, "I'll call her. That way she can't keep me out of the loop for this part. I need to know they're ok."

Duncan hesitated for a long moment during which Andrew could hear his heart pounding in his ears. "Alright, kid," he said finally, "just make sure you do it now, time is short. I'll start pulling up any traffic or security cameras I can find."

"Thanks, Duncan, for everything. You're the best."

"Don't forget it, kid," Duncan said before hanging up. Andrew stared at the address on his phone for a long moment, agonizing over the decision. He should tell Hunter and let the cops handle this, it was their job. A job they were currently refusing to believe was still theirs to do. But going by himself was perhaps the stupidest thing he could do.

"Who was that?" Em's voice asked from over by the door to the sitting room.

"Oh," Andrew said, startled out of his thoughts, "just that friend of mine."

"Did he find Cara?"

"We think so," Andrew said, setting his phone down on the coffee table, "so all I have to do is tell the police and convince them to go find her."

"What do you mean convince?" Em asked warily.

"They think Cara and the others aren't in the city anymore, so they aren't supposed to go looking for her."

"That's stupid," Em cried, "if you know she's here then why wouldn't they go?" Andrew was trying to figure out how to explain it all to Em, but she was just a kid. "Are you going to go get her?" Em asked.

"I...I'm just a regular guy," Andrew said apologetically.

"No, you're not, you tried to save her when she was taken, you got shot and kept fighting for her ever since. Please, go get her back." The expression on her face made any further thought to the contrary evaporate from Andrew's mind. He got to his feet and headed for the door where he had dropped the bag with his gun and spare ammo.

"You stay here," Andrew said firmly, "it might be dangerous. Just stay here and I'll bring her home, I promise." Em beamed at him and swore she wouldn't try to follow. He waited until he heard her lock the door, including the chain, before hurrying over to the elevator. He had left his phone behind intentionally so that Duncan couldn't see where he was going. Thankfully, he'd memorized the address and figured he could make his way there no problem without it.

After a quick report to security that Em was still upstairs and had his full permission to come and go as she liked from now on, Andrew was climbing back into his car. No sooner had he turned it on than a voice came out of the speakers.

"You think I'm really that stupid, kid?"

"Duncan?" Andrew exclaimed, his heart nearly leaping out of his chest, "What the hell are you doing?"

"My job," Duncan said, "I figured this was coming when you didn't call Hunter. I've been looped into our car's Bluetooth system since day one. Now stand down and go back inside."

"No," Andrew said firmly, putting the car into gear, "I'm going to get them back." He'd only gone a few feet when the car sputtered and died.

"You're really not, kid, I won't let you waltz in there like this, you'll only get yourself killed."

"What if it was your son?" Andrew asked, knowing how vicious the question was. "If you had known what was going to happen to him, and you knew where he was, would you really have stood by and let someone else handle it?"

"This isn't your job," Duncan said, obviously angry now, "observe and report, that's all."

"Then why give me all that training? If they'd just wanted an obedient puppet to find information then why train me to shoot, to infiltrate, to survive? I have a real chance to save them, the NYPD is determined to bury their heads in the sand, and everyone else is convinced that they're not even in the country anymore. Let me save them, don't make me have to experience this kind of pain. I know you know how this feels."

"You can't go like this, all you have is a pistol."

"I don't care," Andrew said, "I'm going to-"

"What I mean," Duncan said, interrupting him, "is if you're going to do this, you need the proper gear. Head to 9th and 2nd in Brooklyn, you're looking for Applegate Photography."

"What?"

"Just trust me," Duncan said, sounding suddenly very tired. "I do know this pain, kid, and I wouldn't wish it on anyone. So, if you're determined to do this, I'm going to make sure you have a fighting chance."

"Seriously?" Andrew asked, even as his car turned itself back on.

"You stand a better chance with a covert assault anyway," Duncan said, "if these people heard the NYPD busting down their door, they might just kill the hostages. So yeah, seriously. Start driving, kid, and I'll buy you some time with Hunter, leaving your phone will be a good start and I can play dumb when I need to."

Andrew pulled out of the parking lot and followed the directions Duncan fed him as he drove. Without any trouble, he found the photography studio he was looking for. A little uncertain, Andrew got out of the car and walked beneath the large wooden sign adorned with an apple tree gilt in gold. The door slid open for him, revealing a woman in her mid-twenties sitting at a desk.

"Welcome to Applegate Photography," she said brightly, "Mister Applegate is just finishing up with a client, but is there something I can help you with in the meantime?"

"Uh, yeah," Andrew said, fully realizing how stupid he'd sound if Duncan was wrong, "I was looking to book a wedding photographer for February 30th."

Without missing a beat, the woman smiled at him and gave a little laugh, "You must mean the 28th, but no worries, we'll get you sorted out. Let me escort you to a studio and Mister Applegate will be with you shortly to work out the details."

She got up from the desk and indicated he should follow her. He did so, still a little uncertain, but at least she hadn't laughed him out of the place. He was deposited inside a large studio space with a wide array of lights hanging from the ceiling at various angles. A huge, white backdrop stood against one wall, stretching across the floor to cover some of the concrete slabs. As she left, the woman from the front desk slid a large rolling door shut behind her and left Andrew in relative silence. Ten minutes passed and he was just on the verge of leaving when the door slid open again to reveal a tanned man with slightly graying hair and wire-rimmed glasses.

"Sorry to keep you waiting," he said genially, shifting a camera from one hand to the other so he could shake Andrew's. "I hear you're looking to book a wedding for February?"

"The 30th," Andrew said, trying to make sure there was no mis-understanding.

"Of course," Applegate said with a knowing smile that put Andrew at ease, "let me just get a portfolio for you to have a look at." He then walked across the studio to a set of switches that presumably controlled the array of lights. He flicked certain switches and light began spilling out of the floor around every other set of slabs. With an almost silent grinding sound, the slabs began to rise straight up towards the ceiling.

CHAPTER 39

As THE SLABS ROSE upwards, they revealed racks, shelves, and drawers all ladened with a wide array of guns, knives, grenades, body armor, and even swords. Andrew gaped at it all as they all stopped rising at about shoulder level. It was like he was suddenly standing in the aisles of the world's most deadly convenience store.

"There we are," Applegate said genially, "now for this wedding, are you envisioning photos taken from a distance? Or perhaps something a little more up close and personal for those touching moments?"

"Perhaps a mixture of the two," Andrew said, picking up on the not-so-subtle code he was using, "but either way, I'd like to make sure the guests don't even notice the camera."

"Of course," Applegate said, his smile turning almost sinister, "how big is the wedding meant to be?"

"Honestly we're still working out the guest list, it's difficult to pin these things down sometimes."

"Hmm, well I'm sure it'll be an event to remember. Perhaps I could interest you in something like this." He stepped behind one of the racks and returned with a rifle in his hands. "Steyr AUG bullpup rifle. It has been modified with a longer barrel and extended 42 round magazine. Chambered for the 9mm Parabellum, it should help to not stand out in the aftermath. Simple, versatile, and it will give you crisp images at multiple ranges. You'll notice the selector switch, allowing one to transition quickly and easily between single shots and rapid-fire bursts."

Andrew took the gun and inspected it closely, pulling back the slide, unloading and loading the magazine, and shifting his position. The usual telescopic scope had been modified to include simple iron sights as well. He nodded his approval and handed it back.

"Of course," Applegate said, "all my equipment is customizable to ensure that every shot is one worth taking," he pulled open a drawer to reveal an array of compensators, suppressors, and rail mounted attachments.

"Perfect," Andrew said, "but I wouldn't mind something a little more intimate for the reception. An opportunity to get candids of my guests."

"Absolutely, if you'll follow me." Applegate led Andrew down the room, passing shotguns and even a couple grenade launchers. They came to a display of pistols ranging from tiny Walthers to huge magnums. He reached up and pulled one from the display, handing it to Andrew. "Of course I have a wide variety to offer, but I think this would suit you well. The Sig Sauer M17 military issue. Textured grip with a sharper angle than most offers excellent comfort and precise control of movement. 21 round magazines ensure plenty of shots without pause and of course I have modified it to have a threaded barrel. It comes optic ready to assist with accuracy at range."

Andrew performed similar testing again, making sure it felt alright in his hands before nodding his approval and asking, "As someone who has seen his fair share of weddings, do you have recommendations on changing outfits between the ceremony and reception?"

"Well," Applegate began, lacing his fingers together, "it is a fairly new tradition, all things considered, but one that is worth exploring. For the groom, changing one's jacket can offer greater visual variety while improving functionality and comfort in the long run. Follow me."

This routine carried on for several minutes as Applegate showed Andrew various body armors, knives, smoke, and stun grenades, and made sure there was plenty of spare ammunition. All the while he transitioned smoothly between his metaphors and technical descriptions of the weaponry. It was truly something to behold and Andrew couldn't help but marvel at the mere existence of this place. As a final touch, Applegate would be providing Andrew with a more discreet vehicle into which the chosen gear was already being loaded.

"Now then," Applegate said as the displays lowered themselves back into the floor, "there is simply the matter of my fees. A wedding package such as this is hardly inexpensive, though the quality is guaranteed."

"Right," Andrew said, "I was told to tell you that the apple doesn't fall far from the tree."

A look of something almost like wonder appeared on Applegate's face and he lost all pretense. "So, the old man has finally decided to cash in the favor. I knew his boy, you see, and I always used to say exactly that to him. Tell him hello when you see him again."

"I will," Andrew said solemnly, shaking Applegate's hand again, "and thank you."

The receptionist reappeared at that point and led Andrew out to a somewhat battered Toyota parked in the alley behind the studio. He took the keys from her and climbed in with the duffel bag of gear on the seat next to him. It only took half an hour to get to the warehouse Duncan had found and a cursory pass of the adjacent street revealed a couple of men smoking outside of it and generally trying to look casual despite the cold.

Andrew parked a block away, hiding the car behind a group of dumpsters next to a different warehouse. He'd chosen it because the narrow alleyway would give a prime spot to take out the two guards with plenty of cover in case they happened to notice him. It took a few minutes to get ready, first pulling on the body armor, then securing his weapons in various holsters or harnesses. He positioned magazines and grenades in places he could reach them without being in the way, then pulled the rifle around to grip it tightly. The huge suppressor made the gun slightly unwieldy, but the benefits greatly outweighed the downsides. He had to take out as many of them as possible before they were alerted to his presence. As he was unsure just how many there might be, speed and stealth were his best friends.

With a deep breath and a final check of his weapons, Andrew squeezed into the gap between the buildings. There was barely enough room to walk without his shoulders scraping the walls on either side of him, so when someone grabbed his shoulder, he spun too fast and slammed the gun into the wall as he tried to raise it.

"Jesus Christ," Andrew said in a furious whisper when he recognised Hunter, "are you trying to give me a heart attack?"

"You're lucky that's all I'm doing to you," she whispered back, pulling him back towards his car. "What the fuck are you doing here?"

"What do you think? I'm going to get them. I'm done waiting around for the NYPD to decide they're in trouble. How did you even find me?"

"Duncan told me, idiot, said I either had to arrest you or let you go through with it. He made sure to give you enough of a head start that it forced my hand."

"I'm not leaving," Andrew said stubbornly.

"I know, which is why I chose option three," she said, gesturing to herself. She was kitted out in her own body armor and was toting an M16 in addition to her service weapon. "I know I can't stop you, and I'm not even sure if I want to, but I can't let you go in there alone. So, I'll watch your back on one condition."

"Alright," Andrew said, grinning in spite of himself, "what is it?"

"You cannot, under any circumstances, be seen by Cara, Dirk, or Eliza. I'll be the one to pull them out of there, not you."

"What? Why?"

"Use your brain," she actually poked him in the forehead to emphasize this, "if they see you like this going all Rambo then your cover is blown in an instant. My whole job is pretty much to make sure that doesn't happen. You'll get a call, like the families will, to come and see them once we have them. Agreed?"

"Fine," Andrew said, "now can we do this?"

"Yes," Hunter said, readying her own weapon, "we can do this."

CHAPTER 40

ANDREW CREPT FORWARD IN the alley again, Hunter right behind him, they slowed to a stop near the end so Andrew could peek out. The two men were still there, each of them smoking, breathing out heavy clouds with each breath. Andrew held up two fingers for Hunter who nodded as he knelt into a shooting position. The suppressor slowly inched out of the alley until Andrew had a clear line of sight to both men through the small scope. One had a hand in his coat, possibly on a weapon, while the other lounged casually on a crate next to the door, both hands visible.

"Ready," Hunter breathed from behind him, indicating that she had her own weapon trained on them as well. She would take a shot only if Andrew missed as the NYPD didn't regularly have suppressed weapons on hand. Andrew steadied his breathing and clicked a dial on the scope a couple of notches. These shots were the most important. If he missed and the guards were able to sound the alarm, they would be walking into a meat grinder.

He breathed out slowly, and in the natural split-second pause between breaths, he fired. The rifle jerked back into his shoulder, but the sound was reduced to a far more subdued cracking sound that nevertheless echoed off the brick walls. The bullet found its mark before Andrew had even taken his next breath, splitting through the standing man's skull in an instant. The other had barely had time to flinch before Andrew shifted his sights and fired two shots into his chest. Easier to hit the centre of mass with a more quickly aimed shot. He fell off the crate and onto the ground, obviously dead. Hunter tapped his shoulder and the two of them moved smoothly across the street to where the bodies lay.

"God, I hope you didn't just kill a couple guys on the night shift," Hunter said quietly. Andrew leaned down and reached into the first man's jacket, pulling out a compact submachine gun.

"Not exactly standard for the night shift," Andrew said, quickly unloading the weapon and tossing it out of reach, just in case. Hunter checked the pulse of the second man before grabbing a ring of keys from his belt.

"Alright, let's do this."

"Hang on," Andrew said, peering around the corner of the building, "Duncan said he had dispatch send a unit to drive past the building. Did they report in?"

"Yeah, I checked in with them before I came to get you, they said nothing was suspicious, why?" Andrew waved her over and they rounded the corner, weapons at the ready. He had spotted something blue buried under piles of discarded boxes and tarps. Hunter covered him as he pulled some of the garbage away to reveal an NYPD police cruiser.

Hunter, upon seeing this, helped Andrew pull the largest tarp away from the car. The windshield was marred with a pair of starburst patterns and there was blood splattered inside. Walking to the backseat revealed both officers stuffed inside, clearly dead.

"Jesus," Hunter said, pulling her phone out at once, "you and I are done here, this just got way worse." She didn't wait for a response before making her call and turning away from the scene before them. After giving her name and badge number, she reported the fallen officers and gave the address of the warehouse.

"We have to go in," Andrew said as soon as she hung up.

"Hawk, backup will be here in minutes, they'll storm this place and put them all down if needed."

"Hunter, the fact that there are two cops lying dead here means they know we're on to them. They'll be talking right now about either moving the hostages or killing them. In both cases we need to stop them right now."

Hunter thought for a moment, then acknowledged that there was still a very real danger inside the warehouse and nodded. Using the keys she had taken from one of the guards, she carefully unlocked the side door of the warehouse. Andrew shifted his rifle to his back and drew the pistol from its holster, holding it in front of him as he nodded for Hunter to open the door. This was no different than training, he thought to himself, trying to ignore the knowledge that he'd already ended two lives.

Hunter pulled the door open and Andrew stepped inside, finding himself at the bottom of a set of stairs. A second door led out into the main body of the warehouse straight ahead, but it was chained shut. Pointing his gun up the stairs, Andrew covered Hunter as she closed the door behind them and drew her own pistol. He signaled for her to stop, eyes still on the top of the stairs, and tapped his left hip with a finger. His CIA issued weapon was holstered there, and as it was equipped with a suppressor, he'd rather she use it. Hunter drew it and started up the stairs, Andrew following close behind.

Once they reached the top, they found themselves in an open second floor that must have been used as offices above the warehouse. There was a constant hum of some sort of machinery above them, likely the refrigeration units for the warehouse, but the offices seemed abandoned. Desks and filing cabinets lay overturned and scattered around the room. Hunter started to move into the room, but Andrew held her back, he had heard something. A voice was drifting in from the opposite side of the office space, through a door on the far wall, growing louder by the second. Andrew closed his eyes to listen, translating the Spanish automatically in his head.

"So, what do you want us to do?" the voice was asking, *"Seems convenient that the police came by here right after Pedroso disappeared."* They fell silent as they awaited a response and Andrew peeked out into the office around the corner. A man was pacing

there now, holding a phone in one hand and an SMG in the other. *"I understand, ma'am, we'll take care of them. We will wait for you to cut the feed."*

Andrew's blood boiled at these words and he went into the room out of pure instinct. The man had just turned away from him and so didn't notice Andrew until he was right behind him. A well placed kick knocked the weapon from the man's hand and sent it skittering across the floor. He opened his mouth to shout in surprise or to raise the alarm, but they never found out which because Hunter's foot made precise contact with the man's throat. He fell to his knees, choking and gasping, putting him in prime position for Andrew to kick him squarely in the head. He crumpled to the floor almost soundlessly, unconscious, and barely breathing now.

"Javier," the woman on the phone was saying, *"what's going on? Javier?"* Andrew picked up the phone.

"I must assume that this is Miss Elena Ramos?" Andrew said.

There was a long pause, then, in English, "Your accent is good, but I do not think you are truly a native speaker. What have you done with Javier?"

"He's taking a little nap so can't talk right now," Andrew replied, "I just wanted to let you know your plan has failed. Figured you've earned the right to hear it first."

"I wouldn't count us out just yet," Ramos said, chuckling, "we can be feisty when we need to. I can still see the ones I took on the cameras, so I would not say we have lost just yet. I do appreciate you saving us the trouble of hunting you down. Out of curiosity, who are you? NYPD? FBI? You sound awfully young."

"When you spend so many years committing crimes that hurt as many people as you have, you surely must have known one of your victims would fight back. I'm no one, really, you just pissed me off when you took them. So I'm here to take them back."

Ramos laughed softly through the phone, "Well, I am sorry to have gotten you so upset, we shall make sure to bury you with them." The line went dead and Andrew tossed the phone to the ground.

"Productive conversation?" Hunter asked.

"She admitted to taking them, at least," Andrew replied.

"Hawk, come look at this," Hunter said from near a bank of windows on one side of the office. They were slightly frosted over from the temperature of the cold storage beyond, but they looked out over the majority of the warehouse. Right in the middle, surrounded by tools and building materials, was a much smaller building. The walls were bare lumber, but he knew that the inside had been made to look like a specific room in Colombia. They were being held there. He had found them.

Screens on the outside of the little building showed the camera feed that was being broadcast as well as a few other angles inside. On all of them he could see Cara, Eliza, and Dirk, all still alive and chained to the wall. Huge power lines were running to the building, powering several heaters that blew warm air into the room and kept up the charade. A half dozen men and women were stationed around the structure, all armed and mostly just lounging around playing cards near space heaters. One of them got a call while Andrew watched.

"Shit," he said, grabbing Hunter's arm, "get down." The woman who had gotten the call barked an order and almost as one, the guards turned towards the office windows and opened fire.

CHAPTER 41

BULLETS EXPLODED INTO THE room over their heads, shattering the glass and washing them with a wave of frigid air. Someone shouted something inaudible and the hail of gunfire stopped. The metal wall had offered good cover, but Andrew and Hunter were still surrounded by dents where the bullets had hit. If the wall hadn't been insulated, they likely would have been dead. Stomping footsteps could be heard coming up the other staircase as some of the guards lumbered towards them. Andrew kicked over a desk that had survived the initial destruction of the office and crawled behind it, Hunter right beside him.

"Got a plan?" Hunter asked, ditching Andrew's pistol for her M16. By way of answer, Andrew unclipped a grenade from his belt, pulled the pin, and tossed it over the desk just as the men appeared in the doorway. Thick, billowing smoke erupted from the canister, filling the landing. Andrew counted to three on his fingers and popped up over the desk with Hunter, two large shadows were waving wildly at the smoke, trying to clear it. Hunter released a burst of gunfire at one while Andrew took a few shots with his pistol. Both men dropped to the ground, groaning, then fell still. Silence fell over the warehouse again as both sides waited for the other to act.

"Take a position there," Hunter said, pointing towards the smoky side of the office, "I'll go the other way. On three we open fire from both directions, splitting their attention. Got it?"

"Got it," Andrew said, moving in a crouch to not be seen from below. He swapped out for his rifle again, taking off the suppressor as stealth wasn't exactly an option anymore and it reduced muzzle velocity. He looked across the room at Hunter who did the counting this time, raising her fingers one at a time. In unison they lifted their guns to rest on the shattered window's frames and started firing. Four of the cartel members fell in quick succession but there were more than Andrew had originally spotted. There were at least six more who all dove for cover behind whatever was closest.

Each time one of them peeked out to take a shot, Andrew or Hunter either forced them back or took them out. Andrew tossed three stun grenades into the throng, making a small handful of them stumble around blindly. This made for easy pickings as Andrew squeezed the trigger again and again. Despite the extensive training he had put in, many shots missed, but he still dropped about half of the cartel members.

Hunter snapped her fingers at Andrew and he glanced over, she indicated a spot on her side of the warehouse where a man was hiding behind a forklift. She had no shot on him, but Andrew could see one shoulder. He took careful aim and fired a shot straight through the exposed area, ripping a hole through muscle and making the man fall to the ground. Now visible to Hunter, she fired three shots into his back and he went still. Turning to nod in thanks, she spotted something in the dissipating smoke.

"Hawk," she cried, "on your six." Andrew whirled around, bringing his gun up as he stood, but the woman who had snuck up behind him caught it in one hand, holding it down as the other leveled a heavy revolver at Andrew's head. Hunter made to take a shot but had to fire her next bullets towards another who jumped out to take a shot at Andrew now that he was standing still. The man went down and Hunter turned quickly to fire again, but her gun only clicked. It was empty. Swearing, she reached for her sidearm but knew it would be too late. But apparently it didn't matter.

Andrew twisted, bending weirdly so that it pulled the woman towards the window while also getting him out of the way. The revolver went off, missing Andrew by inches as he wrenched his gun from her grip and hit her in the stomach with it. She made to hit Andrew upside the head with the revolver but he managed to drop his gun to grab her wrist. They struggled for a moment before another shot went off and the woman jerked and fell to the ground. Hunter had gotten her shot off, clipping the woman in the temple. Andrew barely had time to crouch again and catch his breath when the next attacker charged through the door, firing wildly at Hunter.

She was forced to take cover behind a large, overturned cabinet, but the man hadn't seen Andrew right next to him. Reaching to the small of his back, Andrew pulled out a short fixed blade and ran at the newcomer. In the span of two seconds he vaulted a desk and jumped across another, plunging the knife into the man's back at full speed. They tumbled to the ground, Andrew landing on top of him and he delivered another stab to his neck this time. He gargled horribly for a moment, then it stopped as his eyes grew dim.

"That the last one?" Andrew asked, pulling Hunter to her feet as he got back up.

"I think so," she said, brushing herself off. A moment later, Andrew's back exploded with pain as he was thrown forward by the force of a bullet hitting him. The bang it made was almost like an afterthought in light of the excruciating pain of it. Things seemed to slow down as he fell and he could feel the breath being forced out of him by the impact. He slammed into the floor face first as more gunshots rang out over his head. Next thing he knew, Hunter was shaking his shoulder violently, trying to roll him over.

"Hawk? Hawk! Come on, you're alright."

"You think so?" Andrew muttered into the dilapidated carpet, "Why don't I shoot you and you tell me how you feel?" He reached a hand around and felt where the bullet was lodged in his body armor, right in the small of his back. He'd have been paralyzed for sure if not for the vest.

"I think I'm good," Hunter said in relief, "think you can stand?" Andrew nodded and let her help him to his feet. It took a moment for the pain to stop flaring, but it subsided slightly and he stood up straight.

"That'll feel great tomorrow, I take it we missed one?"

"One of the ones who first came up for us," Hunter said, pointing with her weapon at a man wearing his own Kevlar and with a bullet hole in his forehead, "looks like you just shot him in the vest."

"Live and learn," Andrew grunted, "I told Morris that centre of mass only got you so far."

The two of them, Hunter supporting most of Andrew's weight, made their way down the stairs towards the warehouse floor. They had just caught a glimpse of three people huddled together on the cameras, clearly terrified, when the sound of sirens reached them through the warehouse doors.

"You have to go," Hunter said urgently, "they can't find you here."

"I'm not about to outrun them," Andrew said through gritted teeth.

Hunter thought for a moment, "Think you can act natural for thirty seconds?"

"Probably," he said, "why?"

"Because you're going to impersonate an NYPD detective."

CHAPTER 42

IT PLAYED OUT MORE or less exactly like Hunter planned. They quickly scattered Andrew's weapons around the scene, leaving the rifle upstairs with the man on the phone. Their thought was that when ballistics were run, it would look like Hunter showed up to a massacre between rival gang members. After, when the police outside had established their perimeter, Hunter opened the large cargo doors to let them in. There was a slightly tense moment in which Hunter had about thirty guns pointed at her chest, but someone recognised her and she explained the situation. Police officers and a handful of detectives swarmed through the doors, everyone more or less relaxing to do a sweep of the building just in case.

Andrew, meanwhile, slipped away towards the side door away from the dead officers. He waited a full minute after he heard the cargo doors rattle open and then pushed his way outside. Like Hunter had suggested, there was a single partner pair of beat cops who had been relegated to watching this door. Red and blue lights flashed wildly from the front of the building, throwing bizarre shadows in every direction. The two officers, leaning against the hood of their car, stood a little straighter when they saw someone in a Kevlar vest and with a detective's badge around their neck walking straight for them. The badge, of course, being Hunter's meant that he couldn't get close enough for them to read the number.

"You two," Andrew said from far enough away that it wouldn't allow them to see his face well in the relative darkness, "someone was spotted leaving through this door and fleeing the scene. They are likely to be armed and dangerous, so we need you to head down that way and circle around the end of the warehouses."

"Understood," one of them said and the two climbed back into their car and peeled away with a slight spray of gravel. Andrew made his way across the street and into a gap between two more warehouses. Here he was able to ditch the body armor and slip Hunter's badge into his pocket. He dropped the vest into a dumpster before leaning up against it. The cold metal seeped through his clothes and soothed the growing bruise on his back. Letting out a long breath, Andrew kept his eyes glued on the front of the warehouse, waiting for the moment he needed so desperately.

Then it finally came. As a trio of ambulances arrived on the scene, three officers emerged from the warehouse supporting three people in battered formalwear. Hunter had one arm around Cara's waist, they held hands so that Cara could put some of her weight on her. She, like the others, was wrapped in a blanket over her dress but otherwise looked unharmed. Eliza was putting her full weight on the shoulder of the officer helping her and halfway to the ambulance he scooped her up into his arms instead, she seemed to be in shock. Cara was helped up to sit on the stretcher in one of the ambulances where an EMT was already waiting to check on her. It took all of Andrew's willpower not to run to them, but a glance to his hiding spot from Hunter kept him rooted there. It wouldn't be much longer before he would see her properly.

Hunter, after making sure everything was alright with Cara, turned to speak with her captain who had just arrived on the scene. They exchanged a brief conversation before Hunter walked away. This had been part of their plan as well. Andrew walked slowly down to the other end of the alley and waited there; it only took Hunter a couple minutes to pick him up.

"Everything went ok?" she asked.

"Yeah, you'll have a couple pretty confused beat cops but otherwise fine. It was a good plan," he said, handing her badge back.

"You don't have to sound that surprised," she remarked, "but thanks."

"Thank you for getting her out," Andrew said quietly after a while.

"You're the one who found them, I just made sure you didn't get killed. Also, I wasn't about to let Officer O'Connor be the one to bring her out. I'm eighty percent sure he's a cop just so he can play the knight in shining armor with women. He's the one who brought Eliza out of the warehouse."

"Yeah well," Andrew said, genuinely smiling for what felt like the first time in a long time, "she'll eat that up. Wouldn't be surprised if she was playing along just to end up in his arms." Hunter laughed and they drove on in silence for a while. Andrew directed Hunter to the spot where Applegate had had his car parked and they parted ways. He was to head back home and wait for the official call that he could come and see Cara and the others. Hunter, meanwhile, who was supposed to be off informing the families of the rescue, would return to the scene and start the arduous process of laying out their story. The processing and subsequent investigation would be days, but Hunter had Duncan's help to lay the groundwork. They would have a couple of the cartel members' records changed to show affiliation to the Red Cobras, suggesting a turf war gone wrong. Andrew drove home, elated that they had really done it. He knew the shock and regret of what he had done was still to come, but for now, he had done it.

"You look to be in a good mood," Ryan said from behind the security desk as he walked into the building, "any news about Miss Randal?"

"Actually yes," Andrew said, unable to hide his grin, "I just got the call, she and the others were just rescued, all alive and well."

"That's wonderful," Ryan said, smiling as well, "have you seen her yet?"

"Soon, I hope, but at least she's safe." He found Em passed out on the sofa in his sitting room. He contemplated waking her but decided against it in the end. There would be time to tell everyone in the morning. For now, he just wanted the call to come. To keep himself busy, he set about dismantling the numerous photos and reports he'd pinned to his office walls. All of it was pretty much wrapped up now, thanks in large part to Luca's confession. Even Hunter's cold case was solved. All that would be processed and put to bed in the coming days. At around one in the morning, Andrew's phone buzzed on the table where he had left it and he practically dove for it.

"Yes?"

"You can come see her now," Hunter said on the other end, "the Randals just got here, and the other families are on the way. Everyone is healthy and sleeping at the moment, only a little dehydrated from the heat they were pumping into that place." Hunter gave him the hospital and room number while Andrew threw on his coat and hurried back down to the lobby. Ryan smiled in a knowing sort of way, but Andrew barely spared him a glance before he was out the door. Somehow, the media had already caught wind of the rescue and were more ravenous than ever, but he soon left them behind as he weaved through late night traffic. More cameras and reporters were waiting outside the hospital, but thankfully they didn't realize who he was until he had shouldered his way past them and up to the cops waiting at the entrance, ready to hold back the horde.

"Emergencies only," one of the officers said, holding up a hand to block Andrew's entrance.

"It's alright," Hunter said from beyond the blockade, she hurried over and grabbed Andrew's arm to pull him in, "he's expected." The officer nodded in acknowledgement and Andrew let Hunter lead him through the doors and straight to an elevator.

"They've got them up on a private floor," she explained, "apparently limitless wealth and notoriety earns that sort of thing. Easier to keep the media out this way."

"Makes sense," Andrew said, tapping his foot anxiously as the elevator seemed to crawl upwards at a snail's pace. When the doors did open again, he had barely made it a dozen steps off when he was attacked. Margaret Randal had just been coming out of a room down the hall when she spotted him and nearly took him to the floor in a hug.

"I can't believe they're back," she sobbed into his shoulder. Andrew, more startled than anything, patted her on the back gently until George came to save him. He limped over on his cane after leaving the same room and gently pulled his wife from Andrew.

"Come on, Margaret, dear, don't smother the poor boy. I'm sure he'd like to see Caralynne as much as we did." She nodded and buried her face into her husband's chest instead, still sobbing with relief. "She's said she is going to try and get some rest," George said to Andrew now, "but I know she'd like to see you first."

"Thank you, sir," Andrew said.

"Uh, Detective Hunter," George said, "could you help my wife to the elevator? I'd just like a quick word with Andrew."

"Of course," Hunter said at once and took Margaret gently by the shoulders and steered her away.

"Look," George said with a slightly misty expression, "I've already said this to the girl, but I wanted to thank you. She told me what really happened tonight, what you did. You saved my daughter's life."

"I did what anyone would have done." George looked like he would have liked to argue, but merely shook his head.

"I'm glad to see that the company is in good hands at least. We'll see you soon Andrew, now get in there." Andrew nodded his thanks and they shook hands before George left to join his wife. Andrew stared at the door before him for a moment, then pushed it open. Cara was reclined on her hospital bed, asleep. Andrew crept inside and her eyes fluttered open, filling with tears.

CHAPTER 43

"We thought you were dead," Cara said as Andrew approached her, "I saw you get shot when they took us, I got the hood off for a minute, but you fell…" She sat up in her bed, tugging at the IV line in her arm as she reached out a hand for him. Beyond bags under her eyes, she looked as well as she ever did.

"I'm alright," Andrew said, taking her outstretched hands, "just a little sore now. I promise everything is fine. I'm sorry I wasn't there when they found you."

"That's not your fault," Cara said, shaking her head, "I'm just glad you're alright. How are the others?"

"Good, as far as I know, Hunter says they are anyway. Their families should be here soon if they aren't here already."

"Detective Hunter? Is she here?"

"Yeah, she's outside, why?"

"I just need to talk to her, nobody wanted to listen on the way over here."

"I can go get her," Andrew said, making to move away from her, but she redoubled her grip on him.

"Not yet, I need something first," she said, pulling him back to her and grabbing the front of his coat. Pulling herself up to him, their lips met in a long kiss. The tension Andrew hadn't realized he'd been carrying melted away at the contact. Here she was, well and truly alright. When they broke apart, Andrew lowered himself to sit on her bedside.

"Did they hurt you?" he whispered as his eyes finally filled with the tears that he had been holding back.

"Not really," she said, "I think I broke one of their knees when they grabbed me and I got hit for it, but nothing major. They fed us and gave us water; I just don't get why they kept it so hot in there."

"They were trying to make it seem like you were being held in Colombia."

"What? Why?"

"It's sort of a long story, but basically a Mexican cartel convinced Luca Pedroso to betray his own country for money. They made it look like you guys were taken by a Colombian group to spark an international incident. The resulting crackdown would have opened up a chance for the Ramos Cartel to take over the drug trade."

"Jesus," Cara said, leaning back again, "what a convoluted plan just to earn some money and power. What were they going to do with us when the ransom was paid if we were supposedly in Colombia?"

"I, uh, I really don't know," Andrew said, "I've been trying not to think about it ever since we figured out you were still here."

"Who is 'we'? You and Detective Hunter? How did you figure it out?"

"It's a long story," Andrew said again, reflecting that he would have to be very careful how he told it, "You just rest for now."

"I can't yet," she said, sitting up suddenly, "Hawk I have to-"

"You have to rest, we'll deal with everything else later, ok?"

"No," Cara said urgently, trying to get up and out of bed, Andrew held her back by her shoulders and she slumped against him. "Hawk, I've been trying to tell someone for hours, I need to see Detective Hunter. Please."

"Alright," Andrew said softly, brushing hair from her forehead, "I'll go get her, just wait here." Cara nodded and Andrew got up.

He crossed the room and opened the door to find Hunter leaning against the wall there.

"Hey," she said, pushing off the wall, "everything ok?" Andrew waited until a passing nurse had moved out of earshot before answering.

"Yeah," he whispered, "but she really wants to talk to you, to tell you something. Anyway, if it comes up at all, just make sure you take credit for everything I did during all this, yeah?"

"Of course," Hunter said, following Andrew into the room. Cara was upright again and Andrew thought she looked almost frightened. "You needed me?" Hunter asked and Cara nodded.

"There was this man, with the ones who took us," Cara began, "he's still out there."

"Don't worry," Hunter said, "the NYPD is already working to dismantle the Ramos Cartel using the intel we found at the warehouse. Whoever it is, we'll find him."

"No, you don't understand," Cara said desperately, "he wasn't like the other people who had us. He killed the people who kidnapped us, and he only ever visited the place they kept us a couple of times."

"The hitman," Andrew said to Hunter, his eyes widening in realization, "the one Elena Ramos used to kill Alejandro."

"Cara," Hunter said, her tone reflecting the panic Andrew felt for forgetting about him, "how sure are you that he wasn't with the cartel?"

"Very," Cara said, looking a little confused at Andrew's comment, "his voice, it was like velvet, and he had an accent that was some sort of Eastern European. I'll never forget that voice. The things he said, too, made it seem like he was above the rest of them, like he was different."

"Did you ever see him? Was there ever a time when you saw his face?" Hunter asked, leaning in slightly, "We've caught him a couple times on security feeds, but never his face. As far as we can tell he's a ghost."

"Only once," Cara said, "there was a moment when they were bringing us into the warehouse when they took the bags off our heads to push us through the door. I caught a glimpse of him talking to one of the others. He's quite tall, and heavily built, kind of average in general, but he's got this-" Cara jumped slightly at a sound from over by the window. Andrew looked over, having heard what sounded like a breaking China cup. A spiderweb of cracks had appeared in the window, radiating out from a small hole that had appeared there. It wasn't until Hunter had crouched behind the hospital bed and drawn her weapon that Andrew started putting the pieces together.

Slowly, almost painfully, he turned his head to look back at Cara. Crimson red was spreading across her chest, staining the hospital gown she wore. She had a look of mild surprise on her face as she met Andrew's eyes, then slowly rested her head back on the bed, staring at the ceiling.

"Hawk," Hunter was saying from very far away, "Hawk, get down, now!" But he couldn't move. His eyes were fixed on Cara's face, refusing to believe what they were seeing. The high pitched, steady tone of a heart monitor sounded through the room even though the world was ending. It couldn't be real, none of this. He must have fallen asleep waiting for Hunter to call. In a minute, he would wake up next to Em and they would be able to go and see Cara together. But Cara was right there, already dead in her hospital bed with a bullet in her heart.

The second shot only missed Andrew's head because Hunter finally hauled him off the bed and onto the floor. The glass blasted out of the window this time and freeing air swept through the room. Hunter was shouting into a radio, reporting the shooter and requesting backup. They waited there for several minutes, Andrew staring into space while Hunter tried to peek around the bed at the building across the street. When the report came that they'd found the shooter's nest empty, Andrew stood up robotically. The voice coming through the radio in Hunter's hand was still speaking, mentioning a gun and a parabolic microphone pointed at the hospital, but it meant nothing to him at that moment. He didn't want to, but his eyes traveled upwards, over the blood, to Cara's face. He reached out a hand automatically to gently close her eyes before collapsing forward onto the bed, tears streaming down his face. The scream of agony he let out was lost to him in the rush of white noise that was filling his ears.

After all they had been through, after all their work, it had still ended like this. The woman he loved, who he had gone to hell and back to save, was lying dead in his arms. Someone pulled him away from her, strong hands guiding him to a seat in the hallway while doctors rushed into the room, but it didn't matter, it was too late. He stared at the blood on his hands, feeling something inside of him wither. That part of him which had been so brutally damaged when he'd seen Eddie's murder, had finally given up hope and died too.

CHAPTER 44

HAWK WOKE UP A week later in his usual state of misery. He knew that time would eventually get him back to some functional version of himself, but for now he was embracing the horrors he'd experienced. He'd killed people, many of them, to rescue Cara, and their faces haunted him now. He slept infrequently and poorly, but he had made an effort to get some form of rest before today. He glanced over at the picture turned face down on his bedside table and felt a twist in his gut. Looking at her face still brought him fresh waves of agony, but knowing the pictures were still there was almost just as bad.

Hunter had been covering for him, explaining to their superiors that Andrew Hawkins would indeed be mourning the loss of his girlfriend. She had convinced them that he was merely putting on a show for those who were still so interested in the story. Hunter had done her best to help him, but in the end seemed to realize that Hawk simply needed the space for now.

Hawk hauled himself out of bed and tried to rub away the blurriness in his vision, they would be here soon. He dressed a little clumsily as he tried to wake up, putting on the black suit that he'd left out. On the rare occasions he had left the condo in the last week, mostly to give statements to the police, he'd always gone armed, and today was no exception. He tucked his Glock into a shoulder holster beneath his jacket where it would be least visible.

Taking things in little steps was really the only way he was going to get through the day, so he told himself all he had to do was go downstairs. Then, it was make coffee. Force some food down, put on his coat, then wait. The knock on his door jarred him out of the inactive state he'd fallen into in the kitchen. Pulling it open revealed Diane and Em, both in brand new black dresses and coats that Hawk had paid for.

"Hi," Diane said quietly, "are you ready?" Em wouldn't meet Hawk's eye, and it looked like she'd been crying. When he'd had to break the news to her, it broke his heart all over again, but she'd turned up a couple days later. Neither had said anything, she had just needed to be with someone who understood, so he'd been there with her.

"I suppose so," Hawk said, "Ram should be waiting downstairs for us." Diane rested her hand on Hawk's arm for a moment before returning it to Em's back and leading the way to the elevator. Ram was indeed waiting for them in the lobby with the full security team from the building.

"Mister Hawkins," Ryan said mournfully, "the reporters know what day it is and have been gathering all over again. We've had your driver pull into the back lot and we'll clear a path for you to leave."

"I appreciate it," Hawk said in a passable imitation of his own voice. The security moved to flank them as Ram led them to the car and opened the door. As suggested, the media swarm was pressed right up to the gate as they left. Hawk idly wondered if the other tenants of the building were fed up with him yet. They drove through the gate, security carving them a path and showing little restraint as they did so. A couple small scuffles broke out, but they all faded quickly considering the uneven odds.

Once they were free, they drove in total silence, none of them having a thing to say to the others. They all understood what today meant. It was an awful thing, a gut-wrenching experience, but one that could maybe provide an ounce of closure. They left Manhattan, heading for the little town upstate that Mrs. Randal's family was originally from. Apparently, they owned most of the town and had committed to maintaining an authentic image of it. This meant that, quite suddenly, the concrete block strip malls and fast-food restaurants of the highway were replaced by red brick houses with gabled roofs and little shops with swinging wooden signs.

"Here we are, sir," Ram said, breaking the silence for the first time in almost an hour and a half. The car nosed its way between two snowbanks and up the drive of a quaint, stone church that looked like it belonged in an English countryside. A couple dozen cars were already here, their occupants slowly trickling through the wooden double doors. Hawk took a deep breath as they slowed to a stop and then opened his door, reaching out a hand for Em. She took it, still not looking at him, so he couldn't see her tears, and Diane joined them. Together they walked into the little church.

The rich wooden interior was lit by a pair of massive, old-fashioned chandeliers that had been salvaged and wired for electricity, giving the room a soft glow. Most of the attendees were making their way up to the front where the casket waited for them. A large picture of Cara's smiling face was set next to it and Hawk felt his heart twist and his movement grind to a halt. Diane looked over at him questioningly and he shook his head.

"I'm alright," he lied, "you two go ahead, I just need a second." Em gave his hand a little squeeze before letting go and moving forward with Diane. Hawk's head swam with a sudden rush of emotion. He wasn't sure if he wanted to throw up, scream, or just bawl like a child. He stepped out of the way and gripped the back of a pew tightly. There were Cara's parents, greeting guests as Mrs. Randal dabbed her eyes and Mr. Randal stared into the distance between sentences.

"Can't face her either?" someone asked from behind Hawk, and he glanced over to see Dirk and Eliza leaning against the back wall of the church.

"Apparently not," Hawk choked out. The two of them stepped forward and Dirk held out something silver. He took it gratefully and took a big swig of the unknown liquor in the flask. It at least burned some feeling other than crushing remorse into him. "Thanks. Are you two alright? I barely saw you after...well after everything."

"Physically?" Eliza said, "We're fine. In every other way? Not so much. We didn't have any time to process what happened to us before this. I feel like I don't know what to do with myself."

"It'll be alright," Dirk said, putting an arm around her and rubbing her shoulder in comfort, "we're just glad you're alright, Hawk. Cara saw you get shot, so we didn't know if you even made it out of that alley."

"I'm starting to wish I hadn't," he replied, voicing the thing that had been nagging him since the moment the bullet had torn into the hospital room.

"Don't say that," Eliza whispered, her eyes filling with tears, "Cara of all people would have wanted you to be happy." For some reason this made Hawk angry. He supposed that anger was simply an easier emotion to feel at the moment. He was, at any rate, spared the need to respond as the door to the church opened again and Diego appeared there.

"Holy shit," Dirk muttered, "he actually came."

"What are you doing here?" Eliza demanded, drawing Diego's attention.

"I came to say goodbye," he said, wringing his hands.

"No," Eliza snapped, her voice becoming louder and more hysterical by the second, making a few people look around at her, "you don't get that privilege. She'd be alive right now if it wasn't for you and your uncle. Leave, or I swear I'll kill you right here."

"Liza," Diego said pleadingly. When she made no sign of changing her mind, he looked to Dirk and Hawk, but Dirk had fixed him with his own expression of hatred. His head sagging, Diego shuffled back outside.

"That was too far, Eliza," Hawk said, the spark of anger fanning itself to life in his chest.

"Not far enough if you ask me," Dirk said.

"Jesus Christ," Hawk snapped, "how stupid can you get? Diego is not his uncle, and he deserves to be here as much as any of us, and a hell of a lot more than me. He was the one working with the police to gather any and all information about Luca so that they had a tiny chance of finding you. He disregarded diplomatic immunity and put himself on the line for you."

"I don't care," Eliza argued back, "there's something wrong with that whole family."

"Oh, shut the fuck up, Eliza," Hawk was doing his best not to shout, "don't you have some meathead to screw while you wait to inherit your family fortune? And you," he rounded on Dirk, "drinking yourself into a coma on your father's dime is hardly a way to deal with your problems. So, before the two of you start attacking someone who helped save you, you should look at whether you were even worth being saved."

Without waiting for either of them to say another word, he strode out of the church after Diego. The anger felt good, it was cauterizing the wounds, even temporarily. Diego was halfway back to his car when Hawk caught up to him.

"Oh," he said, "sorry, I left before you got a chance to insult me too. Go ahead."

"I figure beating the shit out of you once was enough. I know how much you helped the cops, that by itself was more than those two have ever done. I know it might not mean much, but I think you have every right to be here."

"Thanks, Hawk," Diego said quietly, looking as though a weight was being lifted from him. "I'm sorry for everything that happened."

"Your uncle tried to use you as the fall guy," Hawk said, "that makes it pretty clearly not your fault. Look, I think you should stay, but either way, take care of yourself, ok?" Diego nodded and they shook hands before parting ways. Diego was headed back to the church, while Andrew had spotted someone else at the end of the drive. Leaning on her Chevelle, leather jacket zipped up tight, was Hunter.

"Do I look cliche enough?" she asked as though concerned she was breaking a law.

"Need the sunglasses," Hawk said with a slight smile, "if you're going to be the cop watching the funeral from a distance."

"Damn, knew I forgot something."

"What's up? Did something happen?"

"Nope," Hunter said, hopping up to sit on her car, legs swinging gently, "just here for my friend. Did you see her?"

"No," Hawk said, leaning next to her, "I don't think I can."

"You will," she said, "one day. And she'll be right here waiting for you. When that time comes, if you need company to watch you cry like a man, I'll be right here too."

"Thanks," he said sarcastically, but she knew he meant it.

"For now, I'm keeping the company off your back, but they'll want their own report from you sooner than later. You were never expected to see this much action."

"I did what I had to."

"I know," Hunter said, "which is what I told them, and they agree. So, your current assignment is being modified. You and I will be given a wider license to operate on our own. We even get a budget and Duncan is already rounding up a little support team. All unofficially of course, but you and I will be running a little covert task force designed to stop this sort of thing in the future."

"Wait, seriously?" Hawk asked, not entirely ready to believe her. "But I disobeyed orders from you, broke my standing directive from the company, and instigated a shootout with a cartel."

"Welcome to the CIA," Hunter said, "where that's just called problem solving."

EPILOGUE

TWO MONTHS AFTER THE funeral found Hawk falling back into old routines. He had started running again, first thing every morning. Things had finally been cooling off in the aftermath of the shooting. The Ramos Cartel had all but fallen apart between busts in the US and Mexico inviting federal agents to raid the Ramos compound. Elena Ramos and her top four lieutenants were all behind bars along with around a hundred pushers, cooks, and runners. Hunter had received a commendation from the NYPD's commissioner for her taking selfless action to rescue the hostages. Their story, with a little helpful nudging from Duncan, had been accepted with little resistance. Nightmares still haunted Hawk when he slept, memories of what he'd seen and regrets of what he hadn't, but practice and routine had taught him to put them aside during the day.

He slowed to a jog at his usual spot and stopped to order coffee like he always had, including a blueberry muffin. Brushing snow off a bench on the pier, he sat and placed the muffin next to him. It only took a moment or two before a small hand snatched it away.

"That wasn't for you," Hawk said before sipping his coffee.

"Oh well," Em said from behind him, "ya snooze ya lose I guess."

"How are things out there?" Hawk asked.

"Better, but still a little rough. The Red Cobras are taking over most of the territory that Ramos was holding. The cops are doing what they can but it's impossible to tell when the random other gangs might try to push back."

"And the other kids?"

"Oh, they're alright, still feeling it all, but we look out for each other. You gonna tell me who you really are yet?"

"Nope," Hawk said simply.

"Why do you wanna know about all the gangs and stuff?"

"Just keep an eye out and let me know if anything happens, ok?"

"Yeah, ok. See you tomorrow?"

"Sounds good." Em's footsteps crunched through the snow behind him and soon others were heading towards him again.

"That girl stole my muffin," Hunter complained as she sat on the bench.

"Shouldn't have taken so long to get here," Hawk replied, handing her an extra coffee.

"Sorry, I've been up all night. The taskforce set up to deal with all this has been running overtime for weeks, they're looking for help anywhere they can, so I thought I'd pitch in. Anyway, does she know about you? The real you I mean."

"Nah," Hawk said, waving the thought away, "she knows I'm more than just another rich kid, but that's about it. I think she really just wants to help, even if she doesn't know why. It's useful though, she can get to places I can't without being recognised."

"Just don't mention it to everyone," Hunter said, looking around them, "I can just picture her being dragged in for a polygraph."

Andrew snorted, "So what's up? You sounded cryptic on the phone last night."

"Yeah, well they don't like it when I tell you things over the phone."

"Duncan secures our lines better than Langley's are."

"*I* know that," Hunter said defensively, "but try convincing a room full of suits and power ties of anything and you'll divide them. I'm here to tell you our team arrived in the city today. I'll be meeting them all later on and we'll be setting up more discreet encounters for you and them individually."

"Great," Hawk said, looking forward to being more than a glorified errand boy watching the wealthy, "just let me know where and when. How are they looking so far?"

"Not too bad," Hunter said, pulling out her phone and showing him the photos of a few agents. "A couple are pretty green around the gills, but we picked out these four for you. They're young enough to blend in with you at a club or something. Their covers won't ever be as extravagant as yours, but nice enough to merit you interacting with them regularly in public places." Andrew looked over the photos and raised an eyebrow.

"Not bad, might have to ruffle them up a bit, teach them to take the sticks out of their asses occasionally. What have you got?"

"I got a couple experts in surveillance. Give one a target and not only will they tell you what toothpaste is in their bathroom, but how much is used every night. Total discretion and can blend into almost any environment naturally. Your guys are more the talkative type, these guys maybe speak twelve words a month."

"And Duncan," Hawk asked, "I take it he's still rejected everyone they've given him?"

"So far, yeah. He's gotten pretty protective of you over the last little while, no one seems to know why."

"Perhaps I can shed some light on that," a new voice said as it approached them. Andrew recognized the shaved head and glasses at once. Some deep part of his training told him to stand at the sight of a superior, but he figured a casual greeting would be more appropriate.

"Morris," he said, nodding in greeting, "if you're here to say you told me so, I will throw you in the Hudson."

"No," Morris said, removing his glasses to wipe them with a handkerchief, "I only did what I did to warn you, Mister Hawkins, not to stop you. I had hoped to spare you of the turmoil so many in your position find themselves. I see now that that may have been a mistake. It was not my position to dictate how you carried out your duties and the reports of the incident certainly suggest you were well motivated. I understand that no words I say could possibly rectify the situation so I shall not even try. No, I am merely here to brief you and Detective Hunter."

Hawk thought about this for a moment. Morris was never one to let emotion into the equation but he remembered what Bakowski had told him months back. Hunter was glancing sideways at him now and he realized he'd been staring at Morris silently for about a minute now.

"Right, sorry, go on then."

"Excellent. I have reviewed your new personnel and approved the orders myself. It goes without saying that they are in no way officially here nor will they receive any direct contact from us. Everything goes through you. If any of them, or yourselves, are captured, killed, or questioned, the company will deny you ever existed."

"Understood," Hawk and Hunter said together, they had gotten a similar speech near the end of training.

"We have been keeping tabs on the investigation of the shooting of Miss Cara Randal. While the nest from which the shot was taken held much evidence, none of it could be traced back to a single source. The bullet was a standard caliber fired from a Savage Model 10, both of which can be purchased over the counter from just about any hunting store in the country. The fact that the shooter used a civilian weapon suggests an uncanny level of skill, but we already knew he was no amateur. The good folks in our psychology department started putting together a profile when we discovered something truly disturbing. We already have this man in our system."

"What?" Hawk demanded, nearly propelled from the bench, "You have a name?"

"The Peregrine," Morris said, "real name unknown. He's been on our radar for quite some time now, over thirty years. His first assassination we're aware of shook the company to its core, but in all that time we know nothing about him. The name comes from his calling card, the feather of a peregrine falcon left on each victim. A feather left in the sniper's nest across from the hospital matches the one left on his first victim and several others, including Luca Pedroso whose body was discovered a few days ago. He does, however, seem to only leave the feathers on the targets he chooses, not those he is hired to kill."

"Who was his first victim?" Hawk asked curiously. It surprised him a little that the news of Luca's death had so little impact on him. Not that long ago he himself had wanted so badly to be the one to pull the trigger, now it was as though Morris had told him it would rain tomorrow.

"Theodore Elliot," Morris said soberly. It took a moment for Andrew's memory to conjure up the conversation he'd had with Duncan months before.

"No," Hawk whispered, his eyes widening. Hunter looked at him questioningly and he said, "Theodore was Duncan's eldest son. Joined up with the company and was killed his first week, they nailed his body to the wall as a message."

"You're saying that this is the same guy?" Hunter asked, as shocked as he was.

"That's correct," Morris said, "naturally we tried to remove Duncan from this assignment as soon as we knew of Peregrine's involvement, but he refused outright. We aren't having you pursue this man in any capacity. However, if you would like, we shall keep you in the loop. If you can apply the same kind of motivation you showed two months ago, we may put a stop to him once and for all the next time he surfaces. A last favor to Miss Randal, and an overdue bit of closure for Duncan."

Hawk and Hunter looked at each other and knew they were both thinking the exact same thing. "Sign us up," they said together.

ABOUT THE AUTHOR

Liam has always been a creator .. writing, music, or photography .. they all continue to be his passion. His studies took him from Canada to Ireland where he completed his engineering degree. He currently works as an engineer in Canada where, again, he applies his creative talents through several books.

"After three books in the fantasy world I created, I though it was high time to mix things up a bit and 'The Columbia Conspiracy' is that story. My first foray into the world of spy thrillers introduces the characters of Hawk and Hunter, a pair I plan to write about more."

ALSO BY LIAM BONNER

The Legends of Kalanar – An Epic Fantasy Series
includes:
Shadow's Awakening
Blood of Kalanar
Shadow's Ascension

Manufactured by Amazon.ca
Bolton, ON

33422823R00162